# "A horse can sense when a rider is afraid,"

Sloan explained. "They won't obey anyone who's skittish around them."

Prudence tried to concentrate on his words, but his hand had come to rest lightly upon her shoulder. "What are you doing?" she asked, her gaze trapped by his.

"Talking about horses."

"I mean with your hand." Her cheeks heated. "What are you doing with your hand? A person can't go around doing something so personal to someone else unless...unless..." Unless *what?* her brain demanded.

"Touching your shoulder isn't so personal," Sloan observed, his tone frustratingly casual. "Now say my hand moved down a little lower," he continued, dropping his voice to a whisper. "Well, then you might have cause to complain...."

Dear Reader,

This month, award-winning Harlequin Historical author Miranda Jarrett continues her dramatic saga of the Sparhawk family in *Sparhawk's Lady*, a sweeping tale of danger and romance with a dashing hero who is torn between duty and desire. Don't miss this stirring adventure that was given a 5★ rating by *Affaire de Coeur* and a 4+ rating from *Romantic Times*.

And from author Suzanne Barclay comes *Lion of the North*, the second in her new medieval series featuring two clans of Scottish Highlanders, the Sutherlands and the Carmichaels, who have been fighting for generations.

Our other titles for June include our warmhearted WOMEN OF THE WEST title, *Saddle the Wind*, by author Pat Tracy, and the first Western from author Kit Gardner, *Twilight*, a story of love and redemption.

We hope you'll keep an eye out for all four selections, wherever Harlequin Historicals are sold.

Sincerely,

Tracy Farrell
Senior Editor

Please address questions and book requests to:
Harlequin Reader Service
U.S.: 3010 Walden Ave., P.O. Box 1325, Buffalo, NY 14269
Canadian: P.O. Box 609, Fort Erie, Ont. L2A 5X3

# PAT TRACY

# SADDLE THE WIND

## *Harlequin Books*

TORONTO • NEW YORK • LONDON
AMSTERDAM • PARIS • SYDNEY • HAMBURG
STOCKHOLM • ATHENS • TOKYO • MILAN
MADRID • WARSAW • BUDAPEST • AUCKLAND

ISBN 0-373-28873-5

SADDLE THE WIND

## PAT TRACY

lives with her young daughter in a farming community outside of Idaho Falls. Pat's love of historical romance began when she was thirteen and read *Gone with the Wind*. After reading Rhett and Scarlett's story, Pat immediately penned a hasty sequel wherein the couple lived happily ever after. According to Pat, there is a magic to be found in historical romances that can be found nowhere else, and she enjoys reading the many popular and talented writers who share that magic with their readers. You can write to the author at:

Box 17
Ucon, Idaho
83454

Dedicated to my son, Alan Carl Tracy. I did not have you long, but I loved you dearly.

Sherry Roseberry, Darlene Briar, Martha Tew. Luckily for me you are talented writers, as well as good friends. Thank you for your support and suggestions. I hope I can return the favor.

Special Acknowledgments to Vernon and Pearl Harris for your generous sharing of information on Thoroughbred racing. Your love of horses is clearly reflected in your enlightening conversations and your home. You should charge admission!

# Chapter One

*Port Dodd, Texas—1880*

"Please don't cry, Miss Prudence."

"I'm not crying," Prudence Britannia Abercrombie said, brushing surreptitiously at the tears that had caught her by surprise. "I—I've got something in my eye."

Davy's brown eyes chided her at her less than honest answer. Prudence supposed she should have known that the nine-year-old boy was capable of conveying sympathy and skepticism in a single expression. All the children at Draper House were wise beyond their years.

Prudence sighed and put her arm around Davy's shoulders. Feeling his bony frame beneath his thin cotton shirt shot an arrow to her heart.

"Maybe I am a little sad," she admitted, trying to summon memories of the happy times they'd spent in the now-empty parlor.

Still, the absence of familiar furnishings and the disconcerting echo of her own voice made her feel weepy and fragile. Her gaze kept returning to the brighter patches on the bare walls that marked the places where photographs of her mother and aunts had hung for almost twenty years—pictures of three sisters as young girls in pretty white dresses standing beneath a rose arbor at their English country estate.

"This has been my home since I was five," Prudence confided to the boy at her side. "It isn't easy to say goodbye to it."

Just as the twelve months since Aunt Phoebe's passing hadn't been easy, Prudence mused. Twelve months of scrimping and soliciting donations from their town's four churches and the Women's Aid Society. Of keeping young stomachs full, growing bodies clothed and lengthening feet shod. Lord, just keeping the children in shoes that fit was enough to bankrupt them! Yet she reminded herself that the past year had also been filled with love and laughter.

The responsibility of being the children's sole caretaker was a far heavier burden than she had thought it would be. She had been afraid she would prove inadequate and unable to keep the doors of Draper House open, as her mother and aunts before her had done.

"But you said Amos's farm would be the best place for us," Davy pointed out.

"So I did." All that country air, wide open spaces and gallons of fresh milk. Surely a farm was preferable to their cramped quarters in town. She just wasn't certain the farm was the best place for *her*.

After all, she knew little about raising cows or chickens or, for that matter, planting gardens. She was a city woman. Yet when dear Amos, her late aunt's beau and Draper House's most generous benefactor, had passed away, he'd left his farmhouse and a small parcel of land to Prudence and the children. The generous gift could not be turned down, not when she knew moving was in the children's best interest.

With a parting glance at the parlor, Prudence turned to the doorway. "We'll be fine, Davy."

"Miss Gladys said she was fixin' chicken and dumplings for supper to celebrate us moving and all."

Prudence slowed her step to match Davy's uneven gait. He had been brought to Draper House four months ago by parents who'd decided to pull up stakes and migrate to California. Not meeting her eyes, the nervous couple had said they would send for their crippled child once they were established in their new home. Prudence had suspected then that she might not hear from Agnes or Benjamin Bowcutt again. With an older, strapping son, they evidently had no need for a younger one with a withered leg.

She and Davy stepped into the morning sunlight. Even though Port Dodd was a gulf town, there was no hint today of a sea breeze. The strong June sun warned of the sweltering day to follow.

"Miss Prudence, come on," called little Charlie from the buckboard that waited in front of the house. "We want to go *now!*"

The excited impatience that rang from Charlie's young voice was silently echoed in the eager countenances of the other children sitting in the wagon.

"Is everybody loaded up, Janey?" Prudence asked the four-year-old, blond girl with the calico eye patch who'd stolen a special place in her heart.

"Yes, ma'am," she answered solemnly. "Can we count off?"

"*May* we count off," Prudence corrected her gently. Janey was very proud of her newly acquired ability to count. "That's a wonderful idea, dear. Why don't you lead off?"

"One!" Janey trumpeted immediately.

Prudence assisted Davy into the buckboard.

"Two!" he shouted as he clambered awkwardly in, then reached for the crutch Prudence passed to him.

"Three, four," chimed the five-year-old black twins, Charlotte and Charlie.

"Five," Sarah said with the self-conscious dignity of her sixteen years.

"Six," Richard, their newest addition, called out. Nearly fourteen, he was the oldest boy. Serious, silent, watchful. In the past two months he had carved a place for himself at Draper House with the hard work he relentlessly performed. Even now, he sat in the driver's seat, his rawboned but competent hands gripping the reins of their newly inherited team of horses.

"Seven," Janey piped.

"You were one," Davy informed her with youthful superiority. "You can't be seven, too."

Janey's bottom lip trembled. "I can if I want to."

"You may say as many numbers as you wish," Prudence reassured the girl. "You just need to remember that there's only one Janey Henspeter."

Prudence gathered her black skirts in one hand and climbed next to Richard on the high bench seat. He was already cracking the whip over the broad backs of the plow horses as she adjusted the ties on her black bonnet.

Amos's farm was ten miles north of town. Richard had already made another trip there before dawn, transporting Gladys and Draper House's meager furnishings. Thankfully, Samuel Cheney, their longtime landlord, had shown up in the wee hours of the morning and assisted them in loading their possessions into the wagon.

It wouldn't take long for Gladys to finish unpacking. Prudence had devised the plan as the most efficient means of relocating their place of residence. Pleased that moving day was proceeding smoothly, she nodded at the Draper Street neighbors who had spilled onto their porches to wave goodbye.

Suddenly Prudence found it difficult to swallow. Leaving the only home she'd known since she'd arrived in

America as a child was more heart-wrenching than she'd expected. In an effort to portray a cheerful demeanor for the children, she forced a smile to her lips and added her farewells to those of her charges.

Richard turned the buckboard down Main Street. The boardwalk was filled with Saturday passersby, mostly farmers and their families who had come to town to stock up on supplies and gawk a bit at the fancy airs and clothing of Port Dodd's wealthier residents.

The wagon loaded with children attracted its portion of attention. They fell silent, and Prudence suspected they were uncomfortable at being the focus of so many curious gazes. More than anything, she knew each child was wishing that he belonged to a real family, no matter how poor.

As the wagon rattled toward the edge of town, the business establishments became more humble. Fitch's General Store. Higgens's Livery. The Belly-Up Saloon. Richard drew the slow-moving team to a halt to let three staggering cowpokes amble across the street. Prudence noticed that several other wranglers, their hats pulled low over their faces, lounged in front of the saloon.

One of the men pointed to the stopped buckboard. Another, the tallest of the group, raised his head and looked straight at Prudence. No more than six feet separated them. For a moment she found herself captured by a pair of hard-looking, silvery eyes. Her breath locked in her throat as the force of the unknown man's gaze seemed to take full measure of her—from her bonnet's black ribbons tied securely beneath her chin, to her gloved hands clenched upon her lap. And everything in between!

A burst of raucous laughter broke the powerful spell of the stranger's perusal. A hot flush crept from her collar and moved up her throat to spill across her cheeks. Even in such modern times as 1880, single women were not abundant on the western frontier. She knew it was the scarcity of unmarried females that made her the occasional target of earthy speculation from Port Dodd's male population.

Tall, broad-shouldered and layered in trail dust, the man with the silvery eyes strode toward the horses tied at the nearby hitching post. He must have felt her return stare because he paused and looked at her again from beneath the weathered brim of his dark Stetson.

Fortunately Richard chose that moment to urge their team forward. Prudence turned around on her seat. She didn't want the drifter to get the mistaken impression that she was the kind of woman to encourage a stranger's interest.

She cleared her throat. "I appreciate you driving the wagon, Richard."

His posture was fiercely rigid, as if to relax one muscle would be a dereliction of duty. She noticed that her words caused his cheeks to pinken. He hadn't learned yet how to respond to simple gratitude.

"I can hardly wait till we get there," Charlotte called out. "Gladys says there's chickens and cows and horses and . . . and everything!"

"We can make all the noise we want to," Davy added. "And stay outside all day long."

"There's a swimming hole, too," Charlie contributed. "Amos once said it has water in it all through August even."

As she listened to their excited voices, Prudence told herself again that life on a farm was the best thing for the children. Come fall, the daily drive to the schoolhouse would be a minor inconvenience compared to the abundance of food they would be able to grow themselves. And they would have much more room.

From seemingly nowhere, a horseman on a fast-moving, chestnut-colored mount appeared beside their team. Richard automatically drew back on the reins. Dust swirled up around them. At once Prudence recognized the rider as the tall man who'd been standing in front of the Belly-Up Saloon. Even as she assured herself that the cowboy probably meant no harm, a tremor of distress squeezed her stomach. Neither she nor Richard had a gun with which to protect themselves.

"Excuse me, ma'am" came the low and distinctly western drawl. "I understand that you're Miss Abercrombie, the one Amos left his farmhouse to."

Prudence sat straighter. "That's right."

"I meant to catch up with you sooner," he said, his narrow lips looking grim and implacable amid the black stubble gracing his hard male jaw.

"Catch up with me?" she repeated faintly, not liking the thought of this disreputable man tracking her down for any reason.

His flintlike gaze moved across the children. "I see I didn't make it in time."

"What do you want, mister?" Richard demanded sharply, clearly seeing himself as her and the children's protector.

The hard eyes shifted to the militant boy. Prudence sensed a momentary softening in their stony depths.

"Relax, kid, I'm not here to start any trouble. I just need to talk to Miss Abercrombie."

"What's your name?" Charlotte's voice rang out loud and clear from behind Prudence.

"Have you ever shot anybody with that gun?" Davy asked on the heels of Charlotte's question, giving the stranger no time to answer.

"Sure he's shot somebody," Charlie said. "Probably killed a few, too. I bet he's got notches carved on his gun handle."

"Are you a daddy?" came Janey's soft voice.

"What's the name of your horse? He's a beaut," Davy observed, again jumping into the fray of questions bombarding the frowning rider.

"You sure are dirty, mister," Charlotte pointed out with childlike candor. "Where are you from?"

Deciding it was time to take control of the situation, Prudence clapped her gloved hands together. "Children, please!"

They hushed expectantly.

"My name's Sloan Coltrane," the stranger said quietly. "Over the years, I've had to shoot a man, or two. But I don't take to violence, and no one I ever shot died from his wounds," he continued steadily. "I'm not a daddy. My horse is called Lucky. I apologize for the trail dust, but I've been traveling for better than a week. Had some people I needed to see between here and Galveston."

"That's all very interesting," Prudence said politely, fascinated despite herself by the stranger's laconic way of answering the questions hurled at him. "Why have you stopped us?"

Sloan took off his hat and used his sleeve to wipe his forehead. He wasn't used to the increased humidity that licked his skin like a hot, wet tongue. An unfamiliar sultriness hung in the thick air. One could not ignore it, or the morning sun that bore down on them.

Realizing he'd picked a poor time for his confrontation with the spinster lady and her charges, he decided to move things along. "I needed to talk to you about the farmhouse Amos left you."

The woman's brown eyes become wary. "What about it?"

Sloan smothered a sigh. Damn, he should have written to Miss Abercrombie instead of showing up on moving day to make his offer. He'd been delayed, however, by his brother Jeremy's hasty marriage to Misty Marie.

"I've picked a poor time to introduce myself, Miss Abercrombie, but I'm Amos's nephew. He left me the land surrounding the house he willed to you."

The uneasiness left her eyes. Beneath the unflattering black dress, her shoulders visibly relaxed. "Then we're going to be neighbors?"

He liked her voice. It was soft and coated with an accent he hadn't heard before. She sounded cultured.

Sloan looked again toward the climbing sun. The gentlemanly lessons his stepmother had tried to drill into him over the years prevented him from prolonging this discussion in the rising heat. The children were already beginning to fidget.

"We need to talk, Miss Abercrombie, but it can wait. I'll ride with you to Amos's. We'll settle our business there."

"That will be fine," Prudence agreed, even as her mind raced. Settle *what* business? she couldn't help but wonder. Other than being her new neighbor, she and Sloan Coltrane had no connection whatsoever.

Amos's nephew nodded at Richard, and the young man pressed the team forward. Coltrane and his horse adopted the same moderate pace. From time to time, Prudence found herself casting curious glances at their new traveling companion.

She tried to remember if she'd ever heard Amos mention having a nephew. Amos had been a talker, always having some outrageous tale to share with an obliging listener. With chagrin, Prudence realized that she hadn't paid a great deal of attention to the older man's stories. It was enough that Aunt Phoebe and the children enjoyed Amos's story-telling talents.

"I bet he's a gunfighter," Charlie announced after a few minutes.

"I bet he is, too," Davy seconded. "He's probably filled up whole cemeteries with dead people."

Prudence darted another glance at the man riding alongside the buckboard. She dearly hoped he hadn't overheard Davy and Charlie's remarks.

"Children, let's sing some songs," Prudence suggested brightly. That way there wouldn't be any more unflattering character assessments about Sloan Coltrane, at least not with him in listening distance.

Her suggestion was greeted enthusiastically by the younger children and with groans from the older ones. Nevertheless a chorus broke out. Prudence joined in a bit self-consciously—her voice was a strong soprano and didn't blend well with the children's.

As the dusty miles passed beneath their wagon's slowly turning wheels, Prudence led the youngsters from one song to another. From time to time, Coltrane would turn his head toward her, and she would feel the force of his probing gaze. Something about his stares made her uncomfortably aware of the drabness of her clothing and the dust inexorably settling upon her person. The certainty that her cheeks were streaked with the all-pervasive dust added to her discomfiture. When they finished the last verse, Prudence searched mentally for something else to sing.

The terrifying sound of a rattler, warning of its presence in the brush alongside the road, shattered the momentary lull between songs. Before anyone had time to even gasp, their team and Coltrane's mount were rearing up upon their powerful hindquarters, their loud whinnies revealing their animal panic. The children found their voices and shrieked.

"Whoa! Whoa, there!" Richard yelled, trying to control the terrified team.

The wagon rolled backward, then lurched ahead. One of its wheels hit a hole. Everything seemed to tilt crazily. More screams let loose. Then, without any warning whatsoever, Prudence found herself catapulted from the high seat. A hot rush of air whooshed past her. The knowledge that she was going to hit hard barely registered before her tooth-rattling impact against the sunbaked ground became a reality. A blast of gunfire reverberated around and through her. Her last coherent thought was Coltrane must have shot her. Then everything went black....

"Get back, she needs some air."

The commanding voice seemed incredibly close. Prudence wanted to open her eyes, but the pounding in her head prevented her. She knew she was lying on her back. Something wet and cool was being pressed against her forehead and throat. She sensed she'd been unconscious for several minutes.

"Come on, Miss Abercrombie, it's time to open your eyes and show the children that you're all right."

The damp cloth continued to stroke her throat. The pounding at her temples receded. Her corset, however, prevented her from taking any deep breaths. Prudence silently cursed the garment, wishing that its stays could be magically loosened.

Gradually she realized she *was* breathing easier. The cool cloth moved to the upper swells of her breasts. She murmured her approval. Several more moments drifted by.

Then, as if slammed into her consciousness by the force of a brutish fist, it occurred to Prudence that she was being undressed. By a stranger. In broad daylight. In front of the children!

Her eyelids flew open as she prepared to chastise the person taking such undue liberties, but her gaze was immediately met by compelling silvery eyes. The protest she'd been about to utter fled her thoughts. Disoriented by Coltrane's face being so close to her, all she could do was look at him as he stared down at her, blocking the sun's brightness and covering her with his shadow.

His eyebrows were black and thick and drawn together into a fierce scowl. His nose was carved along strong male lines, and his cheeks and jaw were grazed with the stubbly growth she'd noticed earlier. His lips were narrow, a stark slash of displeasure across his darkly tanned countenance.

Then before her very eyes, the shape and contour of his mouth changed as a slow smile eased its way across his lips.

"Well now, that's better."

## Chapter Two

Sloan found himself contemplating Miss Abercrombie's wide eyes. They were an unusual green-flecked shade of hazel, he discovered. Her head was resting against his right forearm. The bonnet she'd been wearing had flown off, and her hair was splashed across his sleeve.

That she was alive and breathing came as a relief. When he'd seen her bucked from the wagon seat and hurtling through the air, he'd thought she was going to break her neck. In the midst of such a sight, it surprised him that he'd held his aim on the rattler and shot it.

"Want to try and sit up?" he asked when some of the color had returned to her pale cheeks. She nodded.

He noted absently the tiny freckles scattered across the bridge of her nose. Her mouth was softer than it had been when she'd demanded an explanation for his interruption of her journey. She was years younger than he had thought when he'd first caught sight of her in front of the saloon. Using the arm that cradled her neck, he helped her sit up.

"Let's take it nice and easy," he suggested soothingly.

Her gloved hands went immediately to the front of the dress that he'd unfastened, along with the loosened ribbons holding her stays together. He glanced away to give her a moment of privacy, even as the children crowded closer.

"Miss Prudence, are you all right?" asked Janey, the towheaded girl with the calico eye patch, her lower lip quivering.

The question was immediately repeated by the others.

"I'm fine, I'm fine," Prudence kept assuring them in a voice that was wobbly to everyone's ears.

She slipped off her dusty gloves. Sloan saw she was having a devil of a time making her trembling fingers retie her corset ribbons. He helped her the rest of the way up to her feet. She swayed, and he let her lean against him for support. He allowed her a moment to adjust as he reached around her and made quick work of setting her clothing to rights.

The boy with the crutch stepped forward. "Here's your hat, Miss Prudence."

She accepted the dusty bonnet. "Th-thank you, Davy."

As Miss Abercrombie became steadier on her feet, Sloan felt her draw away from him. He dropped his hands from her shoulders and stepped back. The sunlight danced across her abundant dark hair. Not brown, as he'd originally thought, but shot through with fiery glints of red.

"My goodness, what an adventure," she pronounced, shaking a cloud of dust from her black bonnet before replacing it firmly atop her disheveled hair. "Is everyone all right?"

Her question set the youngsters off. The smaller ones crowded around her skirts. She patted their heads and spoke soothingly. The older children inched closer also. She addressed them with quiet composure, taking a moment to hug each of them.

Within a few minutes Prudence Abercrombie calmed her excited wards. Sloan shook his head, then picked up the canteen that had provided the water he'd used to revive her. He returned the container to his saddle, thinking the woman's manner with the children smacked of the female magic his stepmother used to work upon him and his younger sisters and brother.

Sloan retied his bandanna, oddly conscious of the cool moistness next to his throat. He was grateful Abercrombie wasn't the hysterical type. If either Alicia or Lenore had flown off a buckboard, there would have been hell to pay. But then neither sister would have been caught dead riding in a wagon rather than using one of the Lazy J's quarter horses.

"You gotta see the rattler," insisted the black boy who looked about five. "He's a giant!"

The comely, brown-haired girl, whom Sloan guessed to be around sixteen, wrinkled her nose. "Ugh, Charlie, no one wants to see a dead snake."

"Miss Prudence does," he countered, tugging insistently on the woman's skirts. "Don't you?"

"There's snake innards and blood everywhere," the boy with the crutch added with ghoulish gusto.

Miss Abercrombie's feet stopped moving. "Uh, that's all right, I'll take your word for it."

"Mr. Coltrane blasted him to smithereens with just one shot!"

"I told you he was a gunfighter," the crippled boy declared smugly.

Sloan's cheeks grew warm. Since his father's death at the Battle of Valverde when Sloan had been twelve, Sloan had become the man of his family. That meant he'd had to set a good example for his sisters and brother. If one of them heard some kid call him a gunfighter of all things, they would have laughed their heads off.

Sloan felt he needed to set the record straight. Again. For these bloodthirsty little heathens. "I'm *not* a gunfighter."

His denial came out more forcefully than he'd intended, provoking an immediate hush. For all of thirty seconds.

"You're the fastest draw I've ever seen," said Davy.

"Fast and accurate," concurred the oldest boy, eyeing Sloan with open suspicion.

"Children, Mr. Coltrane has already assured us he's not a gunfighter. Now, let's get back into the wagon. Gladys is going to be wondering what's delayed us."

The young people acted as one in obeying the woman's softly voiced command. Ready to remount, Sloan picked up Lucky's trailing reins. The weight of a feminine hand upon his sleeve stopped him.

"Mr. Coltrane."

He turned. "Yes?"

"Thank you."

She was shorter than she'd seemed sitting high atop the buckboard. Her clear gaze met his directly. Sloan could not find one iota of coyness in those intelligent eyes and that was somewhat disconcerting. The single women with whom he was acquainted generally made a habit of batting their eyelashes at him.

"You're welcome, ma'am."

"Having someone like you for a neighbor is going to be very reassuring," she continued in that foreign voice of hers. "Perhaps after you're settled, you might agree to teach the boys how to discharge a pistol."

Sloan recalled his reason for trying to get to Port Dodd in time to stop Miss Abercrombie from moving to the farmhouse. It didn't fit with his future plans that this woman and her band of children become dependent upon him for anything.

"I would have thought that someone in your position would be opposed to violence, Miss Abercrombie."

She regarded him solemnly. Sloan continued to study her upturned face. Her dirt-streaked bonnet was a bit lopsided, and one delicate cheek was smudged with dust. A strange warmth invaded his chest. Something about the woman's bedraggled but plucky bearing moved him.

"I *am* opposed to violence. It has been my observation, however, that upon the American frontier a man must be prepared for any eventuality. A certain prowess with firearms has its place in a well-rounded education."

"The American frontier?" Sloan repeated, not sure he'd heard her correctly.

"Well, yes."

He shook his head. "Ma'am, I'm afraid you've got your facts mixed up. The frontier's gone. It disappeared a long time ago."

She had the nerve to smile at him, but Sloan didn't take offense. Hell, with her sweet accent rolling over him, she could have told him the earth was flat and he would have obligingly listened, before setting her straight, of course.

"I suppose that depends upon your point of view, Mr. Coltrane. From where I stand, however, Texas seems very much an untamed frontier."

To forestall a prolonged debate on the matter, Sloan tipped his hat. It was a tactic he'd seen his father use successfully when he'd wanted to ward off an impending argument with his stepmother.

Miss Abercrombie opened her mouth as if to protest his dropping of the issue; then she sighed. "I suppose we should be on our way."

She turned and strode briskly to the buckboard. The young driver extended his hand to help her. Sloan stepped automatically forward. She looked from the boy to him for a second, as if trying to decide whose help she would accept. He didn't wait for an invitation. He simply curved a palm around her trim waist and exerted the necessary pressure to propel her onto the wagon seat.

The driver scowled at him.

Miss Abercrombie smiled. "Thank you, again."

He watched the buckboard loaded with children move from the dusty clearing. Six of them, he reminded himself, thinking of the silent count he'd taken. And Miss Prudence Abercrombie was their indomitable leader. How did she hold up under such responsibility?

Sloan remembered how his life had changed after his father's death. Initially his stepmother had been responsible for their cattle spread. But somehow things had changed with the passage of years, and by the time he'd reached eighteen, Sloan was the acknowledged head of the Coltrane household.

He'd been the one to oversee the actions of his much younger brother and sisters. He'd been the one who had approved Alicia's and Lenore's prospective bridegrooms. He'd also been the one to try to talk his younger brother, Jeremy, out of marrying so young. Sloan's arguments that a boy who'd just celebrated his nineteenth birthday wasn't ready for matrimony had fallen upon deaf ears. Jeremy had pointed out that when Sloan had been that age, he'd been responsible for the ranch and everyone on it.

Sloan had been unable to refute his brother's words. After all, Sloan had grilled Dan Porter about his intentions toward his stepmother, after accidentally finding them in a compromising interlude in a secluded meadow. At least Dan had understood that it was up to Sloan to watch out for his family, even if Kate had been a trifle upset by his interference.

Now he was free, Sloan thought as he remounted Lucky. Free from the burden of his family. Free from the burden of running the ranch. It had been a burden he had willingly picked up—he did love his family. But he was thirty-two years old, and for the first time since his father's death, Sloan was able to enjoy the heady feeling of being responsible for no one but himself.

He issued a low giddyap and moved alongside the buckboard brimming with children. Nothing and no one was going to interfere with that hard-earned freedom. Never again was he going to worry about setting a good example or protecting those weaker than himself.

For the next few years, he planned on drinking plenty of good whiskey, playing poker until the wee hours of the morning and consorting with loose women. And not necessarily in that order. He also meant to build himself a racetrack that would rival those in the East or the South. In short, he was going to indulge in those pleasurable pastimes that had previously been off limits to him.

He slanted another glance at the spinster who was presently leading her wards in yet another verse of "She'll Be Coming Around the Mountain." The first thing he was going to do was get Prudence Abercrombie and her passel of young people settled somewhere besides Amos's farmhouse. Trying to build his racetrack with them on the premises would be one complication after another. And he was finally, irrevocably, through with complications.

Even as Prudence sang with the children, she continued to be disturbingly aware of Coltrane riding alongside them. The thought of him being their neighbor was strangely unsettling. Something about his rugged bearing made her heart beat a little faster than normal. He was so... so manly. And perhaps beneath the stubble shadowing his jaw, almost handsome?

Her gaze fell to her hands folded upon her lap and the dusty gloves she'd pulled back over them. A certain aura of mystery about him made him seem both dangerous and compelling. The doting mothers and fathers of Port Dodd's single women might want to lock up their daughters to keep them safe from the likes of a man like Coltrane, but Prudence suspected the reluctant parents would soon find themselves issuing dinner invitations at the girls' insistence. It would be like fattening the lamb for the slaughter.

Prudence slid another glance at the solitary rider. If he wasn't already married, he surely would be by fall. She didn't think he was. Married. He had a flagrantly independent manner. Untamed was how he came across to her. Despite the heat, tiny goose bumps danced across her forearms. He'd taken the liberty of unfastening her dress and corset in broad daylight. Purely for medical purposes, of course. But still, such boldness bespoke a rebel nature.

She wondered which Port Dodd miss would ultimately claim him. He probably wouldn't make a satisfactory husband, she decided. Too much of that rebel blood.

Upon reflection, Prudence decided that Marabelle Brubaker would be the most likely candidate to capture Mr. Coltrane's fancy. She was presently away at finishing school but was due home shortly. The girl's parents owned the Brubaker Hotel, Brubaker Mercantile and Brubaker Fishing Fleet. They were among the most generous contributors to Draper House. Marabelle was strong-willed and beautiful. Prudence suspected the combustible combination would appeal to Amos's nephew.

"What's the next verse, Miss Prudence?"

It was the children's sudden silence and not their question that penetrated Prudence's thoughts. "What?"

"After 'she'll be herding nine fine swine,' what comes next?" Charlotte asked impatiently.

"'She'll be tickling ten tan terries,'" Prudence supplied quickly, recalling the final verse that Gladys had taught them just last week. Prudence was grateful that neither the children nor Sloan Coltrane had any idea of the personal nature of her thoughts.

The song ended. Before they could begin another, the buckboard rolled to the crest of a low hill covered in bluebonnets and Indian paintbrush. When they reached the top, Amos's farmhouse came into view. It was a spacious, two-story structure that had been kept in excellent repair. A large covered porch circled the freshly painted building. Its whiteness fairly glistened beneath the morning sun, almost equaling the brightness of the billowing clouds that floated serenely across the limitless blue sky.

The corrals and barns were also in excellent condition. Amos had had everything in readiness for his forthcoming marriage to Phoebe. Prudence's heart squeezed painfully as she remembered her aunt's passing and then Amos's death almost a year later.

Her blurred gaze drifted to the Bartel River that provided water year round. Giant oak and pecan trees grew along its high banks. The sheer beauty spread out before her soothed Prudence's melancholy mood. She'd already said her goodbyes to her mother and aunts. It was time to let go of the grief and concentrate on the present. Country life might be utterly foreign to her, but she had the feeling she was coming home.

For a moment the children, too, were struck speechless by the scene sprawled out before them. Then they started speaking at once.

"Chickens!"

"Horses!"

"Cows!"

"I can smell chicken and dumplings!"

At that outlandish claim, everyone laughed.

"Go faster, Richard!"

"Yes!" came the predictable chorus.

Prudence held on as Richard trotted the team the rest of the way down the small hill.

Gladys Stumple was waiting for them on the porch. In her early fifties, the tall, sturdy woman had been widowed for several years. Aunt Phoebe had hired her shortly after Gladys's late husband's passing.

"Well, it's about time," the housekeeper snorted, wiping her reddened hands on the heavy white apron she wore over her brown dress. "I do declare, I was about to come looking for you-all."

"Miss Prudence fell out of the wagon!" Charlotte shouted. The buckboard barely rolled to a stop in front of the house before she scampered down.

"Mr. Coltrane shot a rattler clean through its eyes," Charlie announced, rushing to the porch.

"Then he started taking off Miss Prudence's clothes," Janey said, as if that embarrassing detail warranted mentioning.

"There was blood and guts *everywhere*," Davy further elaborated as Prudence took his crutch and helped him down.

"Mr. Coltrane?" Gladys inquired, her curious gaze going to Amos's nephew as he dismounted from his horse.

"He says he's not a gunfighter," Davy confided. "But he sure can shoot."

"His horse is named Lucky," Charlotte informed the housekeeper.

"He's not a daddy," Janey said softly.

"And he's never killed anyone—that he knows of," Davy clarified.

"He's so dirty because he's been traveling for a long time," Charlotte explained charitably, lest the older woman have a poor impression of their hero. "He had some folks between here and Galveston he needed to visit."

"He's Amos's nephew, and he owns the land around the farmhouse," Sarah said shyly. "He's going to be our neighbor."

Prudence sensed Coltrane's bemused state as he joined her and the children on the porch. He'd learn soon enough that anything one child knew, the others immediately discovered.

"Well, I'm pleased to meet you, Mr. Coltrane," Gladys said, extending her hand.

"Call me Sloan, ma'am," he returned as he accepted the handshake.

"And you call me Gladys," the older woman ordered firmly. "Now, come inside. I've fixed us up a fine supper to celebrate our first day in our new home."

The children were so keyed up they wanted immediately to investigate their new surroundings. But Prudence said, "Come on, let's enjoy Miss Gladys's dumplings. We have all day to explore the farm."

Fortunately they couldn't ignore the succulent aroma of stewing chicken. In no time at all, everyone was washed up and seated at the kitchen's long pine table. Many of the chairs were mismatched, donated as they were from various households, as were the plates and eating utensils. But that didn't spoil their enjoyment of the meal.

Somehow Mr. Coltrane became seated beside Prudence. She couldn't help noticing he ate three bowlfuls of Gladys's chicken stew. Just as she couldn't help noticing the tiny droplets of water that clung to the ends of his thick, dark hair that lay against his brown shirt collar. He'd washed up at the outside pump and taken the opportunity to liberally douse himself.

His Stetson hung on a hook next to the back door. He looked different without the battered hat. She raised a spoon to her lips and blew softly against the steam while continuing to study him from the corner of her eye.

In the background, the children's voices ebbed and flowed as Coltrane's profile repeatedly drew her curious gaze. Where the Stetson had rested against his head, his dark hair was flattened against his scalp. A narrow scar about an inch long ran from his left eyebrow to his sharply defined cheekbone.

Without warning he turned and caught her studying him. Prudence knew she was blushing and quickly looked away. She told herself that her strong reaction to Coltrane was because of the strangeness of having *any* man seated at their table.

His voice was deeper than any of theirs. He took up more space than anyone else. When he spoke, everyone else quieted. She noticed that most of the conversation was directed to him. Unquestionably, he was the center of attention. Not just for her but for everyone, even Gladys, who kept encouraging him to eat more, even after his third helping. It would be a miracle if the man didn't burst.

She sensed he was a bit uncomfortable with the lavish attention he was receiving. Since his table manners were unexpectedly good, she didn't think he would be self-conscious about that. It was becoming clear to her, however, that something about the present situation disturbed him. More than once she saw him wince when the children mentioned him being their new neighbor. Naturally they were curious about the crops he intended to grow and wanted to know where he planned on building his house, since Amos had left this one to them.

"You can live with us till you get a place built," Charlie offered generously, then turned to Prudence for confirmation. "He can, can't he?"

"I'll be staying in town for the next few days," Coltrane responded before Prudence could answer.

"It'll take more than a few days to build a house," Davy pointed out.

"I'm not planning to build one," he answered cryptically.

"Are you going to live in a tepee, Mr. Coltrane?" Charlotte inquired.

"I'm sure Mr. Coltrane doesn't plan on living in a tepee," Prudence felt compelled to say.

"I'm full," Charlotte announced sleepily.

"Me, too," Charlie echoed.

"Let's go outside and look at the animals," Davy urged.

"Whose chore is it going to be to feed the chickens?" Janey inquired, surrendering to a wide yawn and rubbing her good eye.

"Mine!" several children answered in unison.

Prudence smiled affectionately. Because of the differences in their ages, each of them had unique needs. Yet in other ways they were very much alike. "Let's go upstairs and see the bedrooms first. We'll talk about taking turns doing the chores later."

The sudden scrape of chairs being pushed back resounded through the kitchen. Prudence knew that once they were upstairs with their made-up beds in front of them, it would be relatively easy to talk the younger children into naps. While they slept, the older ones could investigate their new surroundings.

And she could converse with Mr. Coltrane about why he'd wanted to reach Port Dodd before she and the children were settled at the house.

*Organized mayhem,* Sloan thought. All these kids running around like yearlings during spring roundup. How on earth had Miss Abercrombie, at her young age, ended up being in charge of so many children? And where had they all come from, her little band of wounded critters?

As he paced the humbly furnished parlor, he found himself far more intrigued with the woman than with her wards. He'd had ample opportunity to catch her watching him during their noon meal. She acted as if she'd never been around a man before, becoming flustered and flushed by his stare. He paused in front of several glass-domed pictures hanging on the paneled wall. She probably hadn't. Been around a man. *Or with one.*

Something was flagrantly innocent about Miss Prudence Abercrombie. Being saddled with six children of varying ages would more than likely keep her in a maidenly state for the rest of her life. Sloan didn't think there was a man alive who would pursue a woman so burdened. Certainly not with the intention of matrimony.

And he was willing to bet that Miss Prudence Abercrombie wouldn't be susceptible to anything other than that holy state. So she'd die a virgin. With her lovely reddish hair. With her softly shaped lips. With the flawless white skin that he'd glimpsed above her corset.

His brooding gaze wandered to the photographs. Three young women wearing frilly dresses stood in front of a flower garden. Miss Abercrombie resembled them. He wondered how she would look in a pretty summer dress instead of the high-necked black gown she wore.

"Mr. Coltrane, I apologize for keeping you waiting." Her voice drifted into the room like a lilac-scented breeze.

He turned and was greeted by her very direct hazel eyes. Again he was struck by an awareness of the sweetly curved body beneath the drab dress.

"Are you in mourning?" It was a question he certainly hadn't intended asking, but his mouth had nevertheless voiced it.

*Don't answer that,* he wanted to say. A feeling of self-preservation warned him that it would be better if he refrained learning anything of a personal nature about the woman he meant to buy this house from.

She tipped her head, looking much younger without the black bonnet.

"My Aunt Phoebe passed away a year ago."

*A year in black for an aunt?* "You must have been close."

Miss Abercrombie moved to the pictures he'd been studying. "Phoebe is the one in the middle. My mother is on the right. Winifred, my other aunt, is on the left."

Sloan's hostess eclipsed his awareness of the photographs on the wall. "Were the pictures taken back East?"

She shook her head. A lock of hair escaped its restraining pin to join the strands framing her face. "England," she corrected him softly, "on my grandparents' country estate."

*How in blazes had she come to be in Port Dodd, Texas?*

To keep from asking, he pressed his lips together. The less he knew about Miss Abercrombie the better. He was already too curious about her. If that wasn't bad enough, his body was beginning to react to her on a very fundamental level. Sloan gritted his teeth. It was clear he'd been too long without a woman for this spinsterish female to be affecting him so strongly.

He backed up. A part of his reaction was no doubt the result of having unfastened the top few buttons of her dress. Evidently, it didn't matter to his urges whether or not he was undressing a female for passionate or compassionate purposes.

"Well, Mr. Coltrane, aren't you going to tell me why you wished to speak with me?"

He blinked. It was that voice of hers, he decided, that was playing havoc with his common sense. It would be best if he did the talking from here on. "I wanted to reach Port Dodd before you left Draper House for two reasons."

"And they are?"

"First, I wanted to find out how you'd coerced my uncle into leaving you this house."

The color seeped from her face. "There was no coercion involved. Amos left me this property because he wanted to provide a good home for the children."

"I realize that now."

He knew he'd upset her, but she would have been a great deal more disturbed if she knew what he'd originally thought when he'd learned his uncle had willed part of his estate to a single woman. Amos might have been over seventy, but he was still a man.

"I'm glad we settled that. What was your second reason for trying to contact me before we moved?"

"I wanted to spare you the wasted effort."

Her greenish eyes narrowed in her wan face. "What do you mean?"

He drew himself to his full height and assumed the implacable expression he'd used over the years to keep his younger sisters and brother in line.

"I mean I'm going to buy Amos's house from you."

Her delicate eyebrows lifted. "Are you?"

"Before you get completely unpacked," he confirmed.

"You're too late then," she said loftily. "We're already settled in."

He glanced around the tidy room and realized she was right. "That's not the point."

He watched her straighten to her full height. He derived considerable satisfaction that he still towered above her. There was no way this slight woman could intimidate him—as long as she kept her dress buttoned.

"You're right. The point is you may not have this house."

Before he could correct her, the two oldest children entered the room.

"I will join you shortly," she told them. "Mr. Coltrane and I are almost finished with our discussion."

*They were?*

She kept her rigid back to him until they heard the sound of a door slamming shut, then she rounded on him.

Her eyes snapping fire and her pale skin flushed, she raised a finger to his chest. "You may be Amos's nephew, but he left this house to me and the children. I have no intention of selling it. It's perfect for us."

"But you haven't heard what I'm offering—"

"And furthermore," she continued, her small finger almost jabbing him. "I do not care for bullies. Don't you ever again make the mistake of trying to tell me what to do.''

Damned, she was something, with her flashing eyes and her cheeks all rosied up in anger. And that voice of hers! He felt it slide over him like a hot June wind. He steeled himself against its treacherous effect.

"Listen, lady, I've got plans for this bit of land that don't include having a spinster and her flock of misbegotten waifs running wild across it."

Immediately the color seeped from her cheeks.

A hot flush crawled up Sloan's neck, frying his face. He couldn't believe he'd called her a spinster. He'd been raised better than that. Besides, he admitted with a flash of honesty, she wasn't old enough or plain enough to deserve so shoddy a title.

"It really doesn't matter what you want," she said with great dignity, her magnificent voice subdued. "It only matters that I have no intention of selling."

He opened his mouth to offer an apology. She certainly deserved one. She was already sweeping from the room, however, and he didn't think it advisable to stop her.

He might end up saying something a whole lot worse. Like...like asking for just one taste of her lips.

No, he thought grimly as he stalked toward the kitchen to fetch his hat. It would be better all the way around if he kept his runaway mouth as far from Prudence Abercrombie as he could. And his curious hands. And his tightening body.

Miles away.

As he stepped into the sunshine and mounted Lucky, Sloan wondered how the prim and proper Prudence Abercrombie was going to like living next to a racetrack and gambling casino. Unexpectedly, an unholy spark of amusement lightened his mood. She'd be mad as a mud-splattered cat and more than ready to sell to him.

It would be only a matter of time before he had her begging him to buy the place from her. Because he was a gentleman—sort of—he'd pay her the original price he'd intended. When she discovered just how much he was willing to give her, she'd be more than happy to accept his offer and skedaddle back to town.

Sloan didn't make it out of the yard before panicked shouts from one of the children had him turning Lucky and heading in the direction of the river.

# Chapter Three

Prudence's thoughts were caught in a furious whirlwind. How dare Sloan Coltrane think he could order her and the children from their new home! And as for him calling her a spinster...her chest tightened. The truth should not hurt, and he had merely spoken the truth about her single state. Still, his heartless pronouncement stung bitterly.

Bright sunlight coalesced around her. A warm breeze drifted over her. She let the ebb and flow of the children's conversation soothe her jangled sensibilities. From the corner of her eye, she noticed Davy leaning heavily upon his crutch as he gazed in delight at the sluggish brown body of water below them. Surely, Christopher Columbus could not have sighted the New World with any greater degree of enthusiasm.

Then, within the blink of an eye, the bank upon which Davy stood simply ceased to exist. So sudden was his tumble into the river below that the boy seemed to vanish into thin air.

Even before his startled yelp, Prudence gathered her skirts and dashed to the disintegrating ledge. It was an eight-foot drop from the bank to the water. She saw the boy struggling to gain his footing. He'd lost his crutch, which was even now floating downriver.

One thought drove her. She had to get to Davy. The quickest path to the floundering child was in a straight line. Downward. With a jump that caused her heart to leap to her throat, she took that direct route. An inelegant splash ended her descent. Waves of muddy water sloshed over her.

"Davy, grab my hand," she shouted to the floundering boy so that he would know he wasn't alone in his fight for survival.

His eyes went wide in amazement. "Miss Prudence, what are you doing here?"

"I'm rescuing you," she told him reassuringly. Her arms flailed energetically as she imitated the motions she'd seen a sailor employ who'd fallen overboard from the *Majestic,* the ship upon which she and her mother had sailed to America. Prudence suspected that her skirts were a greater hinderance to her than his trousers had been to him. "It's going to be all right. Just kick your good leg and move your arms like I am."

Davy eyed her efforts with obvious misgiving. "You sure are splashing up a storm, Miss Prudence."

"You must, also, if you don't wish to perish," she instructed through a mouthful of gritty water.

"But—"

"Don't argue! Swim for your life!"

"But I can touch the bottom, can't you?"

Prudence stopped kicking. Immediately her heavy skirts pulled her downward as surely as if they were a giant anchor. The water rose to her...waist. Chagrined, she stopped flapping her arms. The slow-moving river gently nudged her. She had to brace her feet against the muddy river bottom to remain vertical, but she was in no danger of being sucked beneath the lazy current and drowned.

"Well then," she began, pushing back a dangling strand of wet hair from her face. "It appears everything is all right. Let us proceed to dry land."

"Miss Prudence, Davy, are you okay?" Sarah called from above.

Prudence shaded her eyes with a dripping hand. Sarah and Richard looked down at them with similar expressions of dismay.

"We're fine," she shouted up to them as she waded awkwardly to Davy. "Here, dear, lean on me," she said, placing his arm around her waist so he could use her support in the same manner he would have used his crutch. "My goodness, country life is just full of adventures, isn't it?"

"What in blazes happened?"

The deeply voiced question had Prudence's gaze jerking toward the bank. Again she shaded her eyes against the brilliant sun. Silhouetted in the noonday glare was a man on horseback. Her spirits sank further.

*Sloan Coltrane.*

Drat the wretched man for catching her in such a distressed condition. She so liked to think of herself as competent and in charge. Yet her brief encounters with Amos's nephew continually portrayed her as some kind of... bumbling oaf.

"We are managing adequately, Mr. Coltrane," she informed him crisply. "You may be on your way."

Trying to dismiss his unwelcome intrusion, she balanced herself against the additional burden of Davy's weight and trudged through the slippery mud. Rude sucking sounds accompanied each step. She could feel the gritty river water seeping through her clothing and walking boots, to her bare skin. Davy attempted to assist her efforts by hopping. Unfortunately each hop impaled him deeper in the river's soft base.

"Giddyap."

The husky command sent a bolt of dread sizzling through Prudence. Her gaze jackknifed to the bank.

Coltrane and his big dark horse were barreling down the gravelly slope.

"Wait! What are you doing?" she demanded as great swells of muddy water surged up around her and Davy.

"Coming to the rescue, ma'am."

His arrogant reply incensed her. "I told you I have everything under control!"

"You've got squat, ma'am," he drawled in a tone that was both disrespectful and bored.

Prudence wasn't precisely sure what "squat" was. But it sounded both crude and vulgar.

Before she could voice her protest, however, he was upon them. He leaned over his saddle and looped an arm around Davy's waist, and Prudence had no choice but to release the boy.

The horse's laboring flanks continued to churn the water around her, whipping it to a loathsome, brackish broth. She staggered, lost her balance and fell backward into the river. Too late she remembered to close her mouth as the dirty water flooded in. She fought to regain her footing. Finally, coughing and sputtering, she was able to stand again, and she pushed back the sodden straggles of her hair.

She wanted to rant her indignation at the insufferable man who'd worsened her predicament, but the angry words died when she caught sight of him carefully lowering Davy to the dry ground above her. As much as she hated to admit it, he looked competent and in control as he sat atop his huge horse. And mostly dry, she noticed with a flash of envy.

She gritted her teeth and waded toward the steep gravelly incline that rose between her and the upper bank. Lordy, she dreaded the thought of scaling it with Sloan Coltrane watching her. Though a short climb, it was bound to be a clumsy and awkward one. Her infernal skirts had surely soaked up a ton of river water.

"Stay put, Miss Abercrombie. I'll fetch you."

She continued moving forward. "I'm managing just fine."

"Anyone ever tell you that you're stubborn?"

His patently smug drawl made her cheeks burn. "You'll find that people are generally too polite around here to make such rude observations."

There, she'd put him in his place without losing her temper.

"Is that so?"

She finally made it to the river's edge. The water only reached to her calves. Gingerly, she picked up her drenched skirts and tried to extricate her mired feet from the voracious mud. She had never been so dirty in her entire life! It seemed especially unfair that Sloan Coltrane should witness this aberration of her normally serene existence.

She blocked out his presence and concentrated instead upon negotiating the distance that separated her from the children.

"Miss Prudence, I think you should let Mr. Coltrane help you," Sarah said after a few minutes. Minutes in which Prudence tried and failed to climb more than a couple of inches up the pebbly slope.

"Or maybe I could pull you up," Richard suggested, moving to the edge of the bank.

"No, get back, Richard," Prudence ordered hastily. "We don't want anyone else falling in."

"Giddyap."

She didn't bother to glance upward. Instead she rested her cheek against the dusty incline and closed her eyes. She knew what was coming. Amos's nephew on an unwelcome mission of mercy. She didn't bother to tell him to go back. As much as it galled her to admit it, she did need his help. Just this one last time, she assured herself. Then she was never again going to endure another encounter with Sloan Coltrane. He would stay on his property, and she would stay on hers.

"Open your eyes, Miss Abercrombie."

Husky male amusement coated the deeply timbred command. With a sigh of resignation, Prudence did as ordered. And there he was—big and intrusive, extending his wide, competent hand. The brim of his lowered hat concealed his expression, but she just knew he was laughing at her. To her shattered composure, it seemed even his horse wore a look of derision.

She had two choices. She could reject his offer, thereby prolonging her ignominious efforts to climb the steep bank while he looked on, or she could end things quickly by accepting his hand and allowing him to pull her onto his horse as he had Davy. She nibbled her lower lip. It wasn't an easy decision, though the grainy taste of river water did assist her in making up her mind.

"Thank you," she said through clenched teeth.

"You're welcome," he replied, leaning over and sweeping her upward.

Various impressions ran riot through Prudence. First and foremost, she was aware of Sloan Coltrane's strength. Beneath the cotton material of his shirt, his hardened muscles worked with seemingly little effort as he lifted her to him. Her second thought was that by allowing him to hold her so closely, she was transferring a significant portion of mud from her to him. It seemed such an intimate thing to do. Get him dirty. A hot flush seared her skin. They were touching in so many places! Her back to his rigid chest. His arm draped with shocking boldness just beneath her breasts. Her backside resting against his lower person.

"Hold on, Miss Abercrombie," he breathed into her ear.

And she had no choice but to turn and wrap her arms around his neck. Then she hung on for dear life as he spurred his horse up the slippery slope. His mount's hooves dug into the shaley soil with lurching blows that threatened to shake her from her unconventional perch. She wasn't afraid of falling—Coltrane's grip was unyielding. Prudence pressed her face against his shoulder. Her nostrils tingled at his frankly male scent. She wondered if the pounding she heard in her eardrum was the thud of his heartbeat or the crazed cadence of her own wild pulse.

For the space of seconds, Coltrane and the tumultuous trip upward became Prudence's entire world. She could think of nothing save the man who held her in his relentless embrace and the wild beast that bore them to the summit. Then as abruptly as it had begun, the journey was over. They had arrived at the top of the bank.

The horse's sides heaved from its mighty exertion. Breathing noisily, it snorted great gusts of air through its flared nostrils. Prudence was breathing heavily, too, though she hoped she wasn't snorting or heaving. Instead, when they finally came to a stop, it seemed as if every muscle in her body was pulsating. She couldn't seem to loosen her death grip upon Coltrane's neck, even though she knew it was time to do so.

"Miss Abercrombie?"

She struggled to compose herself. Still the power of speech eluded her.

"Miss Abercrombie, it's over," he said with unexpected gentleness. "You can let go."

She nodded against his shoulder and tried to relax her grip. Her hands seemed to have a will of their own, however, and she continued to cling to him.

"Ma'am, we're going to take this nice and easy." His broad palm stroked her back. "First of all, you need to open your eyes."

She hadn't realized she'd closed them again. Under the soothing stroke of his hand, she felt herself begin to relax. Gradually her eyes did open. With her nose buried in his shoulder, only a margin of her surroundings lightened.

"There now, that's better, isn't it?"

She tipped her face and found herself staring deeply into Coltrane's glinting eyes. She lost the ability to breathe. She'd never been so close to a man in her life. His hard, bristly jaw, his narrow lips, his chiseled nose, his penetrating gaze that decimated the remnants of her composure. Her mouth went dry as she stared mutely at him.

"Do you think you can stand?"

*Stand?*

*Oh.*

*Of course. As in stand up.*

She'd been able to do that for as long as she could remember. At the moment, however, her legs felt as substantial as partially churned butter.

"I'm fine." The words may have lacked conviction, but they steadied her.

"Sure you are," he said softly. "Let's ride back to the children, and they'll see just how fine you are."

The children? Ride back? For the first time, Prudence took note of their surroundings. She realized the momentum of Coltrane's horse had carried them several yards past Sarah and Richard. His shoulders sagging, Davy sat slumped on the ground. Without his crutch, he was unable to walk. Her arms fell from her rescuer's chest.

A terrible sense of guilt overwhelmed her. How could she have forgotten Davy's predicament for even a moment? He would be feeling awful without the crutch. She knew it embarrassed him terribly when the other children were reminded of his withered leg. The guilt grew. She should have noticed the danger Davy was in and called him back from the bank's edge. Failing that, she should have been able to save both him and the crutch.

"Yes, let's ride back to the children," she said woodenly.

"There's two things you need to know about the country, Miss Abercrombie."

*And I'm sure you're just dying to tell me. . . .*

She tried unsuccessfully to shift her position so she wasn't jammed up so tightly against Coltrane's hard chest.

"First off, there's a lot of erosion around these parts," he continued in that lazy drawl of his. "We don't get a lot of rain. But when we do, it comes down hard and mean. Most of the time that little puddle you fell into is only spit-deep. After a rain though, it turns into a raging river. The crest can even jump its banks. That's what causes the eroding. Keep the children away from this part of the river."

How she hated being lectured by him! Still, she was no fool. She took his advice to heart, though she did need to correct him about one point.

"I didn't fall in. I jumped."

"You *jumped?*"

His obvious incredulity pleased her. It was nice to know the laconic cowboy was human enough to be surprised by something.

"It was the quickest way to get to him."

"How did you plan on getting him back up the bank?"

"I would have thought of something . . . eventually."

"You've got to think ahead, Miss Abercrombie," he chided, clearly not impressed by her initiative. "It's the things that don't seem dangerous that can kill you."

She endured his pithy insights about western living with barely suppressed impatience. She didn't appreciate being lectured as if she were a child instead of an adult.

The heavy arm beneath her breasts tightened as Coltrane shifted his position, drawing her more intimately against him. Instinctively she wriggled away from the shockingly bold contact, trying to erect a respectable distance between her body and his. Draped sideways across his horse, however, she was practically sitting on his lap!

"Relax, we're almost there," he admonished, as if reading her thoughts.

"What's the second?" she asked in a rush, wanting to deflect his thoughts and hers from their near embrace.

"Second what?" he asked softly.

Again, she was certain his deep voice contained a thread of amusement. "You said there were two things I needed to know to stay alive out here."

The man seemed to make a habit of thinking in twos, she reflected gloomily, recalling he'd had a dual purpose for trying to waylay her before she moved into Amos's house.

"The second is that being reckless can get you killed faster than anything I know," he said, his voice devoid of its earlier humor.

"Reckless?" she sputtered in astonishment.

"You better make sure you can save yourself before you decide to save someone else," he growled as they reached the children and came to a stop.

"I was hardly in danger of drowning," she reminded him.

"Not today," he conceded, securing his large hands around her waist. "You might not be so lucky next time."

With a suddenness that made her breath lock in her throat, Coltrane lowered her from his horse and onto the solid ground. She took a couple of shaky steps, then paused and looked over her shoulder.

"What makes you think there's going to be a next time?"

Coltrane eased himself from his saddle and led his horse toward her. "There's some things a man just knows, Miss Abercrombie. Call it instinct."

She'd been right all along. The insufferable man *was* mocking her! Well, she had better things to do than listen to the barely concealed laughter in his irritating, western drawl.

"Davy, are you all right?" she asked in concern as she knelt beside the silent boy.

"He didn't break anything, and he's breathing fine," Richard told her.

"His color's back," Sarah offered. "But he'd probably be more comfortable in some dry clothes."

His head bowed, Davy remained silent. He truly was a mess, Prudence thought compassionately. Streaked with mud, his dirty hair was matted to his scalp. Her heart went out to him. Yet it wasn't like Davy to let a dunk in a river leave him so downcast.

"Why don't you stand back and give him some air" came Coltrane's gruff voice from behind her.

She stiffened, then glanced up. His expression was grim. She noticed that his clothing, too, was now liberally smeared with mud. Then, for the first time, she became fully aware of her own filthy state. Under the blazing sun, her black dress was quickly drying, but the cotton material was caked with a crusty layer of dirt. Talk about messes! She probably looked a fright. Her hand went automatically to her hair. Every bit of it had sprung loose from the twist she'd arranged it in that morning. She could feel muddy tangles and even a twig or two trapped in the slimy mass. Her face was probably as streaked with grime as Davy's.

It was vanity, of course, to consider her appearance at a time like this, but she couldn't help herself. This man had called her a spinster, thereby branding her as being unattractive and undesirable. At the moment, the hurtful words certainly described her.

"We're managing—"

"Just fine," he interrupted with a heavy sigh. "You've told me that before. But what this boy needs is less fussing and more fresh air."

Prudence opened her mouth to tell Coltrane to mind his own business, but before she could do so, he muscled his way between her and Davy.

"Looks like the river got the better of you today, son," he observed conversationally as he hunkered down beside the glum-faced boy.

"Now, see here," Prudence began again. "We don't need—"

Coltrane turned his head. "Why don't you go back to the house and—" his gaze flicked over her "—wash up? You might mean well, but you're in the way here."

*In the way?*

A blade of hot anger sliced through her. She couldn't remember the last time she'd been so furious. She was, after all, the most even-tempered person she knew. Yet this man had her wanting to curse at him before God Almighty *and* the children.

Years of good breeding, however, could not be abandoned in an outburst of temper. She mentally counted to ten. Then to twenty. She'd reached twenty-seven when Coltrane rose abruptly, taking the subdued boy with him.

"You do much riding, son?"

Davy's eyes became the size of Gladys's flapjacks as he looped a mud-splattered sleeve around Coltrane's neck. "No—no, sir."

"Then you're in for a treat."

He carried the clearly awestruck boy to his horse and slid him onto the animal's back. Davy teetered precariously before catching his balance on the saddle horn.

"Hold on," Coltrane instructed matter-of-factly as he mounted behind the boy.

Prudence had no idea if Davy complied, because the two were already on their way to the house.

Several thoughts struck her at once. First, Amos's nephew had been wrong when he'd called her reckless. She didn't have a reckless bone in her body. Many were the times her aunts had told her that she was exactly like her name, prudent. Next, by giving Davy a ride to the house, Coltrane had spared the boy the embarrassment of hobbling there with her and Richard's help. Such attentiveness and compassion on Coltrane's part was surprising. In all fairness, she reluctantly admitted to herself that the good Samaritan was a stranger—she didn't know him well enough to judge the true nature of his character.

As the sun beat down upon her and a nearby fly buzzed overhead, Prudence's physical discomfort grew. From her toes to her scalp, every inch began to itch as the drying dirt chafed her skin.

"It sure was lucky that Mr. Coltrane showed up," Sarah said after a few minutes of silent walking.

*Lucky* was hardly the word Prudence would have used, but she refrained from saying so.

"We've got to be more careful around here," Richard said thoughtfully. "You shouldn't have jumped into the river after Davy."

"I know," she acknowledged bleakly. It was a bitter pill to swallow that Richard and Sloan Coltrane were in complete accord on that point.

As she looked at Coltrane's departing back, she realized the blasted man still had his hat on. Somehow that fact proved the most disheartening of all. Here she was, completely covered in river mud and drying out like an adobe brick on two feet, and he was scarcely the worse for wear.

What a lovely experience it would have been to see the overly confident stranger as disheveled and miserable as she was.

"You're awfully quiet, son. You're not nervous about riding Lucky, are you?"

"No—no, sir."

"You can call me Sloan."

"I don't think Miss Prudence would think that was proper," the boy said quietly.

"No, I don't suppose she would," Sloan agreed.

"Do you think..."

The scrawny boy shuddered against Sloan.

"Do I think what?"

"Do you think she'll send me away now?"

Sloan's heart took a direct hit. "You mean Miss Prudence?"

Davy nodded.

"Because you caused such a ruckus by falling into the river?"

The boy jerked his head in another sharp nod. Sloan remembered what it had been like when word had reached the ranch that his father had been killed in the war. Sloan had been twelve. Nearly a man. He'd felt as if his entire world had come crashing down around him. His stepmother, usually a tower of strength, had sat in the parlor, weeping openly. Alicia and Lenore were there and crying, too. The memory was starkly etched in his mind. The young girls in their Sunday best, clinging to their mother's skirts. Jeremy, just a baby then, somehow managing to sleep through the disturbance.

Sloan had stood in the doorway at the time, a lump the size of Texas stuck in his throat, wanting to offer comfort but not knowing how. He'd vowed then that he'd take care of his family. That he wouldn't let his father down. That he would learn how to run the ranch, the men and the cattle. Oh, there had been a part of him that had wanted to run off and enlist and blast the hearts out of as many Yankees as he could sight in his Winchester rifle. But he'd stayed. Shouldered the load. Because that's what a man did.

As devastated as he'd been by his father's death, however, he'd never once feared that he would be sent away. Like most folks, he'd taken for granted that there would be a place for him at the family table until he was old enough to make it on his own. He glanced at the scrawny lad perched in front of him and experienced a tug of sympathy. By no stretch of the imagination could this crippled child be expected to survive in the world by himself.

"Miss Prudence doesn't strike me as the kind of woman who would send away someone for getting into a spot of mischief. Your tumble into the river was an accident. You didn't do it on purpose, did you?"

"No..."

"Well then, there you go," Sloan said encouragingly. "It was an accident pure and simple."

"Miss Prudence jumped in," Davy informed him, his young voice filled with obvious admiration. "You should have seen her, splashing around something fierce. It was a real sight, Mr. Coltrane."

"I'm sure it was," Sloan concurred dryly, sorry he'd arrived after that part of the adventure was over. "It wasn't very smart of her to come after you, Davy," he felt compelled to point out. "She should have found a rope or a branch to lower down to you. If the water had been deeper and the current faster, you both would have been in trouble."

It didn't surprise Sloan that he was lecturing again. After acting as a substitute father for Alicia, Lenore and Jeremy, he'd become an expert on dispensing advice. That was one of the reasons he'd left home. He was tired of being responsible for everyone's welfare. He'd come to Port Dodd to do some serious hell-raising, not wipe the noses of a bunch of ragtag orphans.

"I guess Miss Prudence kinda lost her head," the boy confided gravely. "She saw me in the water and jumped in before she thought things through." He ducked his head. "It was sure brave of her, don't you think?"

The kid had a point. Miss Abercrombie *had* displayed an admirable dose of courage by plunging into the river to rescue the frail child. Just not much sense.

Sloan resisted mentioning his reservations to his young passenger. Better to let the boy's confidence in his guardian remain unshaken. He didn't want Davy to start worrying about being sent away again.

"She's got real western grit, all right," Sloan admitted aloud.

"We don't got much money," the boy said softly.

"Don't you?"

Sloan didn't figure Miss Abercrombie was in any financial trouble. After all, Amos had left her his farmhouse and a small parcel of surrounding acreage free and clear. The philanthropic gesture shouldn't have surprised Sloan. If he'd been thinking straight, he would have remembered his uncle was a remarkably generous man.

"I lost my crutch." There was an audible gulp, as if the boy were holding back tears. "It was made special just for me in St. Louis, Missouri. I used to have an old stick, but Miss Prudence said it wasn't good enough for me. So...so she saved up and sent away to a fancy hospital, and...and they built it and... and sent it on a train all the way here. It was practically brand new. And I lost it...."

"You'll get another crutch," Sloan promised through gritted teeth, unnerved by the strong swell of sympathy the boy's words unloosed within him.

"I sure hope so," Davy murmured. "We burned up my old stick."

They reached the house. Sloan dismounted and helped Davy down. He didn't let go of him. Instead, he carried the boy to the door, knocked twice and then stepped inside. Gladys Stumple entered the front parlor, drying her hands on her white apron.

"What on earth?" she exclaimed in amazement.

"I fell into the river," Davy said in a small voice. "Mr. Coltrane pulled me out."

"Well landsakes, you're a fine mess. We better get you into a tub full of hot water before you start growing corn in your ears."

"Where do you want him?" Sloan inquired, smothering a grin.

The housekeeper had a fiery gleam in her eyes that suggested she was looking forward to waging battle against the layers of hardening mud coating the boy. Clearly she was the kind of woman who liked a challenge. Sloan had the feeling that Davy was going to be scrubbed within an inch of his young life.

"Bring him onto the back porch," she commanded briskly as she unbuttoned her cuffs and rolled up her sleeves. "Now, don't you fret, child, we'll have you clean in no time at all."

A look of resignation filled the boy's dark eyes. Sloan bit back a chuckle. All things considered, he figured the kid probably preferred his actual dunking to the scrubbing that lay ahead.

"I'd be glad to haul the water for you," Sloan offered, trailing after the woman.

"There's no need," she answered absently. "Amos installed an indoor hand pump." She led Sloan through the kitchen and onto the back porch where she dragged a chair across the wood-planked floor. "Set Davy down here, and I'll fetch the washtub."

Sloan did as ordered. Before he could offer to move the heavy tub for her, the industrious woman was already lowering it into position. He decided Gladys Stumple was as big and capable as most men.

"Appears to me that you need a good washing, too," she observed, eyeing him with the same kind of deliberate purpose she'd displayed toward the boy.

Sloan tipped his hat. "I was just leaving, ma'am."

"Goodbye, Mr. Coltrane," Davy said. A sudden sparkle lit his brown eyes. "Thanks for the ride. It was the best I ever had."

It was probably the *only* ride the boy had ever experienced. A new thought struck Sloan. If he hurried, he might just have a chance of pulling it off.

## Chapter Four

By the time Prudence and the others made it back to the house, Mr. Coltrane had gone and Davy was up to his ears in soapy water. Prudence had been driven crazy with itching as she waited for her turn to wash. But now, a couple of hours later, she was fully refreshed. Her wet hair hung in a single braid that dampened the back of her oldest and most worn gown. She had only one corset, and it was now soaking in a pan of hot water on the stove. It surprised her how much she enjoyed the unexpected sensation of freedom she experienced without the constraining garment.

As she padded across the parlor in her stocking feet, carrying a freshly brewed cup of tea, it almost seemed as if the tumultuous episode at the river hadn't occurred. Except, of course, that Davy was without his crutch and had no easy means of exploring their new home as the other children were doing this very moment under Gladys's watchful eye. He'd been asleep when she'd checked on him a few minutes ago.

She sat in an overlarge chair. Its worn maroon covering made it fit with the room's other mismatched furnishings. She lifted the cup of steamy tea and inhaled the delicate aroma of chamomile. First thing tomorrow, she would take the wagon into town and see Harvey Lexbedder. Surely the carpenter would be able to fashion another crutch for the boy. The device might not have a padded cushion or be as lightly weighted as the lost one, but it would be better than the stick he'd once been consigned to using.

She sipped her tea. Everything would work out fine. Her gaze drifted across their new parlor. She noticed the center picture was slightly askew. Sighing, she sat down her cup and rose. It took only a moment to straighten the tilted frame. As she stepped back to examine her efforts, she nodded in satisfaction. That was how things should be. Neat and orderly. Not chaotic as today had been.

She reasoned that a simple move to the country shouldn't have turned hers and the children's lives upside down. Surely today had been out of the ordinary. Tomorrow would be different. They wouldn't be coping with rattlesnakes, muddy rivers and rude cowboys.

Rude cowboys...

Sloan Coltrane.

Had there ever been a more annoying, exasperating individual? Prudence returned to her chair, picked up her teacup and frowned. She searched her memory for another man who had so upset her usual composure. No other image from her past replaced his. Well, she was done with him. Finished. She recalled his last bit of pompous advice. Imagine him telling her that she was *reckless*. The man was not only irritating, he was a fool.

She looked around the parlor again, pleased to observe nothing amiss. She swallowed the last few drops of tea, then stood and headed for the kitchen. Supper was going to be leftover chicken and dumplings. While Gladys was showing the children the barn and chicken coop, Prudence intended to stoke the fire in the wood-burning stove, fetch the chicken stew from the springhouse and have the stew ready to eat when they returned.

She'd placed several pieces of kindling inside the wood well when she heard a knock at the back door. She started in surprise. Now that they lived in the country, she hardly anticipated unannounced company.

Curious, she flung open the door.

She blinked twice, to make certain she wasn't imagining the unexpected visitor. There before her stood Sloan Coltrane, looking vastly different from how he'd appeared when he'd ridden from the farm a couple hours earlier.

Grim-faced and seemingly more heavily whiskered, he glared down at her. Huge splotches of dried mud covered him. She also noticed that he was hatless.

"What on earth happened to you?"

"I had another run-in with the river."

"But I thought you were returning to town," she said, astonished by the much-transformed sight of him.

"I had some business to take care of first."

"Business? With the river?" she asked, thoroughly confused.

He nodded. "That's right."

It was obvious Sloan Coltrane was in an abominable mood. His eyebrows were drawn into a malevolent scowl. His bristled jaw looked as if it was clenched tightly enough to split down the middle. And his eyes . . . Lordy, his eyes were shooting sparks. She retreated a step from the open door, not certain she should invite him inside.

"Here," he said tersely. "See that Davy gets this."

Her bewildered gaze dropped to his outstretched hands that gripped Davy's crutch. The sight brought a strange fullness to her chest. She could only imagine the effort it had taken Mr. Coltrane to ride alongside the murky river, searching for the missing article. That he'd spent the last few hours performing such a selfless act made her uncomfortable. After all, she'd occupied the better portion of the afternoon thinking dire thoughts about him.

"I—I don't know what to say." She accepted the cherrywood crutch, noticing he had taken the time to wash most of the river's filth from the wood and padded armrest. Her eyes returned to his. "Except, thank you, of course."

His rugged expression remained hard-edged. "You're welcome."

"This will mean the world to Davy," she felt compelled to add, wondering if the man had any idea how important the crutch was to the boy. "He's upstairs. Would you like to take it to him so he can thank you himself?"

"There's no need for that." Coltrane glanced at his mud-caked boots, then to her. "Besides, I'd track a mile of dirt through your place."

He was right about that, she thought, surveying his long legs and broad shoulders. He must have fallen into the river somehow. No other explanation would suffice for his incredibly soiled state. She bit her lip against inquiring about those details or pressing him to personally deliver the crutch to Davy. Despite his act of charity, Coltrane's eyes were cold and hard. The truth was, he resembled nothing so much as a man bent on completing an unpleasant chore.

She had no intention of detaining him.

"Well then, I'll thank you on Davy's behalf."

"You already have," Coltrane drawled.

Beneath the weight of her braid, Prudence felt the fine hairs at the nape of her neck rise. Something about this man's astonishingly deep voice continued to devastate her peace of mind.

As they stood staring at each other, she waited for him to turn and leave. Instead, he continued to look deeply into her eyes. What did he see? What held his unwavering attention? Her appearance was nothing even remotely exceptional. She wondered if he was taking a silent measure of his enemy, the enemy he intended to evict from his late uncle's farm. She licked her lips, trying to think of something socially acceptable to say that would break the unnatural stillness of this bizarre encounter.

"You could offer me a cup of coffee."

"W-what?"

Her brains were as scrambled as the eggs Gladys cooked for them each Saturday.

"Coffee," he repeated softly. "I'd appreciate a cup before the ride back to town."

"Oh."

For some reason the subtle gentling of his formerly harsh expression made her nervous. "Will tea do?"

"Do what?" came his lazy drawl.

"Satisfy you," she said, unnerved by his suddenly obscure manner.

Something about her answer seemed to amuse him. She was certain she saw his lips twitch.

"I guess I'll find out."

"You sound as if you've never tasted tea before," she muttered lamely, moving from the doorway to allow him to enter the kitchen. With a start, she realized she was still gripping Davy's crutch. She leaned it against the wall and stalked to the stove. The kindling she'd placed in it had caught and burned enthusiastically. She carried the white ceramic teakettle to the hand pump and refilled it. Then she sat the kettle on the stove, hoping it would boil in record time.

She moved aside the pan of grayish water in which her stays soaked. When she turned to face Coltrane, she was intensely conscious that she wasn't wearing her corset beneath her dress. Each step she took caused her upper body to bounce. Before Coltrane's arrival she'd enjoyed the sense of freedom, but his presence made her uncomfortable at her unencumbered state. His piercing eyes were so observant that at times she had the feeling he could see right through her garments.

She crossed her arms protectively in front of her dress and continued to eye with dismay the imposing man who stood in the center of the room. A muddy trail of large footprints followed him from the door and stopped beneath his worn boots.

"Sorry about the mess," he said. "I don't expect you to invite me to sit down. I'll just have a cup of that tea and be on my way."

She nodded, her mind suddenly blank. If ever there was a time for a bit of social chitchat, this was it. Unfortunately she couldn't think of anything intelligent to say. The silence stretched between them. She supposed she could always thank him again for tracking down Davy's crutch, but she hated to repeat herself.

*Boil,* she silently ordered the uncooperative water in the kettle on the stove.

"So you drink tea," he observed reflectively. "Is that because you're from England?"

At last, a mundane topic they could discuss without them coming to blows. It stung her pride that he'd been the one to come up with the neutral subject. "That's correct. I come from a long line of tea drinkers," she continued doggedly, refusing to let the tense silence spring up between them again. "I suppose you've always preferred coffee?"

"A man likes to drink something with a little bite to it," he said agreeably.

"Like an unruly puppy?" she mused dryly.

There was a flicker of something in his silvery eyes. That something, whatever it was, caused her toes to curl against the wood-planked floor.

"Of course, if a man is of a mind to sample a really strong drink, his choice is generally whiskey."

She wrinkled her nose. "I've never tasted whiskey, but if it's anything like coffee, I probably wouldn't like it."

He coughed. "Somehow I can't picture a woman like you tossing back a shot of whiskey."

The sudden shrill of the teakettle spared her the necessity of saying anything further. Relieved that their conversation was almost at an end, she removed the kettle from the stove. She opened the cupboard that housed an assortment of battered cups and surreptitiously sought the least chipped of the lot. Her quest was rewarded with a fine yellow vessel that still possessed its handle. She dropped in a few tea leaves, then filled the cheery cup with steaming water. Another quick foray into the cupboard elicited a pretty shell pink saucer. All the while she was aware of Sloan Coltrane's probing stare.

She drew a fortifying breath, then turned to face him. "Here you go."

He glanced down at his dirt-streaked hands. "Maybe I better wash before I get anything else dirty."

A flush climbed to her cheeks. Where were her manners? She should have been the one to suggest he avail himself of the hand pump at the sink.

"Go ahead," she said simply, sitting the cup and saucer on the table. "There's a bar of soap on the sideboard next to the pump. I'll get you a towel."

She opened the deep drawer containing their meager supply of towels, deliberately seeking one without any holes in it. From the corner of her eye, she saw Coltrane prime the pump. Then three grating clangs sounded in rapid succession.

After an initial trickle, the cold water gushed out. In no time at all, he worked up a lather from the lye soap. Riveted, Prudence found herself unable to look away from him as he washed his powerful hands. The gritty bar of soap virtually disappeared within his palms.

Without an invitation from her to do so, he ducked his head under the stream of water until it ran in rivulets down the rugged angles and planes of his face. Earlier that day, he'd performed the same amenities outside. She'd thought little of it. But now, trapped within the same room with him, the ritual seemed both shockingly private and strangely enticing.

"I could use that towel now."

His deep voice spurred her into action. She crossed the kitchen and thrust the faded scrap of material at him.

With an economy of motion, he scrubbed it across his face, then dried his hands. "I feel almost human again."

Prudence said nothing. But she thought he looked more manly, more...splendidly human than any other male she'd ever met.

Abruptly, she remembered that he was her foe, that he wanted to evict her and the children from his late uncle's farm. More disheartening was the memory of his hurtful words in the parlor. He'd called her a spinster. His opinion on that matter had been most direct. He considered her plain and undesirable.

She went to the table and picked up the cup and saucer. "Your tea."

He set the towel aside and reached for it. She noticed that like the bar of soap, the cup and saucer also seemed to disappear inside his broad palms. Incomprehensibly, a shiver tingled along her spine.

He raised the cup to his lips and looked over the rim before drinking. "I guess it can't taste any worse than river water."

She watched him swallow. A mighty scowl seized his countenance.

"I don't mean to be rude, but this stuff tastes like sh...er...I mean it doesn't taste right," he finished weakly.

"Oh! I forgot the sugar," she said contritely. Well, she'd had a lot on her mind, she told herself. It was a perfectly natural mistake to make. It wasn't as if she'd deliberately tried to sabotage his drink.

She picked up a spoon and went to the sugar bowl. She scooped up a generous serving of granules, then cautiously approached the frowning man who towered above her.

"Let me sweeten it for you."

He lowered the cup, and she dropped the sugar into the black tea. She didn't like standing so close to him. He made her uneasy. Still, she took a moment to stir the cup's contents for him. It seemed the least she could do.

She couldn't help noticing his broad chest. It seemed incredible to her that she'd actually been pressed against it when he'd carried her on horseback from the river. The kitchen was silent again. Except for the sound of her breathing. Except for the sound of her heart beating. Except for the sound of the spoon striking the sides of the cup. She felt his breath against the top of her head. This was a far more intimate experience than watching him wash his hands, she realized.

She stepped back, holding on to the spoon as if it were something extremely important that she dare not misplace. "Try it now."

Again he raised the cup to his lips, sipping with noticeable hesitation.

"Better," he growled softly. "It tastes like something my Aunt Eleanor would serve."

"You have an aunt?" Prudence didn't know why the information startled her. Perhaps because Sloan Coltrane seemed so complete and independent.

"What kind of question is that?" he demanded, his manner again hostile. "Of course I have family. It's not as if I was hatched under some rock, you know."

She'd insulted him, she realized with a ripple of shock. Somehow she hadn't thought it possible to wound a man as tough and hard as Coltrane appeared to be.

"It wasn't my intention to be unkind," she said mildly.

His narrowed gaze continued to hold her as he finished the tea, then lowered the cup and saucer to the table.

"I didn't come here merely to return Davy's crutch and drink your tea," he said quietly.

At once Prudence felt her guard go up. Had he come to insist she sell him the farm? Or was he merely here to offer a few more insults?

She braced herself. "You didn't?"

Sloan stared long and hard into Prudence Abercrombie's suspicious green eyes. She acted as if he was going to draw a gun on her. It was his own fault, he acknowledged. He'd put his foot in his mouth more than once around the peculiar woman. There was just something about her that rubbed him the wrong way.

Maybe it was the drab, unappealing clothing she seemed to prefer. Like the godawful dress she had on right now. The only good thing about it was that it'd been through so many washings the color had faded from black to a gun-metal gray. The neck was high enough to satisfy the most vigilant stickler of modesty. The cuffs were buttoned snugly around her wrists, so tightly that even a rambunctious gust of wind wouldn't have an easy time of getting inside. Her waist was trim enough to tempt a man's embrace, but the miserable excuse of the gown she wore gave no evidence of the fact.

That was probably her intention, to use her nondescript clothing as a kind of No Trespassing sign to warn off any man stupid enough to want to get close to her and sample the naked softness of her prissy little mouth. She probably would be horrified to know a man was even thinking about her firmly pressed lips in such a familiar manner. That horror would surely change to outrage if she knew how much he was enjoying the way her breasts jostled beneath her prim bodice.

It had taken him less than a minute to notice that he'd caught Prudence Abercrombie without her maidenly underpinnings, and despite the dress that did everything it could to mask her female form, he was aware of every inch of her body. His challenge, as he saw it, was to finish his business with the prickly woman without betraying what was on his mind.

"I asked you a question," she said, her manner imperious.

Her attempt to bully him failed by virtue of the fact she stood before him with only thoroughly mended stockings covering her dainty feet. He resisted the ridiculous impulse to buy her some new stockings when he returned to town. He could only imagine the kind of righteous indignation a woman like her would visit upon any male crazy enough to offer her such a personal gift. She'd probably order a warrant for his arrest.

"I came here to give you the apology you deserve."

An expression of utter amazement crossed her delicate features. He tried not to feel insulted that she thought him so low as to be incapable of remorse.

"For what?"

"I had no business calling you a spinster," he said levelly.

A bright splash of color washed across her cheeks. "Oh...that."

He'd never seen a woman actually wring her hands, but Miss Abercrombie was doing so right now. Motivated by something he didn't understand, he crossed the kitchen and captured those restless hands.

"I had no right to say that to you," he continued quietly. "You're doing a fine job with these children, and you deserve praise, not contempt, for your efforts."

Her head was bent, and he was unable to read the expression in her eyes. The sweet fragrance of her freshly washed hair drifted to him. He inhaled the scent, her scent, into his lungs and held his breath for a moment before releasing it.

He realized she was trembling. He wondered how often she'd allowed herself to be touched by a man. With all those No Trespassing signs she'd posted, he suspected not many.

"There's no need to apologize for speaking the truth."

At first Sloan wasn't sure he'd heard her correctly. He opened his mouth to ask her what the hell she meant, but he never got the words out.

"It's Mr. Coltrane's horse. I'd recognize it anywhere," piped a youthful voice.

Seconds later Charlie and Charlotte, Sarah, Richard and Gladys Stumple barged into the room.

"Hello, Mr. Coltrane," Charlie said cheerfully, before looking at Prudence Abercrombie. "When's supper?"

"I was just about to fix it," she answered.

Sloan was surprised to catch the hint of a stammer in her aristocratic voice. He glanced to the stove where something gray and grainy floated in an oversize pot. Not exactly a dish to perk up a man's appetite.

Charlie's gaze followed Sloan's, and the boy stepped to the stove where he sniffed the pot's contents. "Doesn't smell too good."

He didn't think it was possible, but Prudence's cheeks became even pinker. "That's not it," she protested. "I was about to warm up the chicken and dumplings we had earlier."

"Then what's that?" Charlie asked curiously, echoing Sloan's selfsame question.

"That's some of Miss Prudence's . . . unmentionables,"

Gladys informed the boy, her tone chiding. "Now, we all have to wash up before we eat, so let's get a move on."

"It's going to take a month of Sundays before Mr. Coltrane will be able to eat, then," Charlotte said, her little nose wrinkled disapprovingly.

"You're even dirtier than before," Janey observed in a voice sweet enough to charm the birds from the trees.

Sloan groaned inwardly. No matter what he did, he seemed destined to make a poor impression on Miss Abercrombie's flock.

"He searched along the river to find Davy's crutch," she explained.

"You must have fallen in," Richard observed.

"Did you?" Charlie demanded. "Did Lucky buck you off?"

"Mr. Coltrane couldn't get thrown off a bucking bronco," Janey countered loyally.

"Anyone can get thrown," Richard said. "You just have to get right back on when it happens."

"Well, what did happen to you?" Charlie asked, pressing again for an explanation.

All eyes turned to Sloan. Mentally cussing himself for not leaving sooner so as to avoid this showdown, he straightened to his full height and decided to take his medicine like a man.

"Lucky tossed me into the brink," he admitted, tucking his thumbs into his pockets as he leaned forward on the balls of his feet.

"You tracked mud across Miss Gladys's freshly mopped floor," Janey revealed to him, as if informing him of a grave crime.

"You'll have to clean it up now," Charlie said sadly. "That's the rule."

Sloan wondered which one of them was going to hand him the mop. He'd obviously toppled in their estimation from gunslinger to floor scrubber.

"He'll have to have a bath first," Charlotte pointed out, a purposeful glint filling her eyes. Her determined look was uncannily similar to the one with which Gladys Stumple had viewed Davy. "Or else he'll just get everything even dirtier."

"The tub's on the back porch," Charlie told him, in case Sloan might have forgotten.

"The young'uns are right," Miss Gladys said. "You definitely need a bath."

Even though Sloan had the feeling he'd have better luck challenging a judge's final verdict than going against Prudence Abercrombie's housekeeper, he decided to try. After all, his goal had been to return Davy's crutch, not get sucked into this tight little circle of misfits. Besides, he still had every intention of getting them off this farm and back into town. His plans for this land simply wouldn't accommodate a bunch of motherless children running wild across the place.

His gaze flicked to Prudence. She was watching him with a knowing expression in her eyes, as if she knew what he was going to say before he said it. He didn't like the idea of her being able to get inside his head and read his thoughts. His thoughts weren't any of her business, he told himself. A reluctant flash of honesty made him admit that he didn't want her knowing just how ignoble some of those thoughts were. He was just a simple man with simple wants.

He wanted to enjoy life and what it had to offer. Fast horses. Good whiskey. Lucky cards. Fat cigars. And frisky women.

Not a single one of his plans involved him getting a bath in this makeshift orphanage. He'd returned the crutch. He'd offered his damned apology. And, even though the stubborn woman hadn't exactly accepted it, he was ready to return to town.

He made the mistake of looking down at the row of expectant faces waiting for his answer. Of course, the oldest boy, Richard, didn't looked particularly thrilled to have him hanging around, but everyone else was looking at him as if his staying to wash up and have supper with them meant something. Or maybe they were just determined to see him mop the floor.

He scrubbed his palm across his whiskers. It was going to be a long, miserable ride to town covered in all this dried mud. He remembered how good Miss Gladys's dumplings had tasted. Just like his stepmother's. Not that he was the least bit homesick. He'd been more than happy to break away from the unrelenting demands of his family. Still, it was a dramatic change to be completely on his own.

But even a man who enjoyed his own company could appreciate a bit of offered hospitality. Another thought struck Sloan. Maybe Prudence Abercrombie didn't want to know how much he was willing to pay for the farm, but these urchins might see things differently. They might like having a potful of money and a house in town. During supper he might just casually mention the amount he planned on offering their guardian.

# Chapter Five

$S$everal things struck Sloan as he took his bath in the washtub on the back porch: Prudence Abercrombie probably had only one pair of shoes and that was why she was walking around the place in her stocking feet. The gray and grainy thing he'd seen floating in the pot on the stove was no doubt her corset, which she also probably had only one of. And he was thinking too damned much about her.

He had a new life and a racetrack to concentrate on. The sooner he got her and her orphans off the farm, the sooner he'd be able to get on with what he'd come to Port Dodd to do.

He hunched forward to run the lathered washcloth between his toes. Without so much as a by-your-leave, the thought of Prudence sitting in the same tub and performing the same act crept into Sloan's imagination. Her toes were probably dainty and pink and each one smaller than his little finger. He thought of the rest of her, remembering well the shape of her legs outlined through her drenched gown. He looked at the bar of soap he'd rubbed across his body and pictured her running that same bar across her breasts. They'd be slick and soapy. Maybe not very big, but they'd feel soft and slippery against his palm. Her nipples would be hard and—

Sloan rose abruptly from the tub. The woman had put some kind of hex on him. There was no other explanation for the way she kept sneaking into his thoughts. Well, he'd had enough of her. Enough of her well-scrubbed face and provocative mouth. Enough of her sharp-tongued words and siren voice. Enough of her plain, ugly clothes and tempting body.

He was a man with a mission, and no *spinster,* no matter how purely female, was going to defeat him. He dried himself quickly as he planned his next move. He would use those kids and her obvious affection for them to accomplish his goal. There was no way she could hold her stubborn resolve against both him and the children. Hell, maybe he could win Gladys Stumple over to his side, too. He'd been told he had a way with women.

A short time later as he sat at the supper table with the entire brood, Sloan tried to ignore Prudence's presence next to him. He discovered it wasn't easy. She was back to sneaking peeks at him again. He couldn't seem to get comfortable in his chair. He didn't know what kind of perfume she wore, but it had a dangerous effect upon him, making him wonder what she'd look like in the moonlight and how she'd feel in the darkness.

"Mr. Coltrane, I sure appreciate you finding my crutch," Davy said for what must have been the tenth time.

Sloan steeled himself against the look of hero-worship in the boy's bright brown eyes.

"You're welcome," he said, feeling awkward under the barrage of thank-you's he'd received.

"Tell us again how you did it," Charlotte urged. "I want to hear the part where you fell into the river."

Sloan smothered a groan. These kids were as tenacious as a vigilante posse tracking down a bank robber. They'd already wrung every bit of information about his afternoon adventure out of him. He decided it was time to guide the conversation where he wanted it to go.

"I just followed the river until I caught sight of the crutch," Sloan explained for what seemed the dozenth time. "That's one of the problems of living in the country," he added in a neutral tone. "There's always trouble around the bend."

"Who's Ben?" Janey asked promptly. "And why's he so mean?"

"Bend," Sloan repeated, emphasizing the last letter. "It means you never know what to expect next."

"Oh," Janey said wisely. "Like when that chicken started pecking Sarah's shoes."

"Exactly," Sloan agreed, satisfied that he was finally getting the discussion on track. "And there's a whole lot worse things than ornery chickens."

"Like what?" Charlotte inquired, her black eyes sparkling.

"Like rattlesnakes," Davy answered, his young voice enthusiastic. "I bet there's more than a hundred of them between here and town."

"I don't like snakes," Janey said softly. "They scare me."

Sloan tamped down the unexpected prick of guilt the girl's worried expression generated.

"There's other things besides snakes in the country," he told them, easing his conscience by telling himself they'd all be better off in town.

"Yeah, there's cows and horses and chickens," Charlie said.

"I was thinking about scorpions, coyotes and flash floods."

"Mr. Coltrane," Prudence Abercrombie began reprovingly. "You're unnecessarily frightening the children."

Her green eyes were sharp and piercing. He had the feeling she knew what he was up to.

"I'm just saying that it's a lot safer living in Port Dodd," he responded innocently. "You can't disagree with that fact."

"But it's no fun living in town," Sarah protested. "We hardly fitted in our house on Draper Street, and here we have lots of room."

"But not much of a social life," Sloan pointed out, suspecting that would be the girl's vulnerable area. She had to miss having friends her own age around. And boys. Sloan remembered how his sisters were always finagling trips into Taylorsville so they could visit their girlfriends and make "moon eyes" at the boys.

"We got each other," Davy explained patiently, as if Sloan had missed an important point. "We don't need anybody else."

"Of course, if you sold the farm," Sloan persisted, committed to laying his cards on the table, "you'd have enough money to buy a bigger place in town, a place with a yard. Shoot, you could probably keep a few chickens."

The silence that greeted Sloan's words was a solid wall of reproach. He glanced at Prudence Abercrombie. Her lips were pursed tightly together. Her eyes flashed fire. He figured she'd deliberately let him run off at the mouth because she wanted to give him enough rope to hang himself. He glanced around the table. From the down-right hostile looks he was receiving, she'd accomplished her aim.

He smiled grimly. He was in this conversation about as deep as a man could get. He might as well throw out the amount he was willing to reimburse them for the move back to town.

"I'm thinking a thousand dollars could buy you folks a fine place, as well as a lot of other nice things."

The silence continued. Thick and accusatory. So much for enlisting the support of the children. Sloan had been at friendlier lynchings.

"Mr. Coltrane..."

Sloan felt all glances swing to the woman at his side. He braced himself for the dressing-down he was about to receive.

"You're right, a thousand dollars is a lot of money," she continued in that damned foreign voice of hers that slithered over his body's most sensitive parts. "But, surely even you must realize there are some things money cannot buy."

She made him feel lower than a snake-oil salesman. Still, he wasn't ready to give up. "Such as?"

"Such as a *home* and family," she answered unhesitatingly.

The very things he'd walked away from, he realized ironically.

"This is a house," he pointed out doggedly, engaging her in a duel of colliding stares. Because they were sitting so close, he could count the tiny greenish flecks in her eyes. "It's built of sticks and nails with a couple coats of white paint. You've lived in it a total of one day. It's no more your home than it is mine."

"It is, too," Charlie protested. "Besides, you can't keep a cow in the city limits, isn't that right, Miss Prudence?"

Suddenly, all around them the children broke into animated spates of conversation. Sloan continued his staredown with Miss Abercrombie, promising himself that he wouldn't be the one to look away first. It was a childish game, he knew. Yet something about this woman provoked him to win at least one battle with her.

"Mr. Coltrane, why do you want to buy our place?"

Davy's question cut through the stampede of other voices. As if by magic, the others quieted.

"Yes, Mr. Coltrane," Prudence said, her eyes simmering with challenge. "Why do you want to buy our home?"

"I'm planning a business venture for the land my uncle left me."

"And for this venture to be successful you need to live in our house?" Her tone was skeptical, her eyes incendiary.

"I need to tear it down," he corrected her.

A half dozen gasps greeted his announcement.

"And why is that?" she demanded coldly.

It amazed him that he'd ever thought her voice alluring. Why hadn't he noticed how brittle and censorious it could be?

"Because," he said, pushing back his chair and tossing his napkin to the table, "the damned thing is sitting in the middle of the racetrack I intend to build."

Prudence also stood. "You want to tear down our home to construct a *racetrack?*"

She made his dream sound as vile as a maggoty piece of beef.

"Along with a fancy gambling hall," he decided to inform her for the sheer pleasure of increasing her indignation. Prudence... She was certainly living up to her name. Prude.

"I suppose you plan to have alcohol and games of chance."

"And the best horseflesh this side of the Missouri."

"Horseflesh that you will, no doubt, whip and abuse."

A hot gust of anger scalded Sloan's skin. Now she'd gone too far. He'd taken a lot of insults from this shrew, but for her to imply that he would abuse a horse was a slap in the face.

"I've never hurt a horse in my life, lady."

"Unfortunately, the horses you intend to race cannot speak in their own defense, but I have no doubt that given a choice they would prefer *not* to dash around a track for the sole benefit of men's greed."

"Well, you're wrong about that. It just so happens horses love to run, and they love to win."

"How convenient for you to have that opinion, since it's bound to make you a lot of money."

He shook his head in exasperation. This was the dumbest argument he'd ever been in. "If you knew anything about thoroughbreds, you'd know they were born to race."

"It doesn't matter what either of us think on the subject. The children and I are united. We intend to stay in our home."

"Fine. You folks better develop a liking for dust. Because you're going to be eating it, drinking it and breathing it. Every time I run a race."

Sloan didn't like the sound of what he was saying, but this infernal woman had pushed him into a corner and he had no choice but to fight back. If he didn't, he'd have her and the children making his life miserable.

He stalked to the back door, reached for his hat, then realized he'd lost it when Lucky had thrown him and he'd fallen into the river. That was one more grievance he laid at Prudence Abercrombie's door. She'd cost him one damned fine hat!

He turned to thank the housekeeper for his supper. She was the only one sitting at the table who wasn't glaring at him as if he'd shot their pet dog. Right on his heels came Prudence. Evidently, she wasn't finished with him.

"Our home will *not* sit in the middle of your racetrack, Mr. Coltrane."

"And why's that?" he asked, curious to hear what she was going to say.

He had no doubt that she thought she could outmaneuver him. That's what made their discussions so lively. That, and her face flushed with color and her pert little breasts, reminded him there was more to this woman than her sharp tongue. Much more.

"Along with this house, Amos left us a right-of-way to the road that runs to town."

She was right. She'd pushed him into another corner. He had no choice but to make things so miserable that she and the children would want to hightail it back to Port Dodd. No matter what, he promised himself, by way of salvaging his conscience, he would pay her that thousand dollars. In the end she would be grateful to him. All right, so he wouldn't hold his breath on that. But one way or another he was going to get her and the children out of his life.

With a final look around the room, Sloan nodded, not trusting himself to say another word. He strode out the back door, letting it slam behind him. He wanted his horse, and he wanted to be out of there.

"Did you hear me?" came that English voice from behind him.

Sloan turned, provoked that she'd followed him outside. He'd had a bellyful of this overbearing woman. "Yeah, I heard you, lady."

She stopped before him, breathless. Dusk was creeping steadily across the landscape. Somewhere nearby a crow cawed.

"You know you can't encircle us with this racetrack of yours."

He hated to concede the point. It had been a fine bluff on his part.

"Like you said, you have a right-of-way to the road," he admitted grudgingly.

A look of satisfaction filled her eyes. It was the last straw for Sloan, who was feeling anything but satisfied.

Without any premeditation upon his part, he reached out.

Prudence saw Mr. Coltrane's hands coming toward her. Her first thought was that she'd incited him to violence—he was probably going to strangle her. His hard fingers curved around her shoulders, however, not her throat.

In the near darkness, she had no way of reading his expression, which was frightening—and oddly exhilarating.

His face loomed shockingly close to hers. "Lady, you can push a man too far."

"I'm not afraid of you."

It was unfortunate that her voice shook, but she refused to betray an iota of her uneasiness before the likes of Sloan Coltrane.

He jerked her to him. She resisted by splaying her hands across his unyielding chest. He increased the pressure of his hold, and the puny distance between them shrank significantly. She braced herself for her first kiss, expecting it to be a brutal ravaging by his hard mouth. She got something shatteringly different.

His mouth was hard, all right. His barely parted lips seemed carved of stone. But it was smooth, polished stone. And he brushed that unyielding substance across her trembling lips. Once. Twice. Three times. The subtle friction sent a rockslide of tumultuous emotions tumbling through her. She felt as if she'd been transported in time and place to the slippery riverbank she'd tried so desperately to scramble up. There was nothing to hold on to, nothing to keep her from sliding helplessly downward. Nothing except Sloan Coltrane's unrelenting grip.

But no, that was then. This was now. Her hands shifted to steady herself. The only thing to hold on to was Coltrane's upper arms.

"Open your eyes."

His gritty voice cut through the confusing haze.

His face was so close she could see the fine lines that fanned outward from the corners of his eyes. His breathing was hard. Heavy.

Slowly, he pushed her back, inexorably increasing the distance between them.

"A word of advice, Miss Abercrombie."

His words set a torch to the tattered shreds of her control.

"I don't want any more of your advice, Mr. Coltrane."

His expression hardened. "Under the circumstances, why don't you call me Sloan?"

Her hands clenched. "If by 'circumstances,' you mean grabbing me and kissing me against my will, then by all means I shall call you Sloan. I shall call you 'Sloan, the Uncouth,' 'Sloan, the Barbarian,' 'Sloan, the Attacker of Innocent Women!'"

"There's no need to get nasty," he said, clearly offended by the names she'd called him. "Besides, by no stretch of the imagination could you call that a kiss. Which just goes to show you need all the advice you can get . . . *Prudence.*"

"Do you think your unmannerly assault has earned you the privilege to address me by my first name?"

His lips curved into an insolent smile. "Nah, what's earned me the right to call you Prudence is that I saved your skin twice today."

"You're addled," she sputtered, wondering where the man got his crazy ideas.

He held up two fingers. "The first time was when I shot that snake."

"If you hadn't waylaid us, that snake would have probably slithered on its way without crossing our path. The horses wouldn't have been panicked. *And* I wouldn't have been thrown from the wagon!"

"That snake was just waiting for a bunch of green-horns to come driving by," he countered, his tone infuriatingly light.

"It's true you helped Davy and me from the river," she allowed reluctantly, "but we were in no danger of drowning. We would have eventually made it to shore."

"A simple thank-you will send me on my way," he said mockingly.

"Then, *thank you!*"

"Just one more piece of business and I'll be out of here." He closed the puny distance between them with astonishing abruptness.

"Wait! What are you—"

His arms came around her waist and hips. Before she could voice another protest, her feet lost contact with the ground and she was being carried back to the house.

"Put me down this instant!"

"Stop wiggling or I'll drop you."

She ceased her struggles and tried to act as if being swept into a man's embrace was the most ordinary of events. Inside she seethed. Sloan Coltrane was rapidly becoming a menace to her sanity. Perhaps it was time she strapped a gun belt to her hip to protect her from his high-handed tactics. The thought of drawing a gun on him was amazingly appealing.

When they reached the back porch, he set her on her feet. She straightened, smoothing her skirts first, then swinging her braid over her shoulder. "Are you going to tell me what that was all about?" she hissed.

"Horse...manure," he muttered succinctly.

Her mouth fell open. "*What?*"

He hitched his thumb through a belt loop. "I know you don't like listening to advice, especially from me. But you should know it's not very smart to go running around outside in your stocking feet. Not on a farm, at any rate. Now, Lucky's a pretty decent horse, but he's not particularly careful about where he relieves himself." Sloan glanced pointedly at her unshod feet. "You were getting awful close to something I suspect you wouldn't want to step into."

She snapped her mouth shut, silently wishing that just once she could get the better of this impossible man. That gun belt was looking more inviting with each passing minute.

"Good night, Sloan." She hurled the farewell as if it were an epithet.

"Good night, Prudence."

It was only after she'd returned to the house that she realized how natural it had seemed to call him by his first name. She suspected that was how she was going to think of him from now on. Sloan. Sloan, the Arrogant. Sloan, the Infuriating. Sloan, the Unrepentant Tormentor of Chaste Women.

Prudence struggled to keep her eyelids open. It wouldn't do to fall asleep in church. Thank goodness the children were restless. Each time they jostled one another it sent a rippling effect along the bench, nudging Prudence to full alertness. The young Reverend Brown wasn't noted for his lively sermons. Chubby-cheeked and shyly serious, he related the story of the Prodigal Son as if he were teaching them their sums. Usually Prudence approved of his undramatic preaching, but after a long, sleepless night thinking about "Sloan, the Frustrating," she needed something more than Reverend Brown's prosaic words to keep her awake.

The early afternoon sunlight that poured into the chapel through the stain-glass windows added to her general sleepiness. She let her thoughts drift to her last disagreeable confrontation with Sloan Coltrane. An invigorating sizzle of anger had her sitting straighter on the hard seat. The man was a brute. The way he'd drawn her into his arms and kissed her had been the most animalistic act she'd ever endured.

And for him to claim that he *hadn't* kissed her, why that was a lie, pure and simple. She might never have been kissed before, but surely she was capable of recognizing one. Especially when it was happening to her. The moment Sloan's lips had touched her, all sorts of alarming tingles and tremors had ricocheted through her. No wonder women were cautioned about letting men have their way. Sloan's way had been darkly stirring, darkly inviting.

With June sunlight pouring into the chapel, Prudence shivered. It had never occurred to her a woman might enjoy the attentions of a rude and arrogant cowboy.

Before she could pursue that disturbing thought, Reverend Brown concluded his sermon and sat down. Pearl Harding rose and raised her ivory music baton. The congregation got to their feet and began singing "We'll Gather at the River."

Prudence added her soprano voice to the others that swelled around her and thought about the sluggish brown river next to the farm, the one she'd done battle with to rescue Davy. Her gaze drifted to him, and she found herself smiling at the sight of his rebellious hair stubbornly refusing to be defeated by any comb. Next to him stood Charlotte and Charlie, their dark faces beaming with joy as they sang. Janey, her flaxen tresses framing her elfin face like an angelic halo, stood next to them. Today she wore an eye patch the same shade of pink as her dress. Then there was Sarah, on the brink of womanhood, her head bent demurely over her hymnal. Richard, stiff and awkward in his hand-me-down suit and his surroundings, acted as if the sound of his voice raised in song was a new experience for him.

A feeling of expanding warmth filled Prudence's chest. Each child was a special blessing in her life, and she would do everything within her power to keep them safe. Even if it meant standing up to Sloan Coltrane. After all, she'd moved the children to the country because she'd wanted to have a better atmosphere than their cramped living quarters on Draper Street. She'd expected them to flourish in their newfound space and freedom.

There was no way she would allow Amos's nephew to destroy her dream by exposing them to the seamiest element of society, drunken gamblers with nary a thought in their heads other than betting on horses or games of chance. Somehow she was going to find a way to stop Sloan Coltrane from corrupting the simple paradise she'd hoped to create for her children.

Prudence angled her chin upward, pouring more emotion into the words she sang. She had right on her side and that meant she *would* prevail over the disreputable Sloan Coltrane. She was certain the good citizens of Port Dodd would see things her way and join with her to drive him from their midst. Let him build his racetrack and gambling casino somewhere else.

# Chapter Six

A cacophonous pounding on his door penetrated Sloan's groggy brain. He opened one eye. A water-stained ceiling came into blurred focus. He raised his hands and cradled his head to keep it from exploding, all the while trying to sort out what was going on.

He was in bed, lying naked and spread-eagled on his back in the room he'd rented above the Belly-Up Saloon. The whiskey that he'd drunk last night made his head pound, and the inside of his mouth tasted like a steer had slept there and had only recently wandered off. In short, Sloan was feeling mean. The last thing he needed was company.

Gingerly he sat up and rubbed a palm across his jaw. It still ached from the brawl he'd taken part in. Experimentally he checked his teeth with his tongue. None of them were loose, so the tooth he'd seen on the saloon floor last night must not have been one of his.

The pounding on the door continued without letup.

"Go away!" New waves of pain reverberated inside his head.

"Sloan Coltrane?"

Sloan swore. Whoever the unwelcome visitor was, he obviously had the right room. "Yeah?"

"You got some company waiting for you downstairs."

"Tell him to come back later."

"Ain't a him. It's a lady!" came the chuckling response. "A *real* lady by the looks of her. If you don't come down, she said she was coming to your room to talk to you. Want me to send her up?"

"Hell, no," Sloan snarled, swinging his legs over the side of the bed. A mental image of Prudence Abercrombie rose full-blown in his throbbing head. He wouldn't be responsible for his actions if he had her alone in his bedroom. He'd probably kill her, and no jury would convict him. He held her completely responsible for last night's fiasco. If she hadn't been imbedded like a burr under his skin, he would have had the enjoyable evening he'd been looking forward to for months, instead of experiencing one of the most miserable nights of his life.

"Tell her I'm coming down."

"She said she'd give you five minutes. Then she's coming up." The man imparted the news with obnoxious good humor.

Sloan swore again and reached for his pants. Prudence Abercrombie in the Belly-Up Saloon. Didn't the woman have a lick of sense? Well, he'd hustle her out of there in a hurry. The woman had no business in a rough and wild place like this, and he was going to make sure she understood that fact in no uncertain terms.

As he jammed his shirt buttons into the appropriate slots, he recalled last night's demoralizing events. He'd smoked the cheroot he'd been looking forward to. No problem there. Then he'd sauntered into the bar and ordered himself a whiskey. It had burned a searing path straight to his gut. Just the way he liked it. He'd enjoyed a second drink, still minding his own business, still savoring being on his own.

He was more than ready to sample the charms of one of the painted gals working the saloon. And he was willing to pay for the pleasure. But when he'd tried to make his selection things started to go downhill. He'd couldn't explain exactly what was wrong, but something sure as hell was. With him. With the gals. He'd looked at the decked-out beauties, waiting for the predictable tug of desire that would point him in the right direction, and, dammit, nothing had happened.

He'd sat there like some old man or an untried boy and…and had looked at the women, thinking things he'd never thought before. Like how some of them didn't look too happy to be there. There was a hint of something sad in their eyes. A couple of the others had been energetic enough, but there had been something forced about their liveliness, as if it were an act.

As Sloan had nursed his whiskey, an unpleasant question had nudged him. Was it possible that the women whose company he'd paid for in the past hadn't enjoyed his attentions? They'd sure acted as if they'd thought he was something special. He knew he'd enjoyed himself. But now as he studied their gaudy dresses and made-up faces, he thought he detected an attitude of distaste on their parts toward the men who approached them. He had the uncomfortable feeling that they'd rather be going anywhere than those upstairs rooms with the rowdy cowpokes draped possessively around them.

Not liking the direction of his reflections, Sloan had turned his attentions to the gaming tables. Figuring that a night of cards and the association of gambling men would clear his head, he'd taken a couple of draws on his cheroot and sat at a table with an empty chair. Introductions had been grunted, first names only. Shorty, Curly, Lefty and Stumpy. The poker had been down and dirty with little conversation during or between the hands, which had suited Sloan's dour mood just fine.

He'd told himself he was having a dandy time, winning more hands than he lost. Gradually, however, he'd become aware that Shorty had an uncertain aim with his chew, Curly could go only about a minute between malodorous belches, Lefty needed to scratch his privates about as often as Curly needed to belch, and Stumpy's greatly obese body stank as if it hadn't been near a tub of bathwater in more than a year. Which it probably hadn't.

Sloan had been ready to call it an early night when one of the men at the table asked him if he'd been able to meet up with the spinster lady who ran Draper House. The last thing Sloan wanted was to discuss Prudence with these lowlifes.

He'd stood and gathered his winnings, indicating with a nod that he'd caught up with her. Stumpy had made the mistake of mentioning that Miss Abercrombie probably wouldn't be too bad, in the dark. Sloan's insides had twisted at the subsequent coarse guffaws that had flooded the table. Lefty made the mistake of suggesting that he wouldn't mind a few minutes with her in broad daylight. She'd probably be so damned grateful for some male attention that she'd—

Sloan's fist had plowed into Lefty's smirking mouth. No mistake there. After that all hell broke loose. More flying fists. Chairs tipping over. Snarled oaths. Grunts. Even a gunshot or two. The sheriff, an unsympathetic soul, had shown up. Sloan had come within a hairbreadth of being arrested. Only some fast talking and handing over his winnings to pay for the saloon's splintered chairs and tables had kept Sloan from being an overnight guest in Port Dodd's jail.

As Sloan descended the stairs two at a time, each thud of his boot sent a jolt of pain through his head. He couldn't believe the contrary female had come to the Belly-Up for another go-around with him. Well, he had a few things to tell her and—

Sloan came to a halt. Amid the shambles of the bar stood his stepmother, Kate Coltrane Porter. He was startled by the pang of disappointment he experienced when he realized there wasn't going to be another showdown with the indomitable Prudence Abercrombie.

"Good Lord, what happened to you?" his stepmother demanded. Both tenderness and exasperation coated the question.

Sloan fingered his jaw and winced. He figured he looked worse than he felt, but not by much.

"Misunderstanding over a poker game," he said.

Not exactly the truth, but that was his story and he was sticking with it.

She shook her head, clucking her tongue at him. "Oh, Sloan, what am I going to do with you?"

A wave of affection warmed him as he stared at the woman his father had married when Sloan was six years old. Beneath a green-feathered hat, her beautiful golden hair was masterfully arranged in some kind of fancy twist. Her moss-colored traveling skirt and jacket looked both stylish and fresh.

"You don't have to do anything with me," he answered. "I've been grown for some time now, in case you haven't noticed."

Kate's blue eyes darkened. "You grew up the day the news came that your father had been killed," she said quietly. "You were hardly more than a boy when you became a man."

He shrugged, realizing he didn't like the sight of his stepmother inside a saloon any more than he liked the thought of Prudence visiting him here.

"Did you come all the way to Port Dodd to tell me that, Kate?"

"It's not such a long trip, not by train, anyway," she answered, dodging the question.

"We've barely said our goodbyes," he pointed out. "Is there some trouble at the ranch?"

She frowned at him. "You might say that."

He suppressed a groan, wishing the pounding in his head would subside. "It's too early in the morning for riddles."

"It's almost high noon," she corrected him disapprovingly. "And there's nothing wrong with a good riddle. If you weren't such an old man, you'd know that."

Sloan could tell by the determined look in her eyes that Kate wouldn't be hurried with whatever it was she'd come to say. Resigned to listening to her at her own pace, he stepped forward and took her arm. "Come on, let's get out of here. There's better places to talk than inside the Belly-Up."

"I haven't had breakfast yet," she informed him, allowing herself to be led from the saloon. "Let's go to the hotel and order us some fried eggs."

This time Sloan didn't bother to hold back his groan as his stepmother's words caused his stomach to roll over. As they walked out into the sunlight, Sloan felt as if his eyes were being stabbed by a hundred sharp daggers.

"You know," Kate began conversationally, her arm still looped through his. "It's a novel experience for me to be accompanied by a man who looks as disreputable as you do. I wonder what they will think of you at the hotel." She threw him an amused glance. "Probably that you're some kind of desperado on the run."

"I just need a shave," he grumbled.

Kate wrinkled her nose. "That would do for starters."

Later, as Sloan watched his stepmother daintily devour a generous portion of steak and eggs, he decided she was probably right about his appearance. He'd received a lot of suspicious glances from the other patrons frequenting the hotel dining room.

"Mmm, this is wonderful. Are you sure you don't want any?" Kate asked as she took another bite of her eggs.

Sloan refused to wince; instead, he took another gulp of hot coffee. "I'm fine."

She laid down her fork and blotted her mouth. "That's really why I'm here, Sloan," she began seriously. "I want to make sure everything is all right with you. You left in such haste after Dan and I were married. I—I wondered if you were upset with us...."

Her words trailed off, and she stared at him as if prepared to hear the worst kind of confession. Sloan smiled. Dear, sweet, determined Kate. She worried about everyone.

"You marrying Dan Porter was the best thing that ever happened to me," he said simply.

"Then why did you leave? The ranch belongs to you. Your father would have wanted you to have it. Both Dan and Jeremy understand that."

"I've had my fill of running cattle," Sloan answered truthfully. "Jeremy loves the ranch. Dan can teach him everything he needs to know to keep it going."

Kate's blue eyes considered him gravely. "I can't help feeling that I've stolen your birthright from you."

"Jeremy is as much my father's son as I am. That means he's just as entitled to have it as I ever was."

"How can you be sure that you won't change your mind? That in a few years the ranch won't become more important to you?"

"I know what I want to do with my life, Kate," he reminded her gently.

Her eyebrows arched. "Race horses?"

"Thoroughbreds," he clarified. "On my own track."

"But why can't you do that in Taylorsville?"

Sloan laughed. "Because I need people to come and watch the thoroughbreds run. A coastal town the size of Port Dodd is perfect for my needs."

Kate frowned. "I wish Uncle Amos had never left you that land."

Suddenly, an image of Prudence Abercrombie rose in Sloan's thoughts, as she'd looked just before he'd bent his head and brushed his lips against hers. The intensity of his desire startled him.

"You know the girls are furious with you for leaving," Kate told him.

"Alicia and Lenore?" Sloan asked in surprise. "They're so besotted with their new husbands they probably haven't even noticed I left."

"You're wrong." Kate's eyes sparkled mischievously. "You kept such a tight reign on them when they were growing up, they want to return the favor."

"I'm not sure I follow you."

"They want to have a hand in choosing your wife."

"*Wife.*" He nearly knocked over his water glass. "I'm not in the market for a wife."

"There's several likely candidates in Taylorsville," Kate said breezily. "You broke a few hearts when you left."

"It's probably a good thing I got away when I did," Sloan said with heartfelt honesty, remembering a couple of the more aggressive females who'd taken to dropping by the ranch around suppertime to bat their eyelashes and coo at him. He'd felt downright hunted his last few weeks at home.

"Jeremy misses you, too," Kate told him.

Sloan laughed. "Now that's a shameless lie. All my brother can think about is Misty Marie."

"I think he needs some man-to-man advice on being a new husband."

"Then I'd be the last person able to help him. Dan's the one he should talk to."

"But Jeremy always felt closer to you," his stepmother persisted. "He's been your shadow ever since he learned to walk."

"It's time he stood on his own two feet," Sloan said gently. "Kate, nothing you say is going to get me back to Taylorsville."

"But look at you," she fairly wailed. "You're sleeping in saloons!"

"Conserving money," he replied succinctly. "I've got everything planned down to the last nickel."

"You've taken to brawling."

"A minor difference of opinion," he corrected her. "Could have happened to anyone."

"You look dreadful. I don't think Port Dodd agrees with you."

"I like it."

"But—but—"

"Give it up, Kate. I'm in Port Dodd to stay. Dan can run the ranch until Jeremy is able to take over. Alicia and Lenore can work their matchmaking wiles on someone else. And my kid brother can figure out how to be a husband on his own."

Kate threw down her napkin. "Lord, you truly are the most stubborn man I've ever known."

"Except for my father," Sloan reminded her.

A look that was both sad and tender crept into her gaze.

"Except for your father," she conceded softly.

Later, as they stepped onto the boardwalk, Sloan was feeling a lot more human. He'd eaten a couple of biscuits, as well as drunk his coffee. The throbbing in his head had diminished to a tolerable level.

"When are you going to start building this racetrack of yours?" Kate asked as she adjusted the rakish angle of her green-plumed hat.

"I'm meeting with my carpenter tomorrow. He has several work crews lined up already. The entire project will be finished in a couple of months."

"You're going to be successful," his stepmother said, sighing, as if imparting bad news.

"I'm going to try to be."

She reached out with her gloved hands, resting them lightly against his arms. "It isn't in you to fail, Sloan."

He smiled down at the woman who was only a dozen years older than he was. "Be happy for me, Kate. I may have left the nest, but, as you said yourself, the train trip between us isn't a long one."

"Just promise me that you'll move out of that awful saloon."

Sloan's smile widened. "The track and stalls come first. Then the gambling casino. I'll have a suite of rooms when that's finished."

"You do have it all planned out."

"Just about," he answered, thinking of Prudence Abercrombie and her little brood planted smack-dab in the middle of his grand dream. "Just about."

"As long as you're happy..."

"I'm happy."

His stepmother tilted her face toward him and rose on tiptoe, planting a maternal kiss on his cheek. Tears glittered in her blue eyes. Sloan hugged her to him. She had been the only mother he could remember having. She'd always been good to him. Always concerned about him, even though the role of stepmother had been foisted upon her at a young age.

"Oh, dear, look at me," she said, stepping back and reaching for an embroidered handkerchief. "I'm making a spectacle of myself."

"You're fine," he said gently, but a flash of movement from the corner of his eye had him turning his head.

On the boardwalk several yards ahead of them stood Prudence Abercrombie, trailed by her tribe of six cleaned and scrubbed urchins. The girls wore simple pastel dresses, the boys white starched shirts and dark trousers that, while patched, were relentlessly pressed. In the afternoon sunlight, they almost sparkled. All except for Prudence. In her drab black gown and old-fashioned black bonnet, she looked like a dark rain cloud.

An unfathomable expression stilled her usually mobile features. She halted in midstride.

"What are you staring at?" Kate asked.

"Prudence Abercrombie," he answered absently, scarcely registering his stepmother's question because he was distracted at the unexpected sight of his newly acquired adversary. He noted that she seemed as unprepared as he was for their next encounter. Her face was unnaturally pale, and she seemed almost transfixed as she stood on the boardwalk.

"Ah, I see," Kate said. "A 'who,' not a 'what.'"

"What?" Sloan asked, unable to pry his gaze from Prudence and her wide-eyed stare.

"I said . . . Oh, forget it. Do you know that woman?" Sloan nodded.

"What is she doing with all those children?"

"They're hers."

"The youngest girl and boy might be," Kate agreed conversationally. "The little black twins, possibly. But the oldest girl is almost a woman, and the tall boy next to her is close to being fully grown. I don't think your Prudence Abercrombie is old enough to be their mother."

"She runs a sort of orphanage," he explained, his attention still riveted upon the woman under discussion. "And she's not *my* Prudence Abercrombie," he tacked on as an afterthought. "She's the one Amos left the farmhouse to."

"Why is she angry with you?"

"What makes you think she is?"

"Because she's coming this way, and she's looking at you as if you were mule pucky."

"Kate!" Shocked, Sloan turned to face his usually ladylike stepmother. "I can't believe you said that."

"I was tired of talking to the back of your head," she responded without a trace of guilt. "Besides, I believe in speaking what's on my mind. It's better for the digestion."

"Mr. Coltrane! Mr. Coltrane!" While Charlie's voice rang out in a friendly greeting, Sloan noted that the rest of the children were regarding him with the open hostility of their benefactor.

"Hello," he responded tightly. Prudence resumed a brisk gait. As she drew closer, she acknowledged his presence with an almost imperceptible nod, obviously intent on walking past him without speaking. That suited Sloan fine. He didn't have a thing to say to the stubborn female. Let her march by him with her nose in the air. He'd intended to ignore her, anyway.

"You look awful," Janey observed sadly. "Did you fall off your horse again?"

Next to him Sloan heard Kate cough. It sounded suspiciously like a smothered chuckle.

"No, I . . ." He broke off, not wanting to explain to the innocent child that he'd been brawling in a saloon.

"He got into a fight," Kate said, clearly suffering no similar compunction to protect the sweet child. "Isn't that a dreadful thing for a grown man to do?"

Janey nodded solemnly. Ahead of her, Prudence had stopped again. It was obvious that she couldn't walk off and leave the girl. Sloan spared her a quick glance. The woman's expression wasn't unfathomable now. It was clear to any and all passersby that she was furious. Her usually tranquil features were scrunched into a downright unfriendly scowl. It annoyed him that she thought she had a reason to be angry with him. He was the one whose dreams were being tampered with.

"What's your name?" Kate asked, as if she was having a soiree in front of the Brubaker Hotel.

"I'm Janey."

"And who are you?" his stepmother inquired of Charlie and Charlotte who'd retraced their steps back to the little blond girl.

"He's Charlie," Sloan said ungraciously. "That's his sister, Charlotte."

"I'm Davy," came the next greeting. "This is Sarah and Richard."

They all stood in a circle around him and Kate. He raised his head and watched Prudence shift from one foot to the other. Obviously she had no intention of joining her band of children.

"I'm very pleased to meet you," Kate said, her blue eyes sparkling with interest.

"You're beautiful," Janey breathed.

"Thank you."

"How come you know Mr. Coltrane?" Charlie asked.

"We're from the same place," his stepmother answered.

"Did he build a racetrack around your house and make you breathe horse dust, too?" Charlotte inquired innocently.

Sloan wanted to find a rock to crawl under.

"I beg your pardon?" Kate sputtered.

"That's what he's going to do to us," Janey elaborated. "Even after he shot a snake to save Miss Prudence."

"And rode his horse into the river to pull her and Davy out."

"And found my lost crutch."

"And ate Miss Gladys's chicken and dumplings."

"And took a bath on our back porch."

"And—"

"Children, that's enough," Prudence said, finally approaching them and cutting off a lengthy chronicle of his misadventures with them. "We need to be on our way. I'm sure Mr. Coltrane and his...lady friend have better things to do than talk to us."

*Snippy,* Sloan thought. The woman was just plain snippy.

"On the contrary," Kate said sweetly, "there's nothing I enjoy better than meeting Sloan's friends."

"We're not exactly friends," Prudence returned coolly. "More like...acquaintances. *Distant* acquaintances."

"Oh, but now that you're neighbors, surely that will change," Kate murmured cheerfully.

Sloan wanted to strangle her.

"Not when he's trying to run us off our place," Richard said hotly.

"I'm not trying to run you off the place," Sloan snapped. "I'm offering you a thousand dollars for it."

"We don't want your stinking money. Right, Miss Prudence?" Charlie asked without a trace of malice in his young voice.

Obviously he was quoting what he'd overheard someone else say. Someone like his precious Miss Prudence.

Sloan tried to ignore the becoming shade of pink that flushed his adversary's cheeks.

"My, isn't this interesting?" Kate drawled. "You must be Prudence Abercrombie. How absentminded of Sloan not to have introduced us sooner."

Absentminded, nothing. He'd wanted to avoid this confrontation altogether. Making polite chitchat with Prudence was a civilized nicety he'd hoped to avoid.

"How do you do?" Prudence's English accent was icy enough to freeze the salty breeze that gusted around them. If it was possible for ice to be green, then that's what her eyes would have been. Green ice.

Kate slipped a gloved hand through Sloan's arm and squeezed him closer. "I'm doing much better now that I know Sloan has made friends in Port Dodd. I've been worried about him getting lonely, being separated from his family and all. You know this is his first time away from home. We were all concerned he'd be homesick.''

A look of confusion thawed some of the ice in Prudence's eyes. ''Family?''

''Why, yes, my dear son has decided to abandon the bosom of his family on some reckless adventure involving horses and racetracks.''

''Sloan is your *son?*''

Sloan found he didn't like being treated as if he were twelve and virtually invisible.

''Kate is my stepmother,'' he said tersely, resenting the fact that he couldn't seem to tear his gaze from Prudence's brilliant green eyes. The salty breeze that swirled around them gently nudged the few tendrils of her reddish hair that had managed to gain their freedom from her unstylish black bonnet. He curled his hand into a fist, resisting the impulse to step forward and whisk the unflattering hat from her head.

He didn't think she'd like it one little bit if he were to do something so rash. She'd probably squawk up a storm of protest.

As he stood in the afternoon sun beside Kate, waiting for Prudence to say something, he watched her slightly parted lips. And remembered. They'd been so soft. So inviting. He hadn't permitted himself to taste her. Looking back on it, he was at first impressed with his own self-control, then impatient with himself for exercising it. If he'd really kissed her, then he wouldn't be standing here being driven out of his mind imagining how it would feel to have his tongue inside her mouth. He'd know.

''What are we waiting for?''

The innocent question came from Janey.

''I think we're waiting for my stepson to stop ogling your Miss Abercrombie'' came Kate's teasing observation.

A scalding flush seared Sloan's cheeks. Prudence's face also reddened.

"What's an 'ogle'?" Charlotte asked.

"We'll talk about it later," Prudence said briskly as she took Charlotte's small hand. "It was nice meeting you, Kate. Come along, children."

There was no goodbye for him, Sloan noticed.

"The pleasure was all mine, believe me," Kate responded warmly.

"Thanks for embarrassing me," he said, watching Prudence and her flock continue on their way down the boardwalk.

His stepmother laughed outright. "Oh, Sloan, if I hadn't seen it with my own eyes, I wouldn't have believed it. You were blushing!"

"Who wouldn't?" he grumbled. "Whatever possessed you to say I was ogling Prudence Abercrombie?"

Kate's smile widened. "I can't imagine what came over me. I'm sorry, Sloan."

He eyed her skeptically. "You don't sound sorry."

"Oh, but I am," she responded, her blue eyes gleaming. "I'm sorry I have to go home and miss all the fireworks."

He took her arm and led her from the hotel entrance. "I'm not even going to ask what you mean by that."

"You mean you haven't figured it out yet?" She shook her head. "That makes it even better."

"What the devil are you talking about?" he asked, not appreciating at all her amusement at his expense.

"Something along the lines of, 'how the mighty have fallen' and 'love is blind.'"

"You're crazy, woman. Love has nothing to do with what's going on between me and Prudence Abercrombie."

"Then you admit that something's going on?" she inquired pleasantly.

"There's nothing going on," he retorted. "You saw her. She's hardly the type of woman I'd..."

His words trailed off.

"You'd what? Court? Woo? Marry?"

He swore, not bothering to lower his voice. There were some tortures so fiendishly devised by women that they could not be tolerated.

"I'm not marrying anyone. I came here to build a racetrack."

"Is there a reason you can't do both?"

"Damnation, yes!"

Kate stopped, forcing him to stop along with her. "You can get as angry as you want to, but that won't change anything. When Dan started looking at me the way you were looking at Miss Abercrombie, I wanted to shoot him. My life was so neatly ordered, so perfectly arranged. The last thing I needed was some dusty cowpoke riding into my life and turning everything upside down."

"What changed your mind?" Sloan asked gruffly, certain he wasn't going to like her answer.

Kate's smile became mysterious. "There are some battles you just can't fight...and win."

"You mean he rode roughshod over your objections," Sloan clarified.

She shook her head. "The real battle wasn't between Dan and me. It was inside myself, and I never stood a chance."

He'd been right. He didn't like her answer. After years of sacrifice, he'd finally managed to gain his freedom from the responsibility of taking care of his family. There was no way he was going to risk that precious, newfound freedom by becoming involved with Prudence Abercrombie. The woman was more encumbered than a mother cat with a litter of newborn kittens.

As long as he remembered that, he'd win the battle his stepmother had lost.

# Chapter Seven

Prudence tried not to feel self-conscious as she walked away from Sloan Coltrane. She was certain he was staring at her, just as he'd been when she'd joined him and his stepmother on the boardwalk in front of the Brubaker Hotel. As much as she tried to, she couldn't be offended at Kate Porter for her blunt way of speaking. Sloan *had* been ogling her, or at any rate he'd been staring at her so intently that she'd wondered if she'd had a smudge of dirt streaked across her face.

Of course, she'd been staring at him, too. He'd looked dreadful! His whiskered jaw was swollen, his wonderful silvery eyes bloodshot and the corner of his mouth bruised. What had happened to him?

When she'd first caught sight of him, the woman he'd been with had been standing on tiptoe, kissing him. Prudence couldn't understand why seeing that had caused her throat to tighten and her stomach to clench. What possible difference could it make to her whom Sloan Coltrane held in his arms in broad daylight on Main Street?

More disconcerting was the wave of elation she'd experienced when Sloan revealed the attractive woman was his stepmother. But it had been there, that sudden lifting of her spirits, that spreading warmth deep inside her. He was her enemy, seemingly fashioned by fate to cause her nothing but irritation. None of it made any sense. The only reason she'd looked forward to seeing him again was to tell him off, but when the moment had arrived all she'd been able to do was lose herself in his relentless gaze.

The children's conversations ebbed and flowed around her as they returned to the farm in the wagon driven again by Richard. There were songs which she absently sang. Lighthearted banter she dutifully laughed over. And yet, some very real part of her had been left on Main Street in front of the Brubaker Hotel. Her sanity most likely, she thought glumly, wishing she could make Amos's nephew disappear in a puff of smoke and have her mind back where it belonged—on the children and their new life in the country.

"I want to see what Mr. Coltrane's building today," Davy announced at the breakfast table.

It had been several long weeks since she'd last seen Sloan. Weeks of frustration and impatience with herself for reliving the feel of his mouth upon hers. Two weeks of lying awake in her bed long after the children had fallen asleep and remembering what it had felt like when he'd swept her into his arms and carried her to the porch. Weeks of knowing she was acting like a fool and being unable to stop herself.

The last thing she needed was for the children to start their familiar chant of wanting to watch what their neighbor was doing on the other side of their property line. It didn't help matters that a conveniently placed hill about four miles from the house provided the perfect vantage point to view the rapidly progressing construction. Sloan had wasted no time in building his gamblers' den.

"We have more useful things to do with our time than spy upon Mr. Coltrane," Prudence stated firmly as she speared a forkful of eggs. She was determined to get her appetite back.

"How about after we finish our chores?" Charlie asked.

"It isn't really 'spying,' is it?" Sarah inquired.

"It's so exciting!" Charlotte exclaimed. "I can hardly wait till they bring the horses."

It was foolish to feel betrayed by the children's excitement at living next door to a racetrack. They were too young to know what lay ahead, but Prudence expected the worst. During the actual races, the noise from the cheering crowds surely would be unrelenting. At night the gaming hall no doubt would be filled with wild and abandoned celebrants. There would be alcohol on the premises. One could count on that. There were bound to be altercations. Probably even a shooting or two.

She shuddered at the thought of her perfect world dissolving into Sodom and Gomorrah. And yet when she'd tried to enlist the aid of the townspeople over the past several weeks to help her prevent the racetrack from opening, they had shocked her by being delighted with the new addition to the community. Even Reverend Brown had expressed a positive attitude about racing thoroughbreds in the area. Prudence didn't know what made that particular breed of animal so special, but everyone seemed to think that Port Dodd had been greatly blessed by Sloan Coltrane's arrival.

"Do you really feel that it would be harmful for the children to watch from the hilltop?" Gladys asked, studying Prudence as if mystified by her reaction to the whole affair.

"Probably not," Prudence said, sighing, knowing the housekeeper was trying to understand what must seem like an overreaction upon Prudence's part to the project.

"Well, don't you think that as long as they get their chores done first, they could spend an afternoon or two watching the carpenters at work? You've got to admit that Sloan hired a first-rate crew. I've never seen buildings put together so quickly."

Even Gladys had turned against her.

Prudence laid down her fork. She valued the woman's opinion and had always admired her practical approach to life.

"I suppose they can watch," she said finally. "As long as they finish their chores and stay on our property."

A cheer went up around the table from all except Richard. The young man alone seemed unimpressed by Sloan and his fancy horses.

It was coming up dusk when Sloan plucked his shirt from the ground and gave the garment a good shaking before putting it on. The workmen were pulling out and heading toward town. Sloan looked approvingly at the almost completed barn and stalls. It had helped to work off his frustrations by throwing himself into the hard, physical labor. The days were hot enough to sweat away any thoughts of Prudence. Unfortunately the sultry nights were long enough to remind him of the last time he'd seen her and the gentle sway of her hips when she'd walked away from him.

His mood had been reflective since that Sunday several weeks ago. He'd heard from his work crew that Prudence had tried to turn the town against him and his racetrack. She'd failed; that much was clear. People in the area were lovers of fine horseflesh and eager to watch thoroughbred racing. He'd already been contacted by several ranchers and businessmen anxious to run their blue-blooded stock.

Sloan stretched and glanced toward the low rise a couple of hundred yards away that bordered his land on the west. Squinting against the dropping sun, he counted five figures. He was getting used to having an audience. Each afternoon now they gathered about this time, evidently to inspect his progress. He suspected they would be a lot more interested when the horses started to arrive. Sloan had debated finishing the gaming hall before running the first races. He'd decided that local interest was high enough, however, to warrant holding his first contest as soon as the viewing stands were completed. That would probably be in three weeks. The house he'd constructed for his good friend and horse trainer, George Washington Curtis, and his wife, Junella, was close to being finished.

A sixth figure joined the group on the dusty knoll. Then, as Sloan watched, they disbanded. He assumed Prudence had come to gather her flock. He wondered if she realized how much he'd altered his original plans to accommodate her and the children. Deciding that the stubborn woman was never going to budge, he'd changed the location of the track and gaming hall, moving them as far as he could from the farmhouse.

He doubted she'd thank him for his consideration.

Or forgive him for messing up her neat little world.

He scowled at the now-empty rise. It was obvious to him that her little world hadn't been perfect when he'd arrived. Clearly, she had barely enough money to eke out an adequate existence.

Telling himself that her money problems were none of his concern, he headed for the small shack he and his workmen had thrown together. Most nights he slept there instead of riding into town. Living conditions were primitive, but he found he liked being close to his land. When the casino was completed, his permanent home would be a luxurious suite of private rooms above the gaming area. He would have other bedchambers available for those wanting to spend the night before heading back to Port Dodd.

His sense of accomplishment grew. Everything was under control. After a bumpy beginning with his neighbor, things were falling into place. He began to whistle softly as he prepared for bed.

"What was it like, riding his horse, Davy?" Charlie asked for at least the third time.

Prudence swallowed the words she wanted to say as she stood in the hallway of the boys' room. Their lamp had been extinguished, and the bedroom was pitched in semidarkness. The only light was provided by the brilliant moonlight streaming through the open window. She told herself it was natural for boys to be excited about the imminent arrival of sleek racing horses in the area. Richard, at least, refrained from talking endlessly about the track that had already been completed. She assumed this was because he was older and less susceptible to the lure of horse racing.

After checking on the girls, Prudence found herself too keyed up to retire to her own room. Instead, she decided to sit out on the porch for a few minutes and watch for shooting stars. Because of the full moon, she had no difficulty maneuvering through the night. She settled herself on the chair, tucking her legs beneath her. The tangy salt air seemed especially heavy. There had been miles of billowing clouds in the sky all afternoon, but tonight she noticed that only wispy tracings of gray occasionally scuttled across the moon.

Crickets chirped. Frogs croaked. She saw what she'd been waiting for, and held her breath at the dazzling descent of a faraway star. For no reason she could comprehend, the sight brought tears to her eyes. Did a star know when it was dying? Surely not. And yet there was now one less glowing orb in the firmament.

Sometimes it seemed to Prudence that she could feel her own life rushing past her, each moment inexorably slipping away. And even though those moments were spent securing a safe harbor for her children, a vague sense of discontent stirred.

This was the only life she'd ever known. Her mother and aunts had raised her to be responsible for the children they took in. Draper House had become her world. It was gone now, no doubt rented by a *real* family. With a start, Prudence realized the name Draper House no longer fit the present circumstances. She wondered what she should call the place Amos Coltrane had left her. "Coltrane House," in honor of the man who'd bequeathed it to her? An unexpected flash of amusement caught her by surprise. People had started calling Sloan's operation "Coltrane Track." How ironic for two totally opposite enterprises to bear the same name.

Prudence shifted her position. She knew she should go to bed. Morning, with its sundry demands, came early. Yet she knew that if she went inside, she would lie awake for hours thinking about Sloan. Why did those thoughts make her feel guilty? What harm was there in being fascinated by Amos's nephew? It wasn't as if anything of a...romantic nature would ever occur between them. She was the last woman on earth a man like Sloan would be drawn to. On the day they'd met, he had labeled her a spinster with shattering casualness.

She remembered the sight of him earlier this afternoon when she'd checked on the children. He'd taken his shirt off to work. Even with the distance separating them, she'd been affected by the sight of his naked torso. Something had squeezed her stomach and clutched at her throat. She didn't know what that something was, but it made her feel vulnerable and threatened. Which made no sense. Not when Sloan was completely indifferent to her.

When she'd returned later, he'd put his shirt back on. It was ridiculous to be disappointed, but nevertheless she had been. Prudence touched a hand to her cheek. How mortifying to admit to herself that Sloan Coltrane had this primitive effect upon her. Thank goodness he would never know what foolish thoughts filled her head. She could well imagine his amusement if, even for a second, he guessed that she was becoming enamored of him. Arrogant man that he was, he would become even more obnoxious.

"Prudence, are you out here?"

At the sound of Gladys's concerned voice, Prudence jumped.

"Yes, I'm over here in the porch chair."

The housekeeper opened the screen door and stepped outside. "I'm worried about Richard."

Letting go of her thoughts of Sloan, Prudence considered the older woman's statement. "He might be a little uncertain, but I think he's settling in."

"I'm not talking about that," she said, crossing the porch. "I know he was spooked when he first came, but he's starting to relax around us. I just came from the boys' room, though, and he isn't there."

"Maybe he's using the facility."

"I checked there, too. I went to the barn. One of the horses is gone."

Prudence rose on unsteady legs. "Where do you think he went? To town?"

Gladys shook her head. "My guess is that he's headed for Sloan Coltrane's place."

Prudence went cold. The last thing she wanted was another angry confrontation with Sloan. "Why do you say that?"

"Just the way Richard's been acting. The others are real excited about them purebred horses showing up, but he's been stewing about it. Because he's the oldest boy, I think he considers himself the man of the house. My guess is that he's gone to set Coltrane straight on a few points."

"Oh, dear."

"Coltrane seems like a reasonable man to me. There's probably no harm in them talking. Might do the boy some good. I just thought you should know that Richard had taken one of the horses." That statement was accompanied by a wide yawn. "Well, good night."

Prudence considered what the housekeeper had told her, but she didn't feel nearly as calm as Gladys. There was no way she could go up to bed without making certain that Richard had returned safely. She walked to the edge of the porch and looked southwest, toward Sloan's property. His place was about four-and-a-half miles away. It would take a little more than an hour to walk there, if she kept a brisk pace. She directed her steps toward the horizon.

Sloan was stretched out on his cot when a fierce pounding sounded against the shack's door. He'd been reading by lantern light, rechecking the plans for the casino. He couldn't imagine who was calling on him so late at night and in such a rude fashion. As a precaution, he withdrew his Colt Peacemaker from the holster slung over the chair next to his makeshift bed.

"Who's there?"

"Richard Beck!"

It took a second for Sloan to connect the name to the boy staying with Prudence. He opened the door. Sure enough there stood the tallest of Prudence's brood.

The first thought to cross Sloan's mind was that there must be trouble of some kind to bring the boy out so late at night.

"What's wrong? Has something happened?"

The gangly youth shook his head, his gaze focused squarely on Sloan's drawn gun. Realizing how threatening he must appear to the lad, Sloan returned the weapon to his holster.

"You're not running away, are you?"

What other reason could the boy have for leaving the farmhouse at this time of night? Though, for the life of him, Sloan couldn't imagine one of Prudence's foundlings fleeing the home she'd so passionately defended a few weeks earlier.

The young man paled.

"No—no, sir." He cleared his throat. "I'm not running away."

Sloan was at a loss. He could hardly offer the kid a drink and invite him to talk. "Come inside and sit awhile."

The boy entered and shoved his hands into his pockets. "If it's all the same to you, I'll stand."

Sloan bit back an oath. He'd thought when he left the ranch, he'd left situations like this behind. Richard bore all the earmarks of a young man with a major dilemma. In fact, the way he was shifting from one foot to the other, he looked suspiciously similar to Sloan's brother, Jeremy, when he'd broken the news that he wanted to marry Misty Marie. Since Richard was a little young to have love problems, Sloan was in the dark as to what the difficulty was. But obviously it was something the kid couldn't talk over with a woman, even one as capable as Prudence.

"How old are you?" Sloan asked finally.

"Fourteen."

He'd been right. The boy was too young to be having woman trouble. That narrowed things down some. "You go riding at night often?"

A strange look flitted across his eyes. "No."

"Then you must have a good reason for being out tonight," Sloan said casually.

"I came to warn you."

The kid's voice cracked. A fiery blush steamed his cheeks. Sloan decided not to take offense. Whatever was stuck in the boy's craw was clearly important to him. Equally clear was that he was nervous about being here.

Still, he'd girded up his courage and come. That said a lot
about his character and the man he would one day become.

"Warn me about what?"

"I—I don't want you to hurt Miss Prudence or...or try
to drive her off her property."

Sloan scratched his jaw. "Did she send you here?"

"No. I came on my own."

"Because you're worried about me hurting her," Sloan
said noncommittally.

"That's right." The boy's chin came up. "You threatened to build your racetrack right around her house."

Sloan ran a fingertip around his open collar. That had
been one of his less noble moments, one he wanted to
forget. "You can see by the way I've laid out the track and
buildings that I'm not going to do that."

"You won't change your mind and switch things
around?"

This time it was Sloan who shook his head. "The track
is going to stay where it is. I've changed my plans so that
the stalls and gaming house are set back from Miss Abercrombie's property line."

"And even if you get mad at her, things will stay that
way?"

Since Sloan planned keeping as far away from Prudence as he could, he didn't figure there was anything she
could do to make him angry enough to tear up his buildings and shift things around, just to make her life miserable.

"The setup will stay the way it is," he reassured the boy.

Mistrust still tinged Richard's eyes, and Sloan wondered about the boy's past. What had made him so cyni-
cal at such a young age? Other questions tugged at Sloan.
How had the young man come to be one of Prudence's
lost sheep? Sloan wondered if the boy was on the run from
something. The law?

Yet, as curious as Sloan was about Richard Beck, he refused to inquire about his past. The boy was a link to Prudence. Upon some deep level that he didn't fully understand, but did respect, Sloan sensed the contrary woman could make him forget the fight he'd waged to gain his independence.

"You ride on home, Richard," Sloan admonished. "You don't want Miss Prudence or Miss Gladys getting worried about you."

"They don't know I'm gone." The boy squared his shoulders.

Sloan figured he was going to issue another warning.

"It ain't an easy world for women alone, especially if they've got young'uns. Every family should have a man to take charge of things." His eyes darkened. "A good man."

Sloan wasn't sure that Prudence would agree with the boy. She appeared to be a woman who could single-handedly run any household. The boy's earnest words made Sloan think that Richard was sharing a bit of personal history from his young life, a bit of painful history.

"Anyway, I intend to look after them."

Without warning Sloan remembered how he'd felt when his father had died. That he was responsible for the others in their household, that he should somehow be able to take care of them. But deep inside he'd known that he was inadequate and unprepared. He'd been scared, but he'd been determined that no one would ever know about his fears. He felt a sudden and profound kinship with Richard Beck.

"When you pick up a burden like that, son, it's a hard one to let go of."

"I won't let Miss Prudence down."

Resolve and something else, Sloan decided, shaped the boy's promise. Maybe he'd been wrong. Maybe a kid of fourteen wasn't too green to have a problem with love. It was clear to Sloan that Richard cared with deep and sweet innocence for Prudence Abercrombie.

"She's lucky to have you watching out for her."

Prudence knew she was lost. What a maddening development. She couldn't quite understand how it had happened. Obviously her sense of direction had become confused in the vast Texas plains that bore no distinctive landmarks, but she didn't know when or how. Good grief, she'd already walked twice today to the small hill that overlooked Sloan's property.

More irritated than alarmed, Prudence sat on a conveniently placed rock and considered her options. She could keep wandering around in hopes that she would recognize a familiar marking, or she could stay put until morning. That was the trouble with Texas, she decided; there weren't that many recognizable objects—like the handy street signs placed at the corners of Port Dodd's thoroughfares. There were only low hills and rolling plains. She looked to the stars and wished she could navigate by them. Aunt Phoebe would probably have been able to manage. She'd spent hours peering through her prized telescope, studying the celestial configurations.

Prudence easily located the familiar star patterns of the Big and Little Dippers, but they offered her no assistance whatsoever in finding her way home or to Sloan's place. She told herself there was nothing to be afraid of. Hopefully, the odd and assorted sounds she heard were made by nonlethal creatures that used the night to forage for food. She was hardly in danger of becoming an evening meal for an armadillo or a possum. She might have been more uneasy if the moon wasn't lighting up the sagebrush landscape.

A moist breeze drifted across her upturned face, offering a mild respite from the heat of the day. She wondered if Richard had returned home. She worried about him more than the other children under her care. He was the newest. He was the quiet one, the one who took the most responsibility upon himself. She sensed he carried secret pains that would remain with him long into adulthood. She didn't know for certain that he'd ridden out to meet with Sloan, but like Gladys, Prudence felt that was his most likely destination. Why? What need could he possibly have to converse with Sloan Coltrane?

The sound of approaching hoofbeats broke the night's stillness. She turned. Twenty yards from where she sat, the silhouette of a rider and his horse came into view.

She scrambled on top of the small boulder and shouted. "Richard! Is that you?"

The horse was reined in by its rider. An instant later both appeared in front of Prudence.

"Haven't you any sense at all?"

Prudence sighed. Why couldn't her rescuer have been Richard? Was it too much to ask to be spared another confrontation with Sloan Coltrane and his disagreeable temper?

"Hello, Sloan. How nice to run into you. You haven't per chance seen Richard, have you?"

"Get down from that rock before you fall and break your fool neck."

"My, it's certainly a balmy night for riding," she observed chattily, having no intention of obeying the man's order.

"Now."

"I'm not sure I like your attitude, Sloan. You're very bossy. Perhaps if you said please . . ."

The rest of her words never left her mouth. One minute Sloan was towering above her on his mount, and the next he was on top of her. His arm came around her waist with disconcerting forcefulness as he whisked her off her perch. He seemed to lower her to the ground and get off his horse in one abrupt movement.

"What in blazes do you think you're doing, wandering around at night?"

"Actually, I was walking to your place," she told him, hugging herself with her arms. He'd released his hold on her, and she was feeling a bit dazed by his habit of laying hands on her and then pushing her from him. "Unfortunately, I lost my bearings."

She hated confessing this aspect of her plight to him, but it went against her nature to lie. Besides, it wasn't a crime to become lost.

"Don't you realize what could have happened to you out here alone?"

It already had happened. Didn't the man listen? Her sense of direction had become mucked up. "I suppose you're going to tell me."

"You could have been bitten by a rattler."

"I tried not to think about that."

"You could have tangled with a coyote."

Just then a coyote chose that moment to howl obligingly in the distance.

"Or you could have become target practice for an outlaw, looking for trouble," he continued darkly.

She shook her head. "The first day we met you informed me that the West was hardly wild anymore."

He swore. She flinched.

"Well, you did say that," she said in her own defense. "I distinctly remember suggesting that you teach the boys how to handle firearms, and you said—"

"Prudence."

"Yes?" She didn't like it when he interrupted her. She liked it even less when he spoke her name with such simmering implacability.

"We're in trouble."

The fine hairs at the nape of her neck rose and she glanced around them. "What's wrong?"

# Chapter Eight

Sloan looked into Prudence's widened eyes and felt like the fool he'd accused her of being.

*We're in trouble....* What had possessed him to speak his thoughts out loud? It was just that she was so determined to win her utterly useless argument that he had suddenly realized how much he wanted to pull her into his arms and kiss her.

She'd scared him, damn it. When Richard had returned to his one-room shack all lathered up about how Prudence had come looking for him and wasn't anywhere to be found, Sloan had thought something terrible had happened to her. Now all she could do was plague him in some stupid female discussion about how the afternoon they'd met he'd told her the West wasn't wild anymore. Women! In two minutes they could do more to destroy a man's concentration than a herd of cattle running off in twenty different directions.

His gaze narrowed. He was thinking thoughts about this prim-and-proper woman that would probably make her hair curl. And she didn't even know it; that's how innocent she was. Here they were alone. It was the middle of the night. Anything could happen. And she was looking at him as if the only thing on her mind was proving she was right, and he was wrong about something that wasn't worth a jug of spit.

"What is it?" she asked again, her gaze darting around them. "What's wrong?"

He deliberately looked over his shoulder, as if double-checking their location. He was stalling, of course. Hell, he didn't know what he was going to tell her. Anything but the truth. Then from out of nowhere a downright evil thought occurred to him. He tried to resist it, but the temptation was just too great. A man could only take so much, and he'd only gotten enough to whet his appetite for more. He wouldn't seduce her, he told himself by way of soothing what had once been a fairly decent code of conduct. He'd just get cozy with her. A few kisses. A few caresses. If anything more happened between them, the choice would be hers to make.

His lie would be a small one, he decided—but necessary to set the stage between them. He'd fought his attraction to this maddening woman long enough.

"I'm afraid we're both lost now, Prudence."

Prudence couldn't believe her ears. Sloan Coltrane *lost?* He'd seemed quite invincible to her. She would have guessed he could be plopped down anywhere on the planet and have navigated his way back to civilization.

"I don't believe it," she said, voicing her astonishment aloud.

He remained silent, and she feared she'd unintentionally insulted him. As confident as Sloan was, he'd probably convinced himself that he had no flaws. Surely it was no easy thing for him to admit he'd become as lost as she was in this vast Texas landscape.

"But then," she continued, "I suppose I know better than anyone how easy it is to become turned around in the darkness."

"That's very generous of you to admit," he said gruffly, turning from her and walking to his horse.

"Where are you going?"

"To get a blanket."

An appalling realization struck her. She was going to spend the night with Sloan Coltrane. If she didn't think of something quick.

"Do you think that's a . . . good idea?" Goodness, she would have never believed her voice could squeak.

"You got a better one?" he asked evenly.

"We could ride double on your horse."

He spread the dark blanket on a relatively smooth piece of moon-drenched ground. "Ride where?"

"Oh, just around. Until we found our way to Amos's farmhouse."

"We'd end up more lost than we are right now. Come morning, we'll know which way is east."

"But . . . but can't you tell by looking at the stars where we are?"

He looked up from where he knelt beside the blanket. "I'm a horseman, not a sailor."

Prudence knew she was behaving badly. Sloan was just being sensible about their predicament, but it was no easy thing to contemplate spending the night, or what was left of it, with a member of the opposite sex. She'd always considered herself modern about most things, but this situation was very much out of her realm.

Why, she was totally at this man's mercy, she thought more than moderately dazed. As a free-thinking woman, she wanted to balk at the vulnerability being woven through her like an invisible but powerful net.

"Then you don't think it's a wise idea to try to find our way back?"

He was stretched out on the blanket now, resting his broad back against the small boulder she'd stood upon to attract his attention.

"Lucky could step in a hole and break his leg."

Her desperate gaze swung to the horse. She supposed
he did need all four legs.

"Come sit with me, Prudence."

She squared her shoulders. She could do that. Sit with
him. They would talk. The night would pass quickly.

She crossed the small distance that separated them and
dropped ungracefully next to him. The ground was hard.
She sat stiffly, wishing that more than a few inches separated them.

"You're favoring your right leg. Did you twist your
ankle?"

Without her permission, he raised the hem of her dress
and cupped her foot in his strong hands. They engaged in
a silent tug-of-war as she tried to pull free from his grasp.

"There's nothing wrong with it," she snapped irrita-
bly. "It's just that I think my shoes shrunk after I fell into
the river. The leather's stiff, and I probably have a blister
or two."

He let go of her foot. She shoved her dress down over
it, sitting with her knees drawn up to her chest.

"Why didn't you ride over to check up on Richard?"

A wave of guilt washed over Prudence. In the tumult of
meeting Sloan, she'd forgotten about the missing boy. "I
don't know how to ride," she admitted absently. "*Did*
Richard come to see you?"

"Twice," Sloan answered.

"What did he want?"

"The first time he showed up to tell me to mind my
manners where you're concerned. The second, to tell me
you'd come looking for him and must have lost your
way."

"They must be so worried about me." She sighed re-
gretfully.

Next to her, she felt Sloan stiffen. "Morning's not that
far off. As soon as they see you're okay, they'll be fine."

"I suppose you're right." She shifted again, finding it impossible to become comfortably settled on the unyielding ground.

"How can you live in Texas and not know how to ride?"

The question was typically arrogant, she thought, wincing as her bottom came into contact with a particularly sharp-cornered rock.

"When you live in town and everything is within walking distance, there's no reason to master the skill."

"You haven't always lived in Port Dodd, not with that accent."

The starry night cloaked them with a mysteriously intimate shroud that seemed to invite confidences. Still, in the short time she'd known Sloan, she'd become wary of his motives. She couldn't forget the anger he'd exhibited when he'd threatened to build his wretched racetrack around the farmhouse.

"I was born in England. When my father died, mother traveled to America to be reunited with Aunt Winifred and Aunt Phoebe."

"How did they end up all the way over here?"

"It's rather a long story," she equivocated, not certain he was truly interested in hearing her family saga.

Sloan turned his head toward her. His silvery eyes glittered like the stars overhead. Despite the evening's balmy temperature, she shivered.

"There's nothing else to do. We might as well…talk."

Prudence experimented with leaning against the rock Sloan was using to support his back. She didn't like the idea of sitting so close to him, but she was finding it impossible to get comfortable any other way. She supposed it was foolish to worry overmuch about sharing a common resting place. Perhaps talking to her companion would divert her thoughts from his disturbing closeness.

"Aunt Winifred fell in love with an American sea captain who was visiting the English countryside. My future Uncle Thomas had come to Bedfordshire to bring news to one of the neighboring families about a son of theirs who'd emigrated to America. Thomas was invited to a soiree where he met Aunt Winifred. Evidently, within moments of their first meeting, they fell in love with each other."

"You sound disapproving."

"Oh, no, it's not that. It's just that from what I've heard, everyone was caught off guard by the suddenness of their attachment to each other."

"Him being a foreigner probably didn't help matters."

"Actually, it wasn't that so much," Prudence confided. "Aunt Winifred was well into her years when she met Thomas. It was generally assumed that she and her two sisters would remain unmarried."

"One of the sisters being your mother?"

Prudence nodded. "The three girls were close growing up. My English grandparents were evidently very old-fashioned. They didn't send their daughters to London for a season. They more or less kept them confined to the countryside. It was all very shocking that Winifred decided to marry any man. I believe she was almost thirty."

"You think someone over thirty is too old to marry?" Sloan asked, his tone clearly offended.

"Not for a man, perhaps." She looked at the velvety sky and swallowed. "But it's different for a woman. Mother was also in her thirties when she married. Father was a widower well advanced in years who had already raised a family of his own. I believe I was quite a surprise to their union. When he passed away, Mother decided to come to America and visit her sisters."

"In Port Dodd," Sloan guessed.

"Uncle Thomas had died at sea. I believe she wanted to persuade Winifred and Phoebe to rejoin her in England."

"What happened?"

"Well, Mother and I settled at Winifred's home, instead. Each of the sisters had a small annual stipend. By pooling their resources they managed quite well. I think they liked the freedom they experienced in America. If they'd returned to England, there would have been innumerable family members ready to oversee their lives."

"I can understand them wanting to be on their own," Sloan surprised her by saying. "Families have a tendency to take over a person's life."

"I think it's just the opposite," Prudence objected. "Belonging to a family gives a person a sense of purpose."

"Do you consider the children you care for as your family?"

"Well, of course I do."

"How did you come to be in charge of them?"

"That's another long story," she answered, suddenly aware that she was no longer leaning against the rigid contours of the rock. Instead, she had mysteriously come to be resting against Sloan's side. He was a lot warmer than stone, and a lot more comfortable. She had never been in a situation like this before. Alone with a man. Her body leaning into his. Darkness shrouding their actions from the rest of the world.

Innocent. Everything about their predicament was purely innocent. Still, a tingling sense of wariness crept down her spine. At least she thought it was wariness. Or hoped so. The women in her family had a tradition of being prudent and rational for most of their lives and then suddenly going against convention. Dear Aunt Phoebe had been close to seventy when she'd become smitten with Amos Coltrane. Evidently the Abercrombie women shared a family legacy of being susceptible to the wrong men. Or was it just that men happened to appear in their lives at the wrong time? Or perhaps the right time?

It was all so confusing to Prudence. Her earliest childhood memories of her aunts and her mother consisted of them being independent and free-thinking. It was difficult, if not impossible, to envision them succumbing to a man. She had never lived in a household with a dominant male figure. She wasn't sure she would like surrendering even a portion of her independence to any man. And yet her mother had. Aunt Winifred had. And if she'd lived several weeks longer, Aunt Phoebe would have. Only her death had prevented her from marching down the aisle with Amos.

A poignant sense of loss on behalf of her aunt smote Prudence. The moon continued to shine. The stars continued to sparkle. And the night continued to envelop her. She wondered if Phoebe and Amos might have a second chance at happiness, in heaven, perhaps.

"Did you change your mind?"

Prudence started. Sloan's husky voice seemed astonishingly close to her ear. "Change my mind?"

"About telling me the long story of how you came to run Draper House?"

Prudence turned her head. It was very close to Sloan's shoulder. Why, if she had an itch on the tip of her nose, she could rub it against his shirtsleeve.

"There was a fire in Port Dodd," she began, hoping her awareness of Sloan wouldn't unhinge her to the point that she did something foolish. Like actually nestle against him.

"They must have rebuilt fast. I didn't see any burned-out buildings."

"This happened fifteen years ago. I was ten years old at the time." She realized from the information she'd just given him, Sloan could figure out how old she was.

Twenty-five. Definitely qualifying for spinsterhood. "Aunt Winifred's home was spared, and she opened it up to the children who'd been left orphaned by the flames. It was to be only a temporary arrangement, until they could be reunited with other members of their families."

"That was very generous of your aunts."

Prudence smiled at the fond memories of her departed relatives. "They were very unusual women, Sloan. I think the townspeople here didn't know what to make of them. They were vocal in their loyalty to the Church of England, yet they took turns attending all the churches in Port Dodd. Aunt Phoebe loved her telescope. My mother liked to sail about the harbor, and Aunt Winifred was a bird-watcher and fascinated by unusual rock formations.

"In all they took in sixteen children after the fire. They were able to return most of them to their relations, but they couldn't find any family to send four of the children to."

"So they kept them?"

"Indeed they did."

"What happened to them?"

"Well, two of them were boys. Quincy is now at the university in Houston. He plans on becoming a doctor. William received a calling to the ministry. Emma Sue is a teacher in Idaho. Margaret Alice is married and a mother."

"And now you've got a new brood of young'uns you're taking care of. Where did they come from?"

"Each of them has his or her own story."

"How did you end up on Draper Street?"

"Aunt Winifred decided to sell her home to provide us with the money we needed to get by, and that's when we rented the house on Draper Street. It was also how we were able to afford the cost of Quincy's and William's education."

Prudence didn't like dwelling on the subject of money. Without Amos's generous bequest, she didn't know what she would have done to maintain a home for the children. While not an immediate crisis, money had become a subtle background concern. They had enough tucked away in an old gray sock under Prudence's mattress to see them through the summer. The fall always brought donations from the area churches. Somehow they managed. There were her monthly meetings with Estelle Brubaker and the Women's Aid Society. Being able to live on the farm was a godsend. They had an abundance of milk, eggs and butter. They'd planted a garden, and it seemed as if every one of the buried seeds had sprouted.

Everything would be all right.

If nothing unexpected happened. Like needing to purchase a new crutch for Davy.

"Are you cold?"

Prudence glanced up at Sloan in surprise. "Of course not. It's a perfect night."

He stared deeply into her eyes, and her stomach took a peculiar lurch. "You just shivered."

His deep voice insinuated itself beneath her skin, and darned if she didn't shiver again. But this time thoughts of money and its scarcity weren't the blame. It was the man sitting beside her with his arm slung around her shoulder that caused her to tremble.

*His arm was around her shoulder....* When had that happened?

"I..." Her voice trailed off.

"You what?"

Prudence opened her mouth to speak, perhaps even to say something rational. But all at once her mind stopped functioning. She had no idea what they were talking about.

The silence grew between them. A feeling of panic welled up inside her. Something was going to happen between them—something she wasn't prepared for. His face was so close, his sharply chiseled features highlighted by the resplendent moon. His eyes continued to stare into her very soul. He appeared to be concentrating intensely upon some weighty matter of the mind.

Prudence's survival instinct surged within her. She sensed she ought to draw away from him. To put some physical distance between them. Yet the moment seemed to consume all her energy. It was almost as if she'd become paralyzed, unable to move as she waited for Sloan to act upon the silent force she sensed gathering within him.

When she could endure his relentless stare no longer, her gaze dropped to her lap where her hands were tightly clasped. He shifted his position on the blanket. Her breath locked in her throat. Mesmerized, she watched his hand move to her lap. His touch was unexpectedly gentle, frighteningly pleasant, as he used his forefinger to separate her hands. His callused fingertip traced an invisible pattern upon her right palm. Slowly, inexorably, Prudence felt the muscles of her body sink into a deep lethargy. She felt his simple touch in the pit of her stomach. She felt it at the tips of her breasts. She felt it . . . between her thighs.

And she felt it within her heart. More than physically, the contact of his work-worn flesh against her suddenly sensitive palm penetrated a place that was as virginal as her womb, a place she had thought no man would ever gain entry. It was a lonely place, but the soil was fertile. There was love and warmth and hope in abundance. Ready to be loosened and set free.

He stroked her palm.

She shuddered and then was embarrassed by her strong reaction to what was surely meant as the most casual contact. Tears pricked her eyes. She sensed there could be great pain in allowing Sloan to continue his simple ca-

ress, just as she sensed no woman ever reached an age
where she was immune to the reactions a man could stir
within her.

Again she was struck with the impression that she
should pull away and end this dangerous interlude. What
stopped her wasn't the pleasure she was deriving from his
touch, but a feeling that the man whose finger was arous-
ing this confusing tempest within her was as needy as she
was for the closeness they shared. He was reaching out to
her. She suspected he wasn't a man to reach out to anyone. That single thought checked her flight.

They were two separate beings drawn together by cir-
cumstance and moonlit darkness. Each of them in their
own way was vulnerable. To draw away would be to reject him. Even though logic advised her to be sensible and
end the encounter, her heart wouldn't allow her to wound
him.

She remembered him riding his horse into the river to
retrieve both Davy and herself.

She saw him when she'd opened her door to him that
same night and he'd extended Davy's crutch to her.

She recalled his face when Janey had asked if he was a
daddy.

Other memories of him being an overbearing bully
flashed through her thoughts, but each of those moments dissolved into nothingness. He touched a place
within her no man had ever touched. And the feelings he
stirred were terrifyingly similar to the love she felt toward
each of her adopted children.

"Your skin is so soft." His low-pitched drawl made her
toes curl inside her shrunken shoes.

"Yours is...rough."

His finger stopped its tingling trek. "Too rough?"

She swallowed. Why did their conversation seem so intimate? So...seductive? "No."

His jaw brushed the top of her head. "I like the way you feel, Prudence."

What could she say to that? The words, *I like the way you feel, too,* were totally beyond her.

"Your hair smells like a flower garden," he continued, his voice a compelling rasp across the height and breadth of her. "Are you comfortable?"

How was it possible to be relaxed *and* alarmed at the same time?

"I'm...okay."

"The ground is too hard for you. Come here. My lap has to be softer."

He suited his action to his words and, before she realized what was happening, she was settled on his lap. He was wrong. It wasn't softer than the ground.

"There, isn't that better?"

*Better?* She choked back a nervous giggle. Better would surely have been for them to be in their separate beds.

"Lean back. I'm not going to bite you."

She found herself turned sideways against him, his wide chest an inviting cradle for her head. Gingerly she rested her cheek against him. The material of his cotton work shirt seemed a fragile barrier between her and his skin. She was fiercely conscious of the hard, muscular flesh that lay beneath the fabric. The steady beat of his heart reminded her that he was a virile male. The firm angle of his thighs reminded her of his strength. His powerful arms reminded her that she was a woman who'd never known a man's embrace.

He rubbed his hands across her back. "Tell me how Richard came to be one of your adopted waifs."

She wasn't certain she could tell Sloan her name at that point. "He just showed up one afternoon at Draper House," she began, drawing a ragged breath. "I'm sure some people in town directed him to our door. He said he'd do any odd jobs we had around the place." She paused for a moment, recalling with vivid clarity how proudly he'd carried himself, despite the uncertainty in his dark eyes. "He's been a wonderful help in the short time he's been with us. I don't know how we got along without him."

"Of course, he could have shown up blind and one-legged and you would have taken him in, too."

There was an edge to Sloan's words that she didn't understand. He sounded almost angry. "If Richard had been so disadvantaged, that would have been even more reason to take him in."

She felt the gentle tug of Sloan's fingers against her hair, and her scalp tingled. "You can't adopt the whole world, Prudence."

"The whole world doesn't want me to adopt it," she answered simply.

"No, I reckon your specialty is taking in Port Dodd's wounded critters."

"They're not critters, they're children."

He tilted her back against his arm. "Tell me this, have you ever done one thing just for yourself?"

Behind his dark head a canopy of stars filled the night sky. She stared deeply into his glittering eyes. Another shiver coursed through her. This one settled deep within her womb.

"I don't know what you mean."

"You're lying. You know exactly what I mean. Have you ever done anything for the sheer joy of doing it?"

She licked her suddenly dry lips. "I flew a kite once."

He smiled abruptly, his white teeth slashing his rugged features. "How old were you?"

"Eight."

"What have you done lately, Prudence?"

She licked her lips again.

He groaned. "That's once too often you've done that."

"Done what?"

"Run the tip of your tongue across your lips."

"I didn't know there was a limit," she said, dazed by the crosscurrents of tingling energy that ebbed and flowed between them.

He lowered his head. "There is tonight, darlin'."

Now. He was going to kiss her now.

The tip of his tongue moved gently against her bottom lip. Her entire body clenched, then relaxed. She'd never experienced anything so shockingly sensuous. Yet even in her innocence, she knew she wasn't experiencing a real kiss.

"I've wanted to do that for the longest time," he murmured, his words strangely slurred.

"What?"

"Taste you."

A primitive excitement grew inside her. Her hands slipped behind his neck and for the first time she touched his hair. It was thick and soft and warm. "Did you like it?"

"It?"

"Me, how I tasted," she clarified breathlessly.

Scandalous, their conversation was surely scandalous.

"I'm not sure. I think I need another sampling."

His mouth lowered to hers. There was a brief testing, as if he was adjusting to her shape and texture. Then, without warning, he deepened the pressure of his lips upon hers. It was as if a dozen shooting stars went off inside her.

His tongue penetrated her parted lips. Bold, possessive, hungry. Not a gentle invasion but an absolute conquest. He demanded surrender, and surrender she did. Not with a white flag. Not with a broken sword. But with a low moan that rippled from her mouth to his.

There was no time to think. No time to catalog the incredible sensations cascading through her. There was only this wild, tempestuous moment. And if she held on tight, she was certain it could last forever.

The kiss, and she was truly convinced this *was* a kiss, unlike the near misses she'd experienced before with Sloan, went on and on. Dimly, she was aware that his hands were fumbling with the buttons at the front of her dress. Dimly she was aware that she'd lost the need to breathe. Just as she was dimly aware that the planets and the stars and the moon continued their individual courses.

It was the shocking touch of his palm against her bared breast that broke the spell. She knew what he'd been doing with her buttons and her corset ties. Loosening them. She realized she most certainly did need to draw oxygen into her lungs. How else could she gasp in indignation?

She pushed against him. "Stop that! What do you think you're doing?"

He was breathing so hard she marveled he could even hear her protest. "You don't want to stop now, honey."

By now his bluntness should have ceased to amaze her. That it didn't, confirmed he had no shame.

"I most certainly do wish for you to stop."

She covered her bared breasts with her hands. How on earth had she gotten into this terrible predicament? Why, if she'd kept kissing him for another few minutes, she'd probably be stripped nude! At that thought, her face burned. She was a mature woman of twenty-five. How could she have let herself be carried away by anything as . . . as foolish as passion?

"Don't cover up, honey. You're beautiful. I want to look at you."

"Ooh! You really are a weasel."

Since she was sitting on his lap, her words lacked the impact they would have carried had they been standing like civilized human beings.

"Calm down, honey. I'm not going to hurt you."

"I am calm. And don't call me 'honey.'"

He continued to stroke her back, even though she was stiff as a poker. She would have jumped off his lap. But she knew if she moved, he'd probably catch another glimpse of her breasts. She really couldn't allow that.

"You don't have to be afraid of me. I would never force you."

"Hah! Don't flatter yourself, Sloan. I'm not afraid of you."

One corner of his mouth tilted upward, as if he were suppressing a grin. She wanted to slap him. Actually, she would have, but there was the tricky matter of keeping her bosom covered.

"It appears to me that you could use some help, Prudence."

"Don't call me Prudence."

"That's your name, isn't it?"

"You've forfeited the privilege," she declared disdainfully, wondering if she could cover herself with one hand while fastening her corset and dress with the other.

"So we're back to Miss Abercrombie," he mused thoughtfully, his manner glaringly unrepentant.

"Help me up," she commanded imperiously.

"Then what?" he asked conversationally, not moving so much as a muscle.

"Then for once in your miserable life, you'll behave like a gentleman and turn your back so I can set my dress to rights."

He continued to caress her back. Through the flimsy material, her body seemed to have developed a mind of its own. And it had decided that his fingers were strong and supple and downright magical in how they made her feel. She could only imagine how they would feel if she permitted him access to the rest of her.

"Do you have any idea how beautiful you are?" he asked.

She wondered if he'd heard a thing she'd said. Tears gathered. No man had ever called her beautiful. Since she knew she wasn't, she'd never been overly distressed by the omission. It hurt her deeply that Sloan thought she was silly enough to believe such a patent lie. But even as she admitted that, she couldn't deny the treacherous yearning his words evoked.

She lowered her head. "I suppose if it's dark enough, any woman would seem beautiful to you."

His hands stilled. Then he used a forefinger to tip her chin upward. "Your eyes remind me of the first tender blades of grass each spring brings."

She stared at him mutely. She hadn't believed Sloan capable of such poetic or hollow flattery.

"Your hair is thick and silky and, when you let the sun find it, streaked with the red of a desert sunrise. Your mouth is soft and sweet and..." His lips hovered above hers. "And I can't get enough of it."

When his kiss came, it was tender enough to free the tears she'd tried to fight. His tongue claimed her with a piercing hunger that shattered her control. Knowing she'd once again been drawn into forbidden territory she loosened the death grip with which she concealed herself.

Sloan groaned deeply within his chest. Somehow their bodies mysteriously aligned themselves with each other. Prudence found herself lying on the ground with him leaning over her.

"Your breasts are beautiful, too. So soft to my touch." The pad of his callused fingertip stroked her. She felt a shuddering, squeezing sensation deep within her. "And your nipples remind me how much we're alike." He bent his head. The brush of his tongue against the distended tips of her breasts made her bite her lip against the exquisite pleasure that rippled through her. "They're hard. Just as hard as I am."

As he continued to kiss and taste this most sensitive part of her, she marveled at her capacity to experience pleasure. She'd hadn't known how wonderful it would feel to be with a man. And yet there was also a definite sense of dissatisfaction as if something were missing. There was a pleasant tingling between her thighs, but there was also a hollowness.

Instinctively she pressed herself against Sloan again, knowing that through him that hollowness could be assuaged. "Oh, Sloan," she said sighing, feeling that she was drifting toward some inexplicable bridge, that once crossed would change her forever. There was the sense that she was nearing some point where there would be no turning back, as if the forces of nature were gathering for an uncontrollable crescendo.

"What is it, darlin'?" His hand had slipped beneath her dress. She could feel the hot imprint of his fingers on her thigh.

*No turning back...* The momentous words tumbled like the swirl of raging rapids through her thoughts.

"I never knew it would feel this way."

His caress continued upward. Her entire body seemed to hold its breath. It took every bit of her concentration not to squirm.

"What would feel this way?"

"You. Me. This."

His warm palm cupped her most private place. And it didn't matter that she tried not to, she still squirmed. She pressed herself even closer to his renegade touch.

He rubbed the heel of his palm against her, and she shuddered. This time the pleasure coursing through her was almost unbearable.

"*This,*" he said, his voice hoarse, "is what it's all about."

"Between a man and a woman," she whispered, her throat tight.

"Between you and me," he corrected her gruffly.

"I love you, Sloan."

The minute the words escaped Prudence's mouth she wanted to call them back. For one thing, they weren't true. She most certainly *didn't* love Sloan. Not in the way her mother must have loved her father, or in the way Winifred and Phoebe had loved the special men in their lives. The truth was she didn't *want* to love him. He was too bold for her tastes. Too wild. Too reckless. Too... uncontrollable.

But she did want to satisfy the incredible hunger he had unleashed within her. What a dreadful indictment of her lack of character.

Horrified at this admission of her carnal nature, Prudence wanted to hide that sad discovery behind a wall of outraged modesty.

But she could not.

She had gone too far.

## Chapter Nine

Sloan saw the haunted look in Prudence's eyes and silently cursed his lack of control. He was a bastard. That was a bitter truth for a man to acknowledge under any circumstances. It was even worse when he'd tried to take advantage of a respectable woman like Prudence Abercrombie.

He got to his feet, doing his damnedest not to stare at her lovely breasts. "You were right before. We should call a halt to this."

"Sloan—"

"I'll turn my back so you can fix your clothes."

A heartbeat of silence passed. His forehead broke out in sweat. What would he do if she begged him to finish making love to her? He didn't think he had it in him to turn her down. But only a gold-plated bastard would take advantage of an infatuated female.

"It's a little late for that," she muttered, also rising to her feet. "You've already seen a goodly portion of my attributes."

It took a moment for her words to sink in. Unaccountably, he was nettled by her equanimity.

He decided to do a little jabbing of his own. "In that case, would you like my help?"

Even though his back was to her, he knew she was glaring at him. Good, he'd get her angry and she'd forget any nonsense about being in love with him. In love with him... Sloan jammed his fingers through his hair. Good Lord, he didn't relish the thought of breaking this woman's heart.

"Sloan, there's something you ought to know."

She was going to tell him again that she was in love with him. It was crazy, but for a moment he felt a surge of pure joy. Then sanity surfaced. Being in love with a woman like Prudence would mean marriage and a ready-made family of *six* urchins. He wasn't ready to lose the freedom he'd so recently gained.

"You can tell me later. It's time we got you home."

He darted a quick glance in her direction and was relieved to see her breasts were tucked inside her chemise. Her fingers were practically flying up the front of her dress as she buttoned it. Okay, so maybe he wasn't relieved. Maybe he'd like to continue looking at her perfectly formed bosom. Maybe he'd like to see the rest of her, too.

Maybe he'd lost his mind. He scowled. She'd done it to him.

"It's those hideous black dresses of yours," he said, speaking his thoughts aloud.

He ripped the blanket from the ground.

"I beg your pardon?"

"You heard me." He secured the rumpled blanket to his saddle and turned. "Let's get out of here."

When she didn't move, he curled his fingers around her arm and pulled her to his horse. He didn't loosen his grip as he bounded onto the saddle. Less than a second later he had her sitting in front of him.

"I don't see what my dresses have to do with anything."

"Then I'll explain," he said, pleased he'd diverted her thoughts from another declaration of love. "They're black and they're ugly. Whereas you, Miss Abercrombie, are a fine figure of a woman. Naturally when a man looks at you, he doesn't want to see a high-necked, long-sleeved, frumpy black scrap of cloth covering you up. So he makes it disappear in his mind. And all he sees when he looks at you is your naked flesh."

Her gasp of outrage soothed his ragged sense of control. He was still hard and hurting, and, with her pressed against him, it was all he could do not to rein in Lucky and start things all over again. Only this time, his damned honor wouldn't keep him from claiming her fully.

"I bet you didn't even know a man could do that," he continued, his voice sounding harsh to his own ears. "Well let me tell you, we can. We do it all the time. Especially with little prim and proper virgins who don't know up from down and would probably faint dead away if a man really said what was on his mind."

"Are you finished?"

Her calm tone made him grind his teeth together. Either the woman had ice in her veins, or she was as skilled at hiding her feelings as a professional poker player.

"No. Now, take your hair—"

"You said you liked it!" she protested with an angry wail.

"Yeah. I like it. Down around your shoulders. Your bare shoulders. But that's not how you wear it. Oh, no, not you, Miss Abercrombie. You take that pretty mane and bunch it up into a tight little knot on the top of your head. Just plain orneriness, if you ask me."

"Well, I haven't asked you."

"Of course, it's none of my business if you want to walk around looking like someone's sainted grandmother."

She made a choking sound.

"The point is . . ." He broke off. For the life of him, he couldn't remember the point he'd been trying to make. All he knew was that he was angry, and it was her fault.

"Pray continue," she urged, her English accent making the invitation sound like a command from royalty.

"I've had my say," he muttered.

"And you've made your feelings crystal clear."

He had? "Then that's that."

"Not quite, Mr. Coltrane." She sat ramrod stiff in front of him. "I understand that you blame my humble mode of dress and my conservative hairstyle for provoking you into becoming an animal."

He frowned over her head. He didn't like being called an animal. It came uncomfortably close to describing how violently he'd wanted her. He kept his silence, though. Better to let her vent her anger and get it over with.

"But there's something you need to understand. I don't know what possessed me to say that I loved you, when in fact all I feel toward you is a strong personal loathing."

He should have been glad that he'd succeeded in making her so mad that she no longer thought she was in love with him. Somehow, however, *glad* was the direct opposite of how he felt.

"I suppose I was caught up in the moment," she went on to say. "It was the most astonishing thing, really. I've never experienced . . . er . . . physical ardor such as what happened between us. It's quite inspiring, isn't it? No wonder so many poets have written about it. Anyway, in the . . . passion of the moment, I lost my head. I apologize for misleading you. But considering your grossly insulting rudeness, I'm sure you'll understand me not holding my breath for you to forgive me."

He knew his mouth was hanging open. He'd never been cut so low by another human being. And to have been done so by this petite, prissy-mannered female knocked the air from his lungs.

They rode in silence across the slowly rising plain. Before long, Amos's farmhouse came into view.

"There's one more thing, Sloan."

"What's that?" he asked, bracing himself for another go-around with his passenger.

"You are a low, vile, despicable cad."

"Anything else?"

"Yes. You knew all along the direction you needed to travel to return me home, but you lied about it. I can only conclude that you did so to... to assault my person in a carnal fashion."

Now she was making him mad. "Well, ma'am, there might be some truth to that. Isn't it lucky for both of us that you enjoyed it so much?"

"Ooh!"

He leaned forward to whisper in her ear. "I did you a favor, honey."

"Hah!"

"I showed you what you've been missing."

"Your generosity is overwhelming."

"And I stopped because you said you loved me, and I didn't want to take advantage of you."

He heard her suck in her breath. Maybe he'd gone too far, but Prudence had a way of pushing him to the far fences.

"You may not believe me," he added, "but I do respect you. If it weren't for you, the children you've taken in would probably be dead or wandering the streets begging for handouts. You're a good woman, Prudence Abercrombie."

"I'll accept your respect," she said coolly, already trying to pull away from him and dismount, even though they had a few more yards to go. "But I'd appreciate it greatly if you'd never speak to me again."

"Hold on, I'll help you down."

She turned on him, her eyes blazing. "I don't want your help! I just want you to stay away from me and the children."

They engaged in a brief wrestling match. Lucky got disgusted with their antics and started sidestepping.

"I said to hold still!"

"And I said I don't want your help!"

"What's going on?" came Gladys's curious voice.

Sloan looked toward the house and realized the front door was open. They'd drawn a crowd.

"Miss Prudence, you're back!" Charlotte cried happily.

"What happened?" Davy asked, yawning widely. "Did you get lost?"

"Yes, she got lost," Sloan took great satisfaction in answering as he forcibly helped Prudence to the ground. "If I hadn't found her, she'd still be twiddling her thumbs, waiting for someone to rescue her."

Prudence stalked to the front porch.

"Well then, thank you, Sloan. We appreciate your help," Gladys said warmly. "Richard will be greatly relieved. He's still riding around, looking for Prue, but he's been coming to the house every so often to see if she's here. He'll probably be showing up again in a few minutes."

"I'll say good night, then," Sloan said flatly.

He turned Lucky toward home. The children's various goodbyes followed him out of the yard. Prudence's aristocratic voice was noticeably absent.


"Serve Miss Abercrombie another piece of cake," Estelle Brubaker, plump and serene, instructed the serving girl dressed in a gray gown and crisp white apron.

"Thank you, but I'm really quite full," Prudence said as she took another sip of tea.

On the second Tuesday of each month she took tea with Mrs. Brubaker and the women serving on charitable committees of the various churches. The Brubaker parlor was filled with lovely and fragile artifacts from the finest Eastern stores. As she glanced at a delicate vase resting upon a marble column, Prudence couldn't help but think that the hand-painted object probably cost more than what it took to run her household for a year.

"Marabelle, darling, come in and say hello to the ladies."

Young, beautiful and vibrant, Marabelle Brubaker was home from finishing school. Her lustrous blond hair was cleverly arranged in cascading curls, providing a magnificent frame for her perfect features. Her saffron yellow dress consisted of narrow ruffled tiers that were drawn upward and gathered snugly at her tiny waist. Being in the same room with the lovely young woman made Prudence feel like an old crone. She brushed her fingers against the black material and remembered Sloan's derogatory comments of last week. She'd been too proud to tell him that she didn't have money to buy new clothes and had been wearing black since her mother's death over five years ago.

"My mother likes to show me off," Marabelle confessed with disarming humor. She entered the room and turned slowly. "She also likes to show off my new wardrobe." The girl crossed the floor and placed an affectionate kiss on her mother's upturned cheek. "Now, my manners are something Mother isn't quite so fond of showing off."

Everyone laughed. Prudence felt about two hundred years old. She couldn't even imagine how it would feel to be so young and carefree.

"Marabelle, behave yourself," the older woman admonished, beaming with open pride at her only daughter.

"Yes, Mama," she replied dutifully, her blue eyes twinkling with infectious good humor. When her glance fell upon Prudence, the girl's smile widened. "Oh, this must be a meeting to provide funds for Draper House. Prudence, how have you been? How's Janey?"

"She's doing fine."

"How many orphans do you have now?"

"She has six," her mother answered. "Though I'm quite sure the last young man who showed up is old enough to be on his own. Really, Prudence, there's no need for you to take in everyone who shows up on your doorstep."

"Richard does so much work around the place, I feel as if I should be paying him," Prudence said, feeling obliged to defend the boy. "Welcome home, Marabelle."

"It's wonderful to be back." She snatched a crumb of white cake from the serving tray and popped the morsel into her mouth. "What's this I hear that you've moved?"

"It's true," Prudence confirmed. "Amos Coltrane passed away and left us his farmhouse."

"I'm sorry to hear he died," she said, her lovely features sobering. "I imagine the children love living in the country."

"Well, if you ask me, I think it's scandalous," Mrs. Brubaker sniffed. "I don't wish to offend you, Prudence, but the way your aunt was carrying on with Amos was quite... Well, I don't know exactly what to call it in polite society."

"You already said it was scandalous," her daughter pointed out. "But I think it was most romantic. Just think, even though they were greatly advanced in years, they still fell in love."

The room became uncomfortably silent. No one ever challenged Estelle Brubaker's opinions. Not her friends. Not her husband. And most certainly not one of her children, even her well-loved daughter.

"Ah, the young, they have quite an imagination, don't they?" the matron inquired with surprising mildness.

Prudence concluded that Estelle was so happy to see her daughter that she was allowing the girl some extra latitude in expressing her opinions.

"What is the name of your institution now?" Marabelle asked as she sat in the unoccupied chair next to Prudence.

"It's hardly an institution," Estelle protested.

"It certainly is," her daughter corrected her. "Prudence Abercrombie provides a valuable service for Port Dodd. Why, she's an institution herself. I don't know what we would do without her. How many families are willing to take in unwanted children?"

Prudence didn't know if she liked being referred to as an institution. Even though she knew Marabelle was praising her efforts, being called an institution made her feel a thousand years old.

"We haven't come up with a new name," she confined herself to answering.

"Hmm, you can't keep calling your establishment Draper House if you don't live on Draper Street, can you?"

"I suppose not," Prudence agreed.

"I know. Why don't we name it The Abercrombie Home?"

"Goodness, that won't do," the girl's mother protested. "Prudence is far too young to have the home named after her."

"I don't know what age has to do with it," Marabelle mused. "Besides, Prudence has been caring for the children on her own for the past year. You wrote me so yourself, Mother."

Prudence's gaze kept pivoting between the two women. It was an unnerving experience to be talked around as if she weren't even present.

"Still, there's the matter of continuity," Estelle noted. "When Prudence goes to meet her Maker, the name would lose its meaning. No, I do believe we should change the name of Draper House to Brubaker Place. After all, our family has contributed the most heavily to the children's welfare in the past and will continue to do so in the future."

Prudence was taken aback by the older woman's dispassionate reference to her own demise. Estelle made it sound as if death lurked around the next corner.

"It's Prudence who does all the work," Marabelle pointed out as she leaned forward and patted Prudence's knee. "Has Janey enjoyed receiving the letters I mailed to her?"

"They're her most prized possessions. She keeps them tucked under her pillow."

Marabelle smiled warmly. "I can hardly wait to ride out to your new home. How are Charlie and Charlotte doing?"

"Really, Marabelle, we hardly need a name-by-name accounting of their lives," Estelle commented testily as she set aside her teacup and signaled for the maid to carry it away.

Marabelle winked at Prudence. "Forgive me, Mother. I've been away so long I've forgotten what constitutes a proper subject for conversation at one of your afternoon teas."

"Today we are discussing the inconsiderate manner in which Prudence's children have been wearing out their shoes. Really, my dear," the older woman said, frowning intently at Prudence. "They must learn to be more responsible."

Prudence bit her lip against pointing out that it was hardly the children's fault that their feet were growing. It wouldn't do to offend Port Dodd's leading social matron. Not when the woman did contribute to their needs, though not quite as generously as she'd indicated to her daughter.

"We will endeavor to be more careful," Prudence assured her.

"We've had enough talk of shoes," Martha Larsen said, her voice pulsing with excitement. "Marabelle, have you heard about the racetrack that's being built?"

The girl nodded. "It's all Father's been talking about."

"Mr. Coltrane is bringing in thoroughbreds," Dixie Scott told them.

"He's the most fascinating man," Delores Martin said, sighing. "When he first arrived in town, he seemed quite rough and unrefined. But I saw him at the bank yesterday, and he had decidedly improved the quality of his dress. He looked very handsome, very dashing."

"He comes from a sound family," Estelle remarked. "George has investigated his background. He's one of the Houston Coltranes. His father was a war hero, and his family owns one of the largest cattle ranches in Texas. He's single," she finished with a significant look at her daughter.

"I'd heard that," Delores added casually. The woman had two unmarried daughters and no doubt considered Coltrane a potential suitor for one of them. "Howard has invited him for supper one evening next week."

Prudence would have loved to have told the women present that Sloan Coltrane was a vile and brutish deceiver of women. That he had no scruples, no code of honor, and would take shameless advantage of any woman unfortunate enough to cross his path.

Of course, she did no such thing. For if she explained that she had been alone with him in the middle of the night and had allowed him to partially undress her, her reputation would have been as shredded as her dignity. So she sat there in Estelle Brubaker's elegant parlor and kept her lips firmly sealed. The young women of Port Dodd were going to have to find out for themselves that a wolf in sheep's clothing had infiltrated their neighborhood.

"Are you still opposed to the racetrack, Prudence?" Delores asked.

"I don't condone gambling," she answered honestly. "Certainly not in my own backyard."

Estelle laughed. "You just don't understand men, dear. Even the finest and most upstanding gentleman has needs we women don't. They do like their cheroots and their port. Try and curtail their card games and a most distressing argument ensues. At least when the racetrack opens, we will know where our men are. It will keep them innocently occupied."

"I intend to go to the races myself," Delores announced. "My family hails from the South, and there's a long tradition of soirees and galas associated with the running of thoroughbreds."

"That's true," Estelle observed reflectively. "When Harvey and I toured England, we attended the races sponsored by the gentry. Gracious, you should have seen some of the gowns. They quite took my breath away."

The conversation continued to swirl and ebb around Prudence, but her thoughts weren't on fancy English day dresses. She was thinking about the man who'd kissed her with such dark and heavy passion. His boldness. His intensity. His renegade touch. He had held her in his powerful embrace and transported her to trembling excitement. She glanced at the faces of the women who animatedly discussed sponsoring a ball to herald the opening of the racetrack and wondered if they'd experienced the same thrilling sensations that Sloan had stirred within her.

Of course, they were married women and entitled by both the laws of the land and God to rightfully enjoy such passion. Prudence shifted uncomfortably on her chair. She had accepted that no man would wish to marry her as encumbered as she was with responsibility. But only after her incredible nighttime encounter with Sloan did she fully realize what she had sacrificed. There were aspects to the marital state she had never considered. Aspects that explained why Aunt Phoebe, even at her advanced age, had spurned convention and allowed herself to be courted by Amos Coltrane.

"Prudence, did you hear me?"

Prudence felt a tug on her hand and looked into Marabelle's clear blue eyes. "I beg your pardon?"

"I asked if it would be convenient for me to drop by tomorrow to visit the children. I brought gifts from New York."

"Tomorrow will be fine," Prudence answered, but as she stared into the girl's lively features a sense of foreboding stirred. When Sloan laid eyes upon the beauty, what would he think? Her gowns were colorful, her hair artfully arranged and her laughter infectious. Jealousy was a sin frequently warned against, but Prudence knew that was exactly what she was feeling. Jealous. She chided herself for her weakness. It was hardly Marabelle's fault that she had been blessed with beauty and a generous spirit.

Besides, what did it matter if Sloan Coltrane fell head over heels in love with the girl? He meant nothing to her. He was a mean and dishonorable man. It wouldn't matter to her if she never saw him again.


"It took you long enough to get here," Sloan said by way of greeting to his old friend George Washington Curtis.

"You be nice to my husband," Junella said laughingly, accepting her companion's assistance as he helped her to the train platform where Sloan had been waiting for them. "He's come a goodly piece to work for you."

They were an attractive couple and drew several curious glances from others on the platform. Born into slavery, George had once been responsible for an entire stable of thoroughbreds for his Southern owner. After the war, George and his beautiful wife had migrated to Texas, seeking a new life. Sloan had been impressed by the older man and had hired him to break and train the ranch's stock of working horses. It had been a step down for George, but he and his wife had seemed happy enough to settle in Taylorsville.

Sloan figured a major part of his own love for thoroughbred's came from his association with George and from hearing the man sing the praises of such famous horses as Herod, Eclipse and Byerly Truck. One thing was certain when he'd decided he was going to leave the ranch and have his own racetrack: George Washington Curtis was his first and only choice to care for and train his horses.

"You tell him, Junella," George said, a wide smile wreathing his face. "Sloan Coltrane's got to be the pushiest boss man I ever worked for. I just hope he's got a fit place for us to live."

Sloan grinned. He hadn't realized how much he'd missed his friend's good-natured ribbing. "You've got the best house on my property."

George shrugged. "That's right generous of you."

"Of course, it is the only house right now," Sloan admitted with a chuckle. "Tonight, though, I've decided to put you and Junella up at the Brubaker Hotel. We'll have supper there and talk about old times."

"Oh, Lord, what's wrong?" Junella asked, her eyes sparkling with mischief. "You must be softening us up for some bad news."

"No, everything's going fine." If one didn't count his miserable debacle with Prudence Abercrombie the other night. "The truth is I'm just glad to see some friendly faces."

"Then you're about to be real happy because we didn't come alone."

Sloan was reaching for the valise George had set on the platform when Junella's words stopped him. He looked up in time to see two well-dressed young women descend from the train.

"Sloan!" They rushed forward and reached him at the same time, almost knocking him over. "We missed you so much, we decided to pay you a visit."

"Alicia, Lenore," Sloan said in disbelief. As much as he loved his half sisters, he wasn't sure he was glad to see them. Mischief and disorder usually followed them wherever they went. "What are you doing here?"

"We just told you," Lenore returned, the yellow feathers on her pert hat dancing. "We've missed you and came to see if you were all right."

"After Mother's report, we were worried about you," Alicia added.

"Mother's report?" Sloan asked guardedly.

"She said you'd been in a drunken brawl," Lenore explained, her tone disapproving. "We've come to make certain that you haven't gone to hell in a hand basket, which Hortense Tittle says often happens when a man is left to his own devices."

Sloan shook his head. Hortense Tittle was Taylorsville's resident harridan and a man-hater, to boot. He couldn't believe his sisters would credit anything she said.

"And that you haven't taken up with loose women," Alicia continued. "Hortense says most men do. If they get the opportunity."

"I've been breaking my back building my racetrack," Sloan said, amazed that his well-bred sisters would think him capable of moral depravity. After all, he'd practically been a father to them.

The train whistle shrieked. Lenore slipped her hand through his arm. "We can continue this conversation later. We need to get our baggage from the train before it pulls out."

They'd brought *baggage?*

# Chapter Ten

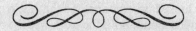

"It was very kind of you to invite me to dinner." Prudence seated herself in the chair the waiter pulled out for her and smiled at Marabelle. "Especially after the wonderful shopping trip you sponsored today."

Marabelle grinned. "What's the point of having money if one doesn't spend it? I've often thought that instead of the monthly Women's Aid teas Mother conducts to address the particular needs of the children, you should be provided with a yearly operating budget."

"That would certainly be an improvement," Prudence agreed. "Though I do appreciate your mother's efforts on our behalf," she added hastily.

"Mother has a good heart. I love her dearly. But she does like to...er...lord it over people." Marabelle accepted the menu the waiter handed her and smiled sheepishly over it at Prudence. "I'm a lot like her."

Prudence couldn't help returning the smile. Marabelle Brubaker possessed an irresistible streak of good-naturedness.

"Good heavens, who's that handsome man?" Marabelle asked, her gaze drifting beyond Prudence to someone behind her.

Prudence turned. Striding across the hotel dining room came Sloan Coltrane in the company of two lovely young women and a black couple. "If you mean the man in the suit, it's Amos Coltrane's nephew."

"*That's* Sloan Coltrane? No wonder all the mamas in town are talking about him. He's very striking."

"So's a rattler," Prudence muttered, returning her gaze to her menu.

"You don't approve of him?"

Prudence looked up, embarrassed that she'd spoken her hostile thoughts aloud. Still, the truth was the truth. "He might be dressed like a gentleman today, but he's an ill-mannered ruffian."

"Oh, that's right, I'd forgotten you were opposed to this racing venture the whole town's buzzing about."

"It's more than that," Prudence felt compelled to explain. "I feel he's a bad influence on the children. All they talk about are those blasted thoroughbreds. You'd think they were flying horses the way everyone is carrying on."

"Well, prepare yourself because he's coming directly to us. I wonder what he wants to say to you?"

"No doubt something rude and insulting. He doesn't enjoy my company any more than I like his."

"Miss Abercrombie."

It was a statement, not a question. Prudence looked into the watchful eyes of the man who several nights ago had kissed her so passionately and touched her so intimately. Her grip tightened on the hand-printed menu. She mustn't think about that now. Mustn't think about the heat and hunger he'd unleashed upon her. Mustn't think about how her body had opened up to him as if it were a drought-parched piece of earth and he was a spring rain.

She inclined her head. "Mr. Coltrane."

He had the temerity to smile at her. Her cheeks immediately warmed.

"Prudence." Amusement laced his husky drawl.

Obviously he was mocking her. Her chin angled upward. She had no intention of revealing how much his silent laughter hurt. "Sloan."

Dimly, Prudence was aware that his dinner companions and Marabelle were looking back and forth between them with the greatest curiosity. It became of paramount importance to reveal none of the humiliation and anger she felt toward this man, especially not in so public a place.

"You're looking particularly lovely tonight."

The bald-faced lie took her breath away. Compared to Marabelle and Sloan's female friends, she resembled a common crow that had wandered into a flock of elegantly plumed peacocks.

"Thank you," she said through gritted teeth. Maybe if she ceased talking to him he'd go away.

"Aren't you going to introduce me to your friend?" he inquired with maddening politeness.

It shouldn't have surprised her that even in the company of two beautiful young women, he would want to make the acquaintance of another. Obviously the man was a lecher of the worst sort. "Marabelle Brubaker, allow me to introduce Sloan Coltrane. You've heard me mention him."

Marabelle made a strange choking sound, but she managed to keep her smile in place. "I've heard a great deal about the racetrack you're building."

"You'll be hearing more," he acknowledged confidently, turning to the man who stood next to him. "I'd like you to meet George Washington Curtis and his wife Junella. George is my horse trainer."

As Marabelle exchanged greetings with the couple, Prudence glanced at the two comely young women in the group. She thought she knew everyone in Port Dodd, but they were strangers to her. It did seem a bit much for him to be in the company of two women at the same time. But

probably a low-down sort like Sloan didn't adhere to the
social stricture that required a man to escort only one
woman at a time.

"And this is Alicia Jenkins and Lenore Breathwait,"
Sloan continued. "My sisters."

It took a moment for the last two words to sink in.
Prudence didn't know that she believed him. It was quite
a coincidence that every attractive woman in his company was somehow related to him. Still, a feeling of relief
washed over her, followed immediately by a sense of impending doom. She didn't want it to matter to her with
whom Sloan kept company.

"It looks like you ladies were about to order your
meal," Sloan said after they'd traded a sociable spate of
hellos. "We don't want to intrude."

Prudence opened her mouth to suggest he leave, then.
Before the words were spoken, however, Marabelle was
gesturing to the empty chairs at their table.

"Oh, please, join us. I'm terribly curious to hear about
this racetrack you're building. I understand it's on Amos
Coltrane's land and right next to Prudence's place."

In horror and disgust Prudence watched as another table was placed next to theirs. Sloan seated his sisters on
one side of him while he claimed the chair next to her.
George and Junella sat next to Marabelle. Prudence
gnashed her teeth together. It just wasn't fair that she kept
running into this rude man. She glanced at him from beneath her lashes. Was he just too dense to realize that she
didn't want to spend any more time with him? Or was he
contrary enough to enjoy provoking her whenever the
opportunity presented itself?

The conversation continued calmly enough with Prudence maintaining her silence. When her meal arrived, she
sliced and chewed each bite with grave concentration.
Thankfully, her presence at the table went virtually un-

noticed and no participation in the animated conversation was required from her.

"How long are you going to be visiting Port Dodd?" Marabelle inquired of Sloan's sisters.

"Not long at all," Lenore, the petite blonde, answered. "Unfortunately we have responsibilities at home."

"We would stay longer if we could," Alicia said. "Naturally we don't like the thought of Sloan being on his own."

No doubt they feared he would disgrace the family name.

"The truth is, he made our lives miserable when we were growing up by always keeping us under his eagle eye," Lenore volunteered cheerfully. "He was the one who decided what young men could come calling and which ones were to stay away."

"Now that he's getting on in years and will probably marry soon, he's moved away." Alicia frowned. "And that doesn't seem fair at all. We should be able to help him select his life mate, just as he helped choose ours."

Sloan's dark eyebrows converged over his nose. "I'm not getting married."

"You see," Lenore said. "It's just when a man starts spouting such nonsense that some woman snatches him up."

George laughed outright. "That's the way it happened to me. I was just minding my own business. Junella came along, and before I knew what hit me, we were 'jumping the broom.' A man don't stand a chance when a woman makes up her mind that he's going to be her husband."

"George! Shame on you for telling such an outrageous story. Why, my papa tried to run you off with a shotgun, and you wouldn't stay away."

"I couldn't." He shook his head sadly. "A man just doesn't stand a chance against that female magic you ladies work."

Junella's eyes shone with suppressed laughter. "Oh, hush, George. If you keep making up such tall tales, these good women will think I married a fool."

"Well, one thing's for certain," Sloan said, his voice edged with determination. "If I ever do decide to marry, I sure as blazes won't let my sisters pick the woman."

"Oh, but we'd do a good job for you," Lenore protested. "We understand you."

"You just think you do," he growled.

"We know what qualities a woman would have to possess in order to be compatible with you," Lenore said, undeterred by her brother's clear aversion to the topic under discussion. "First of all, she would need the patience of Job, because being married to you would require a saintly amount of patience."

"And she would have to love horses," Alicia added.

Lenore nodded. "That's right. She would have to be an expert rider."

"She'd probably have to be beautiful, too. I can't imagine Sloan with an ugly woman," Lenore mused, her lovely brow furled in concentration.

"And she couldn't be too prudish," Alicia remarked. "Sloan does like his cheroots, his liquor and his card games."

"And he swears a tad too much for a truly devout Christian woman."

"Damnation, I don't swear!"

At the outrageousness of that statement, the entire table burst into laughter. Except for Prudence. She didn't feel like laughing at all. Sloan's sisters had just described Marabelle Brubaker as the perfect choice for him, and herself as the worst possible wife. Again she tried to tell herself that nothing about Sloan Coltrane mattered to her.

But the message rang hollow in her mind. And in her heart.

"Miss Brubaker... It is 'miss,' isn't it?" Alicia asked with artificial casualness.

Marabelle nodded, her blue eyes sparkling. "Yes."

"Do you ride?"

Marabelle nodded with mock graveness. "I'm accounted an excellent horsewoman. You might even call me an expert."

"That's very interesting, isn't it, Sloan?"

From Sloan's disgusted expression, Prudence assumed he didn't like the direction the conversation had taken any better than she did.

"*If* I married," he said, his voice a low growl, "I wouldn't give a damn about whether or not my wife knew one end of a horse from another."

"Really?" Lenore questioned, her tone dubious. "And why is that?"

"Because, dear sister, I consider myself fully capable of teaching her to ride."

He reached out absently and stroked the back of Prudence's hand. Startled by the unexpected contact, she nearly leaped from her chair. What on earth was he up to, making such a provocative gesture with the whole world looking on? All right, so it wasn't the entire world. But goodness, the other five people sharing the table with them surely noticed that his fingers were leisurely caressing her hand.

"But she would have to be beautiful, wouldn't she?" Alicia insisted. "I mean you wouldn't fall in love with a plain woman."

"I have no intention of falling in love with anyone. But rest assured that if I did, she would be beautiful...to me."

Prudence felt an alarming softening of her insides. The intensity and depth of Sloan's hard stare was focused squarely upon her.

"And her degree of saintly patience?" Lenore prodded. "You can't disagree that you would demand an extremely compliant wife."

"On the contrary," Sloan said quietly. "I would expect any wife of mine to stand up for herself. And if I was behaving like a jackass, she would be the first to let me know it."

"It sounds like you're describing my Junella," George said, gazing affectionately at his wife. "She sure does know how to keep me on the straight and narrow."

"There, you see?" Alicia said approvingly. "Even the best of men needs a good woman looking after him."

"What I see," Sloan muttered wryly, "is that I should have settled a lot farther from Taylorsville, like maybe on the other side of the ocean."

Lenore poked his arm. "You know we would still come visiting, no matter where you moved. You're our brother, and family is supposed to stick together. That's what makes it such a blessing in a person's life."

"More like a curse," Sloan countered.

Prudence thought about the children under her care and knew that Sloan was as wrong as a man could be. Family was everything. And if a person didn't have one, they were truly adrift in the world.

"I know Jeremy misses you like crazy."

"He's got Misty Marie now. She's his family. He should be happy enough."

"Well, there's a problem of some kind. And he won't discuss it with us," Alicia said, her playful manner becoming more serious. "When he comes to talk to you about it, please be sympathetic, Sloan."

"Good Lord, is he coming to Port Dodd, too?"

"Probably sooner than you think," Lenore retorted. "What did you think would happen when you left Taylorsville, that we would forget about you?"

Prudence could tell from Sloan's rueful expression that he'd probably hoped that very thing.

"I figured you'd be so busy living your own lives that you wouldn't have time to interfere in mine."

"Hah! You're a fine one to talk about interfering in other people's lives, after riding roughshod over us when we were growing up."

Sloan's features sobered. "I just did what I thought needed to be done."

Lenore and Alicia exchanged meaningful glances.

"We merely wish to return the favor to you, dear brother," Alicia said.

From the determined glint in her eyes, it was obvious to Prudence that Lenore was in complete accord with her sister's statement.


"When is Miss Marabelle going to get here?"

"That must be the hundredth time you've asked, child," Gladys said, her tone affectionately scolding. "She'll get here when she gets here and not a minute sooner."

Hoe in hand, Prudence stopped on her way to the garden as she passed the front porch. In anticipation of Marabelle's arrival, Janey was dressed in her Sunday best. The special bond between the young woman and the girl had once caused a twinge of jealousy in Prudence. With time, however, Prudence had realized that it wasn't a betrayal of Janey's feelings toward her for the girl to love someone else.

"I bet she's going to bring us some presents," Charlie said confidently from his perch on the porch railing.

"Of course she will," Charlotte said. "She always does."

"I hope it's peppermint sticks," Charlie said, looking wistful. "I surely do love peppermint sticks."

"Where are you going with that hoe?" Gladys demanded from her position on the rocker. "The children worked that garden patch this morning."

"I just thought I'd see if any weeds escaped their notice," Prudence said mildly, not having wanted to draw attention to her efforts.

"But we already did the bestest job in the whole world," Janey protested. "You said so yourself."

"That's right," Charlie agreed, his young face puckering with a disapproving frown. "You said we passed inspection with flying colors."

Prudence lowered the hoe. She always tried to be inconspicuous when she followed up after the children, but this time she'd been caught.

Gladys rose from the rocker. "Honey, you're going to drive yourself crazy trying to make everything perfect. Any of those old weeds that escaped this time, the children will surely get tomorrow. You've been working too hard as it is. Come sit for a spell and have a glass of lemonade."

"Sarah made it, and it's delicious," Charlotte pronounced, smacking her lips.

Prudence walked to the porch and leaned the hoe against the railing. Gladys was right; she had been driving herself too hard. It was just that she needed to do something to keep from thinking about Sloan Coltrane. Working herself to a state of near exhaustion seemed the only way she could rid him from her mind. And even those efforts hadn't succeeded.

"I guess a glass of Sarah's lemonade would hit the spot," she said brightly, wiping her brow. "My, it's going to be another scorcher today."

"It sure is," Davy agreed, hobbling over to the porch and lowering himself to sit on the wood-planked steps.

"It's bound to hit the century mark," Gladys observed. "It would be a fine day to visit the seashore."

"Can we?" the children cried in unison, their voices shrill with excitement.

Prudence shaded her eyes against the sun's burning glare and looked skyward. There wasn't a cloud for a hundred miles. The rain that had threatened several weeks ago had never materialized. "I suppose we could pack ourselves a lunch and take the wagon," she said casually. "If everyone wants to, that is."

"Oh, we do, we do," the children shouted.

"But what about Miss Marabelle?" Janey asked in concern.

"We'll wait for her," Prudence answered. "I'm sure she'd enjoy a day at the seashore, too."

"Well then, let's ask her 'cause here she comes," Charlie said.

Prudence glanced toward the road. A surrey pulled by two chestnut horses headed toward their yard. Immediately Prudence noticed that Marabelle wasn't alone. A man was driving the gaily trimmed rig. Conflicting emotions swept through Prudence. Excitement at the opportunity of seeing Sloan again. A sickening feeling of jealousy lodged in the pit of her stomach that he was with Marabelle. And dread at the realization of how much it meant to her.

"Why, she's got Reverend Brown with her," Gladys said. "My lands, I didn't know they were keeping company. I never saw a more unlikely couple."

Prudence pressed a palm against her queasy stomach. It *was* the Reverend and not Sloan driving the buggy. A giddy wave of relief raced through her, followed by an icy shaft of fear. It shouldn't matter whether or not Sloan Coltrane took a surrey ride with Marabelle Brubaker.

She and Sloan meant nothing to each other. Why, they were virtual strangers and on opposite sides of the fence about his bringing horse racing to Port Dodd.

And yet, as she spent the day at the seashore with Marabelle, the Reverend and the children, her thoughts and her heart were far away from the sound of the waves and frolicking laughter. More times than she could count, her gaze strayed inland to the property she couldn't see and the man she couldn't forget.

Gladys had been right about Reverend Brown and Marabelle being an unlikely pair. And yet they had looked surprisingly right together, two dissimilar people making a charming couple.

The next morning after another sleepless night, Prudence joined the children at the breakfast table.

"It's here," Richard informed the table at large.

"What's here?" Prudence asked, suppressing an embarrassingly wide yawn.

"Where have you been?" Gladys inquired tartly. "On the moon?"

*How did you know?* Prudence was tempted to ask.

"It's the first racehorse," Charlie said around a mouthful of flapjacks.

He was so obviously thrilled by the news that Prudence refrained from telling him not to talk with his mouth full.

"He's a beauty," Richard said. "A real thoroughbred. You know it just by looking at him, without anyone even telling you he's a purebred."

"When did you see him?" Davy demanded.

"This morning. I was exercising one of our horses and happened to be riding by Mr. Coltrane's spread."

"Were they racing him on the track?" Davy wanted to know.

"Nope. He was in one of the corrals. I figure he came on the same train as that horse trainer fellow, but today was the first time they had him out of his stall. He looks mighty fine, let me tell you."

"I want to see him," Charlotte said.

"We mustn't make a nuisance of ourselves," Prudence reminded everyone at the table, her voice firm. Sloan had made it abundantly clear he didn't want the children pestering him.

"But if he invites us to see the new horse, can we go?" Davy persisted.

"If Mr. Coltrane gave us an invite, it would only be neighborly to accept it," Gladys said smoothly. "Isn't that right, Prudence?"

Prudence shot a silent look of impatience at the housekeeper. Gladys stared back at her with a benign expression of innocence that didn't fool Prudence for a minute. The woman was shrewd enough to know that the last thing Prudence wanted was to see Sloan again. Yet, as she reflected upon it, Prudence decided the chances were slim that Sloan would ever extend an invitation for them to tour his racetrack. Feeling that she was on safe ground, she smiled at the hopeful faces around the table.

"If Mr. Coltrane asks us to see his new horse, then of course we'll accept his gracious invitation."

Charlotte and Janey clapped their hands while Davy and Charlie let loose a couple of loud hurrahs. Even Sarah and Richard looked excited at the prospect of seeing a genuine thoroughbred racehorse. For the life of her, Prudence couldn't understand what the fascination was with the four-legged creatures.

"Then it's settled," Gladys observed in satisfaction.

"It's settled that we will *wait* to be invited," Prudence clarified.

Later that afternoon Prudence went to the knoll that overlooked Sloan's land to collect the children for supper. The weather was beginning to turn ominous, but none of them wanted to leave. Evidently there were now *two* thoroughbreds on the premises, and they didn't want to miss the opportunity of seeing them run on the track.

"Come along," Prudence instructed them. "It's getting windy. A storm must be coming. Besides, supper is ready, and you need to do some studying."

"I'm not hungry," Davy said.

"It's summertime, we're not supposed to study any lessons in the summer," Charlie objected.

Prudence put her hands on her hips in exasperation. She had been far too lax with the children's schedule, and now she was paying the price. It was a mutiny pure and simple.

"We need to prepare now for when school commences in the fall. Not only that, the weather is changing," she told them.

Janey's bottom lip quivered. "I bet Miss Marabelle would let us stay. *She* likes Mr. Coltrane and his horses."

Prudence took the blow heart-center. As far as she knew, she'd never been compared with anyone else and come up short in any of the children's estimations.

"I have no way of knowing what Miss Marabelle would do in this situation. But as long as you're under my care we shall do things my way."

"And your way is just fine," Sarah said softly.

"It sure is," Richard agreed. "Come on, pumpkin, we can see the horses again tomorrow."

With her little nose in the air, Janey accepted Richard's hand and turned toward the farmhouse.

Prudence stared after their departing backs with a lump in her throat. She wasn't prepared for the sense of hurt she experienced at being criticized by one of her children. And even though she told herself she was overreacting, the sting of tears built behind her eyes.

The truth was that Gladys was right. She did want everything to be perfect. Herself. The farm. And the children themselves. And, of course, nothing could ever be perfect. That was the way life was. Because if the world were a perfect place, each of the children under her care would have a loving mother and father.

A surprisingly cool gust of wind buffeted her. She looked at the sky. Instead of its usually clear blue color, it had deepened to a turbulent gray. Giant clouds sped across the limitless horizon. It had been weeks since the last rain had fallen. She wondered if the coming storm would give them a reprieve from the sultry days and nights.

Before heading back to the house, she glanced in the direction of Sloan's property. A man on horseback was riding toward her. She had the insane urge to run, even though she knew it was Sloan and not a desperado who approached. She held her ground as the wind pelted dust and rocks against her legs and arms.

"What—"

She intended to ask him what his hurry was, when he leaned over his horse and swept her into his arms.

She was so stunned by his unexpected action that she hung limp for a moment while trying to collect her senses.

His mount pounded the ground for a few more yards. Sloan kept looking over his shoulder. She had just summoned enough air into her lungs to ask him if he'd lost his mind, when he brutally reined in the horse and leapt down, taking her with him. The rocky earth came up abruptly and slammed against both of them. They rolled over each other. The whole world seemed upside down. They came to rest with him on top of her, pressing her into a gully where rocks dug hurtfully into her back.

She gulped a ragged breath and got a mouthful of Sloan's musky scent. She felt as if she were in the river again and drowning. He was everywhere and nothing made any sense. Least of all the thunderous roar coming toward them.

# Chapter Eleven

Sloan shielded the woman beneath him. He didn't want to think about how small and fragile she felt. He hoped to hell his own body would be enough to protect her from the black, dirt-belching twister he'd seen tearing across the horizon toward her. The ground shook beneath them. It sounded as if the earth itself were being split in two. Suddenly the air seemed to be sucked from Sloan's lungs. A roar blasted his eardrums. Dirt and rocks slammed into his back and legs.

And then it was over.

His ears popped, and in its own way the subsequent silence screamed as loudly as had the surly twister.

"Prudence, are you all right?"

He raised himself above her limp form. Her face was pressed sideways into the dirt. Her hair was a tangle of pebbles and dust, and her eyes were closed. "Prudence," he commanded sharply, "open your eyes and tell me you're all right."

"You're always telling me to open my eyes," she said, still lying in a flattened heap against the ground.

Her mumbled complaint sounded like music to his ears. She was fine.

"You miss a lot of excitement when you close them," he pointed out, spitting a mouthful of Texas grit from his mouth.

"And there's always plenty of excitement when you're around," she muttered as she pushed herself to a sitting position. "What happened?"

"You mean you don't know?" he asked, incredulous that she could live in this part of the country and not understand its dangers.

"You attacked me?" she asked, brushing the dust from her hideous black dress with trembling hands.

"A twister as big and as mean as any I've seen just ate up a few miles of Texas," he growled through a jaw clenched tight enough to snap off a gun barrel. As far as he was concerned, Prudence Abercrombie needed a leash and a full-time handler. She was clearly a menace to herself.

Sloan got to his feet. His new hat was nowhere to be seen. He squinted and slowly turned. There was no sign of Lucky. A sickening feeling got loose in his belly as he imagined his big-hearted horse swallowed up in the deadly twister.

"Oh."

His gaze jerked back to Prudence. She was still sprawled on the ground and about as disheveled as a woman could get and still have her clothes on.

"I was at the bottom of the hill and looking up when I saw it coming toward you," he told her, fighting back the naked terror that had tunneled through him when he'd realized the peril she was in.

"I . . . I guess I was looking the wrong way. I didn't see it coming."

"I shouted at you to take cover, but you must not have heard me."

"I didn't." She hugged her knees to her chest, and Sloan wondered if the reason she didn't get to her feet was because she was too shaken to stand on her own. Suddenly her face whitened. "What about the children? Do you think—"

"The twister was heading due south," he reassured her. "Tearing off in the opposite direction of your place."

"Thank God," she whispered, trembling visibly.

Sloan continued to glare down at her. He didn't like the feelings she made him feel. He didn't like thinking about what would have happened if he hadn't been able to save her. He didn't like thinking how vulnerable she looked with her hair straggling every which way and her black dress torn at the shoulder. He didn't like seeing her with dust streaking her face and her hands.

"Come on, let's get you back to the house before the rain hits."

"What rain?" she asked, her expression bewildered.

A fat drop of water struck Sloan's cheek. "The rain that's going to soak us to our bones if we don't get a move on."

He looked up the hill they'd tumbled down. He figured it was more than four miles back to her place. As if gored by a long-horned steer, the late afternoon sky opened up and a deluge of water poured down on them.

He leaned forward and grabbed her hand. "Come on."

He kept a firm hold of her even after her skin became slippery with the rain that washed down over them. They really couldn't run over the uneven ground that in seconds had become muddy and slick, but Sloan made sure they kept a brisk pace. By the time they reached his shack, their clothes were plastered to them.

He opened the door and dragged her inside. The rain's deafening racket lessened only slightly. It was mostly dark in the one-room building. In the meager light he was able to ignite the oil lamp on his second try. His hands were shaking, but he figured it was more from the scare of almost seeing Prudence eaten alive by the twister than him actually being cold.

"W-what is th-this place?" she asked, her teeth clattering like a señorita's castanets.

"My house, until I get the casino built," he answered succinctly, realizing for the first time that he'd managed things so that he and Prudence were alone. She was going to have to shed her wet clothing. He hadn't planned things this way, he assured himself. Hell, he'd just been performing an act of Christian service.

"Who's going t-to live in the other house you built?" She stood with her arms wrapped around herself and a sodden lock hanging down the middle of her face.

"It's for George and Junella."

"Th-that's very generous of you."

"Prudence."

"Y-yes?"

"It's time to take off your clothes."

Her water-spiked lashes trembled. "P-perhaps you could give me a blanket to wrap myself in. I'm sure I'd be w-warm enough."

"Now, Prudence, you've got to be sensible about this. If you stay in those wet clothes, you'll get pneumonia and die. Then who would take care of your little band of wounded critters?"

Her huge eyes flashed green fire. "They're not wounded critters!"

"Stop stalling and take off your clothes." He unfastened the first button of his shirt. "Do you want to see who can get naked first?"

"You're horrible!"

"Naw, I'm just too practical to freeze to death when I don't need to."

"Perhaps if you built a fire in that stove, we wouldn't need to undress," she said stiffly.

"The fire comes after we're both wrapped in dry blankets."

She nibbled her bottom lip. Until that moment, Sloan could have honestly claimed he wasn't aroused physically, that he was just doing what needed to be done to keep them both healthy. For no reason he could comprehend, the sight of her even white teeth worrying her pouty lower lip made him grow hard. He gritted his teeth. Damn it, he'd had no intention of taking advantage of her. He'd learned his lesson the last time they'd been alone. She wasn't the kind of woman a man seduced and discarded. She came with baggage. His only concern today had been for her welfare. Until now.

"The least you can do is turn your back."

"Now, why aren't I surprised you feel that way?"

She raised her chin.

He swore to himself. The day Amos had willed him this piece of land, he'd willed Sloan endless aggravation.

"I was going to tell you the same thing," he said, pronouncing the bold-faced lie without a flicker of remorse. "I'd appreciate it if you wouldn't watch while I take off my britches."

She spun around as if she'd been lassoed and jerked in the opposite direction.

"You are a crude and brutish man, Mr. Coltrane."

"You're welcome. I hope I'm around the next time you need your soft hide saved."

He watched her stiffen at his insult. Well, she deserved it. He was no more crude or brutish than the next man. Hell, he was probably better than most. But of course, Miss Purity hadn't been around enough men to know when she was well off. Well, that was her problem, not his.

He got out of his clothing in record time, while his reluctant guest drew out her undressing process until it became torturous for Sloan to watch. And he did watch. As long as one of them had their back turned to the other, he figured . . .

The truth was, there was no way he could resist looking on as she peeled the abused black dress from her wet skin. An indefinable feeling of pleasure and pride stirred as he looked at her beautifully formed body. She was so soft, so sweetly curved. Her undergarments were plain with nary a ribbon or a ruffle, but the simple white chemise and drawers emphasized the womanly contours they covered. He could see through the flimsy wet fabric to the pink skin beneath. She had a narrow waist and gently flared hips.

He swallowed. Hard. She was everything a man could want in a woman. He remembered the night they'd had dinner at the hotel. He'd wanted nothing more than to make his interfering sisters, George and Junella, and Miss Brubaker disappear so he could be alone with Prudence. Well, he had her alone now. And all he was wearing was a scratchy blanket. He waited a heartbeat to see if she would slip out of her underthings. She didn't. Instead, she reached for the blanket on the cot next to her and wrapped the gray strip of material about her.

"What about the fire?" she asked.

He turned quickly and moved toward the stove. "Coming up."

"I suppose they're going to be worried about me at the house," she said forlornly.

"They probably will be," he conceded gently. "But they won't come looking for you until this rain lets up."

As if to strengthen his comment a blast of thunder exploded overhead. Prudence jumped. Sloan curved his hands into fists to keep from crossing the small distance that separated them. If he drew her into his arms, it would be for more than offering comfort.

"How about some coffee?" he asked, picking up the full pot. "It isn't that old."

"I suppose tea is out of the question," she murmured.

"Your choices are whiskey or coffee," he said, wondering how it was she could still seem like such a lady when she'd been reduced to a rough blanket.

Prudence stared at the bare-chested Sloan and wondered how on earth it was possible for her to converse civilly with him. He was so rawly masculine, and it seemed shockingly provocative to her. She was convinced he wore nothing under his blanket. And here they were, alone, practically nude and talking about coffee. She shook her head, thinking it might have been better if she'd been swept up in the twister Sloan had saved her from. At least then she would have had a reason to feel as if she were spinning out of control toward a terrible fate.

If *anyone* ever discovered she'd spent this time with Sloan at his place in a semidressed state, her reputation would be irreparably damaged. Why, the good people of Port Dodd might even decide she was unfit to act as guardian to the children she'd taken in. And yet, Sloan was acting as if this were a perfectly ordinary social call. She shook her head.

"It's not that difficult a decision, Prudence."

She blinked. "What isn't?"

"What you'd like to drink."

"Oh. Coffee, of course."

"Of course," he returned with what she detected as sarcasm. "I should have known better than to think you'd like a belt of whiskey."

"You have a peculiar way of speaking, Sloan," she observed as she unobtrusively tried to adjust the blanket that seemed to be drifting inexorably downward. She'd knotted it above her breasts, leaving her shoulders bare but giving her the opportunity to have her hands free.

He sat the pot on the stove. "How's that?"

"You don't say you would like a drink of whiskey, you refer to it as a belt or a shot. Don't you find that peculiar?"

"How many years have you lived in Texas?"

"Twenty, but you knew that already," she answered, perplexed by the humor glinting in his silvery eyes.

"Then what's peculiar is that you still speak with an English accent and you don't understand the way Texans talk."

She frowned at him. "I was raised in a household of Englishwomen, and they rarely referred to imbibing spirits in belts or shots."

He arched an eyebrow. "*Rarely?* I'd say never."

"I suppose I was isolated growing up," she admitted, fiddling with the blanket's edge.

She thought she saw a trace of pity in his gaze and straightened. "Perhaps by the time I'm eighty, I'll have your colorful way of speaking down pat."

A sudden grin slashed his rugged face. "I bet you will."

There was something so utterly captivating about his amusement that Prudence felt her heart skip a beat. Again a terrible sense of foreboding filled her. She was enjoying herself far too much with this man. She reminded herself that she would be better off lying broken and unconscious in a rock-strewn gully than if she were caught with Sloan. Somehow the inner warning couldn't stop her from smiling back at him.

He turned his broad back to her and with splendid male grace poured two mugs of coffee. She accepted hers gratefully, hoping it would give her hands something to do other than fuss with the blanket.

She took a cautious sip of the steaming liquid and singed her tongue.

"Careful, it's hot."

Like most of Sloan's warnings, it came too late. She cradled the hot cup in her hands and cast about for something innocuous to say. The silence was dangerous to her peace of mind.

"The children say you've got two thoroughbreds now."

"What were you doing on the hill?"

The statement and question were pronounced at the same moment.

"You go first," he said with more politeness than she'd thought him capable of demonstrating.

Because standing before him seemed unnecessarily awkward, Prudence sat in the chair next to the table. "The children can't seem to think or talk about anything besides your fancy purebred horses. I was on the hill because it was time for supper, and I was afraid they would stay there all night if someone didn't fetch them."

"They're welcome to visit anytime they want," he offered generously.

Prudence frowned into her coffee. It was the very invitation she'd hoped he wouldn't extend. When she glanced at Sloan, something akin to grief touched his eyes.

"Is something wrong?" she asked, wondering what was behind the look of pain etching his features.

"I don't know if Lucky made it."

A chill squeezed her heart. She hadn't for one moment thought about Sloan's horse.

"It's my fault," she said miserably. "If I hadn't been daydreaming I would have seen that twister coming and...and..." She broke off, not knowing what she would have done.

"It's no one's fault," he countered tightly. "If Lucky lives up to his name, then he'll have beat that mangy twister. When the rain lets up, I'll go looking for him."

An enormous crescendo of thunder rattled the shack. Prudence flinched, splashing hot coffee on herself.

Immediately Sloan was beside her. "Did you burn yourself?"

It was too much for her. His warm, callused hands holding hers. His naked chest scant inches away. His scent, primitive and male. His rough voice sliding over her like golden honey that had been set afire.

She tried to draw away.

"Prudence, look at me."

At least he hadn't told her to open her eyes. They were wide open and focused on his hands.

"I can't."

"Why not?"

His deep voice was a silken scrape.

"I—I'm afraid," she admitted.

He used his knuckles to force her to raise her chin. Her breath locked in her throat. His eyes were hard with a look that, even in her innocence, she recognized as arousal.

"I don't love you, Sloan."

His eyes crinkled at the corners. Her stomach slid to her toes.

"There're some things you don't tell a man unless he asks," he said.

"I just wanted you to know. I was wrong when I told you that I did."

"You already explained that. You were feeling things you hadn't experienced before."

She nodded, unable to speak.

"Are you feeling that way now?"

She closed her eyes, then immediately snapped them open, lest he accuse her of cowardice. *I'm all hot and slithery inside,* she was tempted to say, but knew that doing so would cause nothing but trouble.

She was a prudent woman, after all.

"I'm feeling—" she searched her vocabulary for something that would suffice "—fine."

The pitiful word, of course, in no way described how she truly felt.

"Well there's fine and then there's *fine,*" he said, his words a lure to lascivious thoughts.

She couldn't believe how much she wanted to reach out and touch his chest. Just to see how the bristly hairs would feel against her fingertips. And the dusky skin that encircled his tight nipples. She would like to touch that, too.

Another thunderous pounding shook the shack. This time Prudence didn't flinch. Instead, she gazed unwavering into Sloan's eyes. She was old enough to know the facts of life. She had never thought she would experience them, but she considered it her duty to instruct the young women who left her care when they reached maturity. Reverend Brown had been the one to inform the young men leaving Draper House about their proper role as morally responsible citizens.

Sloan's thumb continued to massage her clasped hands. He was telling her something with his eyes, something she wanted to deny but couldn't. There was passion in this small room. Ripe and ready to explode. It was as if it had a living force of its own and was enveloping them within its sizzling currents. Compared to its raw power, the energy expended by the twister seemed insignificant.

There was more pounding.

It was in Prudence's chest and in her loins.

"Sloan, are you going to open this door, or do I have to break it down?"

Sloan's head jerked around, and Prudence jumped to her feet, looking for a place to run or hide.

"What are we going to do?" she wailed faintly.

He took a step toward the door. Her desperate plea stopped him, making him turn toward her. "There's no place to hide, Prudence."

"But there has to be! I can't be found like—like this," she said, gesturing wildly to both of their states of undress.

"We came in from the rain," he replied calmly.

"We took off our clothes!"

"Not all of them," he interjected. "You kept your underwear on."

"My reputation will be ruined!" she wailed, still keeping her voice low.

"Jeremy won't say anything."

"Jeremy?"

"I'd know my brother's voice anywhere. God only knows why he's standing outside my door in this downpour, but he is and I have to let him in."

"You can't!"

"Prudence..."

"What?"

"I don't have a choice."

"But... but I don't want your brother to see me like this."

He looked at her as if she'd sprouted an extra head. She didn't think she was being the least bit unreasonable. "Maybe I can hide under the bed."

"Sloan, for hell's sake, I'm going to drown out here! Let me in!"

Another pounding assaulted the door.

"You're not going to crawl under my bed!"

"Why not?" She moved closer to the small bunk. "I think I can fit. I'm really not all that big."

"Honey—"

"Don't call me 'honey.' Not under these circumstances," she cried.

"We didn't do anything wrong."

"Only because we were interrupted!"

His eyes caught fire. "Is that right?"

"You know it is. I was seconds away from throwing myself into your arms and making an absolute ninny of myself."

"Well now, that's right interesting to know. For next time."

"There isn't going to be a next time!"

"Sloan!" came another bellow from outside.

Prudence looked around the room desperately and was suddenly struck by a bolt of pure inspiration. In one corner, a sizable cupboard was pushed up against the wall. There was a foot gap between it and the adjoining wall. She could easily wedge herself into the corner.

"Hand me my clothes," she ordered as she dashed to the miraculously provided space and pressed herself flat against the wall.

Gazing at her with a look that was heavily laced with male frustration, he did so.

"Now what? Don't you think my brother's going to notice a half-naked woman right off when he comes in?"

"I'm not half naked! I'm semiclothed," she corrected him. "Now, throw that old coat over me. It's big enough to conceal me."

"Prudence, I don't think this is a good idea."

"Don't think. Act. The moment calls for it."

"My brother's bound to spend the night. Do you intend to stand in the corner all that time with my coat thrown over you?"

"When it stops raining, take him with you to look for Lucky. I'll use that opportunity to dress and return home."

"What's going to stop you from getting lost?"

"I'll worry about that later. Now, open the door for your brother before he knocks it down."

Sloan regarded her for another half moment before the cheerfully lit room disappeared beneath the folds of his musty greatcoat.

Prudence heaved a sigh of relief.

Her reputation had been saved.

And Sloan's brother wouldn't think she was a trollop.

# Chapter Twelve

Jeremy swept into the room on a gust of water and wind. "What the hell took you so long?"

"I was asleep."

"I could have drowned out there!"

"That's the risk a man takes when he comes calling in the middle of a rainstorm," Sloan retorted in disgust, trying to keep his gaze from drifting to the corner where Miss Prudence Abercrombie had decided to conceal herself. He still couldn't believe he'd let her talk him into such foolishness. His brother certainly wouldn't tell anyone he'd seen her here. Anyway, by morning Gladys and the children would know where she'd been. The way those kids blabbed every bit of information they knew, it wouldn't be long before the story spread farther.

Sloan really didn't think her reputation would be damaged. He couldn't imagine anyone thinking Prudence could behave in a less than proper fashion. She was a lady through and through. And he'd beat to a pulp any man who claimed otherwise.

"Is that coffee hot?" Jeremy asked, shucking off his wet clothing. Water cascaded off him as if he were a pup shaking himself dry.

"Hot enough."

"Good, pour me a cup."

Sloan did so, trying to gauge if the rain had lightened any. It sounded as if it was coming down harder than ever.

When Jeremy was stripped down to his skin, he looked around the room. "Got an extra blanket?"

"Yeah." Sloan walked to the bed and stripped off the top cover. "Here."

Jeremy sat in the chair that Prudence had so recently vacated. "Why are you living in a shack?"

"It's only temporary," Sloan told him. "When the casino's finished, I'll have a suite of rooms there."

He sipped his coffee. "You built George's place big enough for a family of six."

"I wanted them to have plenty of room."

"Yeah, but it's not as if they're going to have kids. You know Junella's tried for years to have young'uns."

"I figured they would have room for any family that might come visiting."

Jeremy laughed. "You sure didn't do that for your own family."

"I wasn't expecting them to show up before I got the gaming hall finished."

"Mother was worried about you."

"I'm doing fine."

"Lenore and Alicia said you were acting peculiar."

"They said you were having marital problems," Sloan returned, his ear cocked to how hard the rain was pounding the roof. "They just like to have something to fret about. Women are like that."

"What if they're right?" Jeremy asked, his jaw sinking toward his chest.

"I'm not acting peculiar!"

"Yeah, well, that's all and well for you, but have you thought that maybe I *am* having myself some of those marital problems?"

Sloan looked guiltily at his brother. He hadn't really believed Jeremy was having any trouble. "What's wrong with Misty Marie? Are you sorry you married her?"

"No."

Sloan's patience frayed. How could he help his brother with his problem when all he could do was think about Prudence hiding behind that blasted coat? He rubbed his jaw, wondering if any man in creation had been as besieged as he was.

"Jeremy, don't you think you could have talked to Dan about this? Now that he's married to your mother, he's kinda like a father to you."

Jeremy's face turned brilliant red. "I—I couldn't talk to him about . . . this."

"Are you sure you can tell me?" Sloan asked. Judging from the scarlet blush sweeping his cheeks, Jeremy was as miserable as a motherless calf. "I'm not married. I can't give you any advice on being a husband."

"You haven't been married, but you've . . ." Jeremy stared glumly into his coffee.

"I've *what?*" Sloan demanded, his patience snapped clean through.

"You've bedded your share of women."

Sloan's feet slammed down as he shot to his full height. "What the devil do my . . . mating habits . . . have to do with you and Misty Marie?"

Hell, there had to be a better way of describing what a man and woman did together in the privacy of a bed-chamber than calling it "mating habits." But for the life of him, he couldn't think of one. His gaze swerved to the corner where Prudence huddled behind his coat. Lord, she was getting an earful.

"I've heard the talk around the Golden Slipper and the Pleasurely Palace. Those gals would give it to you free, even if you didn't have the money to pay for it."

Sloan felt his face turn as red hot as his brother's. He stalked over to where Prudence was hiding and pitched his voice as low as he could and still have her hear him.

"Are you ready to show yourself?"

He didn't add, now that his reputation had been blasted to smithereens and he'd been all but branded a libertine by his own brother.

"Don't you dare remove this coat," she whispered back. "I'll never forgive you if you do."

"Sloan?" His brother's voice was hesitant.

"What?"

"Why are you talking to your coat?"

Sloan swore softly and succinctly before turning to face Jeremy. "I'm not. I'm talking to myself."

"Don't you think that's ... peculiar?"

"What if it is? Doesn't a man have a right to do what he wants in his own house?"

Jeremy cast a jaundiced looked around the humble room. "You mean in his own shack?"

"Right." He strode back to his chair and sat down, picking up his coffee. He was convinced the rain was lightening up. "So what's the story between you and Misty Marie?" He swallowed a mouthful of coffee.

"I think I'm doing something wrong in bed with her."

Sloan choked, then coughed. His eyes were watering when he spoke. "Why do you say that?"

"Because she doesn't act like she enjoys it when...I'm inside her. She just smiles a brave little smile, like she's doing her duty as a woman and a wife. I figure I'm doing something wrong, and you can tell me what it is."

Sloan had trouble looking his brother in the eye. He realized for the first time how difficult it had been for Jeremy to bring up this subject with another human being. It took guts for a man to confess something so personal to someone else. His gaze swung to the corner he'd just left. It was up to Prudence whether or not she revealed her presence. In the meantime, he intended to be completely honest with his brother. And pray the rain let up.

"Has she always acted this way?"

"Well, we waited until we were married before we... uh...did it."

"That's good." *You're a better man than I am, brother.*

"But we did a lot of kissing and touching. She really seemed to like that. She still does. She makes these little sighing sounds that drive me crazy until all I can think about is getting inside her. But then when I do, she just sort of freezes up. I want her to like it as much as I do."

"That's good." Sometime soon he was going to have to think of something else to say.

"The thing is, I want you to tell me how to make love to my wife so that she does enjoy it."

Sloan was humbled by his brother's faith in him, but he didn't feel up to the challenge of helping him solve his problem. After all, he'd never made love to a woman that mattered. He'd bought and paid for physical pleasure.

Would Prudence like having him inside her?

"Well?"

Sloan closed his eyes and imagined himself in that narrow bed with Prudence. "You need to make sure she's ready for you...to enter her."

"Why are you whispering?"

Sloan hadn't realized he was. He cleared his throat and began again. "She should be moist and moving her hips against yours, as if she's inviting you inside. And even when you are...there, you've got to keep kissing and touching her. You need to go slow. A woman takes longer than a man to warm up. Her nipples will get hard. Use your tongue on them. She'll like that. Remember to keep talking to her, too. Tell her you love her, that she's beautiful, that you need her. Give her time to catch up with you. If you get things right, she'll finish before you."

Sloan swallowed. "There's a place, a small nub at the crest of her opening. If you rub that careful like, she'll all but explode."

Deep silence filled the room.

Sloan realized it had finally stopped raining. He didn't dare look in the blasted corner. He'd probably see Prudence lying on the floor in a dead faint. He got to his feet and began sorting through his clothes for a dry pair of pants.

"Thanks, Sloan."

"You're welcome."

"What are you doing?"

"Getting dressed so I can go out and look for my horse."

"How'd you lose him?"

"We got separated in the storm."

"I've never known you to be thrown, big brother."

Sloan reached for a shirt. "Happens to the best of us."

"I'll come with you."

"Fine." When he was dressed, he opened the door and let his brother proceed himself outside. "I forgot something. I'll be right out."

He stepped to the corner, pulled down his coat and stared into brilliant green eyes. "I'm sorry you had to hear that, but Jeremy wasn't going anywhere until I answered his questions. I figured you could interrupt us any time you wanted to."

"He's very lucky to have you for a brother."

Sloan wished he knew what she was thinking behind those glazed eyes of hers. "Stay here until I come back for you. I don't want you trying to walk back to your place in the dark."

"But—"

"I'll see that Jeremy spends the night at George and Junella's place. Neither he nor they will know that you were here." His gaze dropped to the upper swells of her bosom, where the blanket didn't reach. "But I'll remember you were here. All the way till Judgment Day."

When Sloan stepped into the night, a single truth tore through his mind. What he'd described to his brother was how he would make love to Prudence, not how he'd coupled with the women he'd paid for. He suspected there would be a world of difference between the experiences.

Prudence paced Sloan's one room abode. She'd put back on her damp clothing, tidied her hair with his comb and straightened things up a bit. She'd performed the latter activity because she'd needed something, anything, to take her mind off Sloan's earthy description of how a man made love to a woman. She might have known the basic facts of male and female intimacy, but to hear Sloan put it into words, his words... She shivered. She'd wanted everything he'd described. She'd ached for it, in places she'd hardly ever thought about.

The door to the shack slammed open. Prudence's gaze shot to the open doorway. Sloan stood there, looking almost uncertain. Then, within the blink of an eye, he was inside and shutting the door behind him.

"Did you find Lucky?" she asked, anxious to know if his horse had escaped the twister's path.

Sloan nodded. "He was standing in front of his stall when we went to saddle Jeremy's horse. He wasn't pleased to have been left to the mercy of the elements, either."

"I'm so glad he's okay."

Sloan's eyes bored into her. A strange kind of energy seemed to fill the shack. He looked like a man who had something to say but couldn't find the right words.

"Is Jeremy settled for the night at George and Junella's?" she inquired casually, seeking any means possible to avoid an uncomfortable silence between herself and Sloan.

"He decided to ride into town tonight so he'd be able to catch the eight o'clock train home." Sloan's silvery gaze flashed fire. "He wanted to get back to Misty Marie as soon as possible."

Prudence blushed and looked away from Sloan's intense stare. She supposed something ought to be said about what she'd overheard, but she couldn't bring herself to mention the intimate sexual details Sloan had discussed.

"Since the rain has let up, I'd like to go home now."

"I figured you would," he said quietly.

"Will the trip be too much for Lucky after his adventure?"

"I saddled up another horse," he informed her, his voice devoid of feeling.

She glanced up. "One of your thoroughbreds?"

He surprised her with a smile. "A man would have to be crazy to ride double at night on a thousand-dollar horse."

"They cost a thousand dollars?" Prudence gasped, astonished by the vast amount someone would pay for horseflesh.

"Some do. The ones that can run like the wind and have the heart of a champion."

She shook her head. "It's hard to imagine an animal being worth so much."

"Look what folks charge for a purebred breeding bull," he pointed out. "Some animals, just like some people, are worth whatever it takes to possess them."

Goose bumps rose on Prudence's arms. "You can't possess a person. The War Between the States made that illegal. It's in the Constitution now."

"I'm not talking about slavery," he said. "I'm talking about what happens between a man and a woman."

As Prudence reflected upon the subject, she decided that there could be an almost master-slave relationship when a man and woman made love. There had been a point when Sloan had kissed her breasts that she'd felt enslaved by the primitive yearnings unleashed within her body. She stared deeply into his eyes and wondered if he'd felt the same aching need she'd experienced.

"I'm ready to leave," she said softly. Her hands trembled and her knees shook. It occurred to her with savage clarity that if she didn't escape this room now, in a few minutes she might not want to.

While Sloan had been checking on his horse, Prudence had realized she was grateful his brother had interrupted what she was certain would have resulted in her and Sloan becoming lovers. So reckless an act could cost her everything. Her own self-respect. The respect of the townspeople. The guardianship of the children. Sloan threatened everything she was, as a person and as a woman. And because he made her dizzy with desire whenever they were alone together, she had made the only sensible decision where he was concerned.

No matter what bizarre circumstances might thrust them together, in the future she would always keep her bodice buttoned and her corset fastened!

"Here," Sloan said, crossing the room. "You'll need this to keep you warm."

It was a shock when he wrapped his coat around her, the one she'd hidden behind earlier in the evening. She slipped her arms into the spacious sleeves and felt as if she were being embraced by Sloan. His scent was there, along with the pungent aroma of cowhide.

During the ride back to the farmhouse, Prudence passed the time by silently singing all the verses to "She'll Be Coming Around the Mountain." She thought it was the safest method of keeping Sloan Coltrane pushed to the back of her mind. That way she wouldn't be affected by how it felt to have his strong arms encircling her and his substantial chest pressed against her back. She thought it was a brilliant strategy until they reached the yard.

But then her mind capriciously reminded her that she and the children had been singing the same song the first time she'd met Sloan. Unwillingly, she was reminded of all that had transpired between them. And what would *never* happen between them. A quiet sadness filled her heart. Her world and Sloan's were a million miles apart.

He was a man indifferent to family and responsibility.

She was a woman to whom family was everything, and responsibility was part and parcel of that everything.

Yellow streams of light shone from the house's windows.

"It looks like they waited up for you."

Sloan's husky voice made the inside of her ears tingle, a feat she hadn't even suspected they were capable of. "I hate knowing they've needlessly worried about me."

"Family does that," Sloan said, his tone gritty. He eased her from the horse, then stepped beside her.

She started to walk toward the house, then stopped and turned. "Thank you, Sloan. You saved my life."

"It was my pleasure, ma'am."

She'd been feeling incredibly sad a moment ago, but his lazy Texas drawl brought a smile to her lips. "Good luck with racing your horses."

He tilted his head. "Are you sure you mean that?"

"I can see how you've laid out your track and the other buildings. They aren't going to pose a hazard to the children. In fact, they will be delighted to know they've been invited to tour your place. They really want to look at those fancy horses of yours."

"But you won't be coming with them, will you, Prudence?"

It surprised her that he knew her so well. "No, I'll let Gladys act as chaperon."

"You're telling me goodbye, aren't you?"

She shivered. The man really was uncanny in his observations. "I—I'm afraid of what happens to me when I get too close to you, Sloan. I have a world here. A safe world. It's the only life I've ever wanted for myself, and I don't want to lose it."

The expression in his eyes was enigmatic. "And I'm a threat to that life?"

"You know what's happened between us so far. It's more than what's proper for a woman like me."

"A woman like you?"

"A woman with a certain position in the community," she explained through a painfully tight throat.

"I want to call you a coward," he said slowly, as if measuring and weighing each individual word he used. "But the truth is you've got more courage than anyone I've ever met. You speak the truth, no matter how... hard...it might be. You lay open your feelings like you're spreading out a poker hand after the last man's raised and called. And it doesn't seem to matter if you're holding the winning or the losing hand. That takes guts."

It was the crudest compliment she'd ever received, but it made her heart soar. "Thank you."

"There's something you need to know about playing cards, though."

The skin on the back of her neck prickled. "What's that."

"There's always another hand."

He stepped forward with an abruptness that startled a gasp from her and pulled her into his arms. His head lowered with the swiftness of a striking predator. And his kiss. It was hotly possessive and made a ruin of the wall she'd tried to erect against him.

She should have struggled, of course.

She didn't. Instead, she held on and...and...went along for the ride. It had to be as wild and daring as any thoroughbred's dash to the finish line.

After a time he let her go. She swayed against him.

"Prudence..."

"Hmm..."

"Are you going to be able to stand up on your own?"

There was enough self-satisfaction in his voice to stiffen her spine. She opened her eyes, wondering when she'd closed them.

"Certainly."

"Then I don't need to carry you inside?"

Oh, he was a contrary man.

"Not this time," she answered with a toss of her head as she turned toward the house again.

"That's what I figured."

She heard the creak of saddle leather and knew he'd remounted. When she reached the porch, she couldn't resist turning to watch him ride out.

He was on his horse and it was moving. Toward the porch.

"What are you doing?" she asked in consternation.

"Seeing you safely inside."

She grinned at him, amazed at how his unpredictable nature buoyed her spirits. "You're such a gentleman."

"I can be when the occasion calls for it," he said cryptically.

"And that happens maybe once or twice a year?"

He shook his head. "I don't do my reckoning by the year."

"You don't?"

"I do it by the woman," he said softly.

*What did that mean?*

The front door opened before Prudence could inquire.

"Land sakes, where have you been?" Gladys stepped onto the porch with a raised lantern. "We've been worried sick that twister got a hold of you."

"It almost did," Prudence said. "If it hadn't been for Sloan, I'm sure I would have been killed."

The housekeeper looked toward Sloan. "Come inside so you can warm up and we can thank you properly."

"Thanks for the offer, but I'd better be on my way. It feels like more rain is on the way."

"Miss Prudence! Miss Prudence!"

The children flowed out the door around Gladys.

"We were so scared you'd got eaten by that trickster," Janey cried, her small arms encircling Prudence's legs.

Prudence reached for the railing to steady herself.

"It was a twister," Charlie corrected the girl. "And it wouldn't have eaten her, it would have carried her up into the sky."

Prudence knelt beside the trembling child. "I'm fine, sweetheart. There's not a scratch on me."

Well, perhaps there were several scrapes from her tumble down the hill with Sloan, but there was no reason to dwell upon them when she'd been delivered safe and sound from the tempest. She glanced over Janey's blond head and saw Sloan's retreating figure. She wasn't certain how she would survive the tempest in her heart.

"Miss Prudence, did you see it?" Davy asked. "Was it huge?"

Prudence reached out to give Charlotte, who'd also crowded close, a hug, then she rose. "I'll tell you all about it when we're inside."

"You haven't had your supper yet," Gladys said. "Come into the kitchen and we'll feed you."

At the housekeeper's suggestion, Prudence's stomach perked right up. Hot food sounded wonderful. The children followed close at her heels. Though they should have been in bed, she decided it wouldn't hurt for them to stay up late one evening. She'd come frighteningly close to losing them, and it felt good to have them close by.

"Where's Richard?" she asked as she sat at the table.

"He and Micah waited for the rain to quit. Then they went out looking for you."

Poor Richard, this was the second time he'd gone out to search for her after dark. It took a minute for the second name Gladys had spoken to register.

"Who's Micah?"

"My brother," Davy announced, his voice filled with obvious pride. "He's come to fetch me."

Prudence felt as if someone had slammed a fist into her stomach. She had been so sure that Davy would stay with her until he was fully grown. When the Bowcutts had abandoned their younger son in Port Dodd, they had done so with a finality that had made Prudence feel contempt for them. Clearly, she'd been wrong about their intentions.

"You mean your folks have settled in California and they sent Micah to come and get you?"

She couldn't believe how much it hurt to lose one of her children. It didn't help to know that she should have been happy for Davy being reunited with his real family. But even the stab of guilt she experienced wasn't enough to make her willingly let go of the boy. She'd come to love him. As deeply and devotedly as any mother could have.

She forced her lips to form the shape of a smile, but inside she felt cold and hollow. "I'm ... I'm delighted for you, Davy."

A look of pain darkened the boy's eyes. "My folks still don't want me." He raised his small jaw. "But Micah wants me. He's says we're brothers and brothers stick together. He says he got a job on a ranch in Arizona, and the head man said I could live with him and his missus. It's all settled. Micah and I are going to take the train there."

Prudence felt ashamed of the sense of relief that washed over her. There was no way anyone could expect her to entrust Davy to a boy that was only a few years older than he was.

Gladys carried a steaming bowl of beef stew to the table. "You'd best wait till you meet Micah before you make any decisions about Davy's future."

Prudence's gaze flew guiltily to the older woman. She sensed the housekeeper knew exactly what she was thinking, that Davy belonged with them no matter what. She refrained from pointing out how irresponsible it would be for her to send the boy off without any guarantees about his future or his safety. The excitement and hope shining in Davy's brown eyes made her hold her tongue.

There would be sufficient time to resolve the boy's future calmy and prudently. Sufficient time to convince everyone, even Davy's brother, that a young child needed a secure home in which to grow up.

She picked up her spoon. "I look forward to meeting your brother, Davy. I'm very impressed that he traveled all this way to find you."

"He loves me," Davy said, his voice filled with heart-wrenching awe. "He told me so, straight to my face."

Prudence glanced at the other young faces at the table. A poignant look of wistfulness tinged Janey's good eye. Charlotte and Charlie looked as if they were listening to one of the bedtime stories she read to them each night. Even Sarah's expression was dreamy. Evidently it didn't matter how old someone was. The thought of having a family, or even one family member, say that you were loved evoked a keening sense of belonging.

Belonging...

As she looked around the table again, it struck Prudence that none of these children truly belonged to her, that as much as she might want it, they weren't her family. And that each of them needed and deserved their own mother and father. She hadn't been nearly diligent enough in trying to find individual homes for them, she realized. She'd accepted their presence in her life as natural, her love for them sufficient to raise them.

But they didn't belong to her.

And if Micah was determined to take Davy with him, she didn't know how she could stop him. She laid down her spoon.

"What's the matter, Miss Prudence? Aren't you hungry?" Charlotte asked.

"Not very," she answered softly. "I guess I'm more tired than I realized."

Janey's bottom lip thrust out. "Too tired to tell us a bedtime story?"

Prudence shook her head. "No," she said thickly. "I'm never too tired for that."

## Chapter Thirteen

"So you see, Miss Abercrombie, I have a place for both Davy and me to live," Micah Bowcutt stated with simple but unshakable resolve.

The morning after her tumultuous encounter with Sloan, Prudence sat in the parlor trying to assimilate everything Micah had told her. From the young man's resolute posture and unyielding stare, she sensed she would be unable to change his mind about taking his brother with him.

Her hands curled into fists even as her stomach tightened. She wanted their private discussion to be at an end. She wanted to tell him to go away. She wanted him to leave Davy where he belonged. With her. But the words stuck in her throat.

As much as she wanted to be otherwise, she knew she had to be fair to Micah and fair to Davy. Who would have ever guessed that it would hurt so much to be fair? Still, a part of her refused to give in without a fight. An honest fight, she decided, trying to compose her arguments against Davy being taken from her.

"How old are you, Micah?"

"Seventeen," he answered, his brown eyes unflinching.

"Don't you think that's awfully young to take on the responsibility of caring for a child?" she asked gently.

"Maybe," came the flat answer. "But he's my brother, and he belongs with me. With his family."

"But he wouldn't be with his family, not really," she pointed out. "From what you say, your mother and father haven't changed their minds about Davy living with them."

Micah's Adam's apple worked. "Their decision has nothing to do with me and Davy."

"I admire your brotherly loyalty, but Davy is happy here with us. He's a member of our family. We love him." Her voice wavered. She swallowed. "He's safe here. There's plenty of space, and he's sure to get three meals a day, every day. He has other children that he's become close to. They accept him just as he is."

"Ma'am, I know what you're saying is true. And I thank you for the care and love you've given my brother." This time it was Micah's voice that cracked. "But I love him. Ever since he was a baby, I was the one who looked after him. I've got good and steady work waiting for me in Arizona. My boss, Mr. Yates, and his missus know about Davy, about his leg. They're good people." The young man squared his shoulders. "I swear to you that he will have a good home."

She wanted to continue the argument, to force the boy to admit that Davy was better off staying with her. But in her heart, she already knew that Micah Bowcutt would not leave Port Dodd without his brother. Even though the sense of loss she felt was tearing her apart, she also knew this special young man would protect Davy, and that Davy would ultimately be happier with his own kin.

"Have you..." Tears burned her eyes. It hurt to breathe. "Have you thought about settling in Port Dodd? There's room for you here."

"I know you don't think so, but I'm a man fully grown, not one of your orphans." A look of stubborn pride tinged the young man's eyes. "Besides, I've given my word to Mr. Yates. I couldn't let him down."

"I see."

"When I showed up last night, I planned on taking Davy with me right away, but I can see now that it's going to take a few days for him and you to say your goodbyes. I'll send a telegraph to Mr. Yates and let him know that I've been delayed."

"Thank you," she whispered hoarsely.

"Ma'am?"

"Yes?"

Micah stood. "I want you to know that I think you're a right fine woman."

She didn't think she could manage another "thank you." She settled for a nod.

"You've been a better mother to Davy than his own ever was. Mrs. Yates is a good woman, too. She's got two daughters, but she's got love to spare. She's a lot like you."

The young man plopped on a battered hat and left Prudence to her thoughts. She stood upon unsteady feet, drawn to the picture of her mother and her aunts. As she pressed her fingertips to the domed glass, she wondered if the hole in her heart left by Davy's absence would ever heal.

Why did things have to change, and why did those changes have to cause such pain? She supposed it helped to know that Davy was going to a good home, that he was going to be able to grow up with a brother who loved him. She turned from the picture. It just didn't help enough to take away the ragged sense of loss.

"Are you sure you don't want to come with us, Miss Prudence?" Charlie asked for what must have been the fiftieth time.

The children were loaded in the wagon and in high spirits about their coming visit to Coltrane's track. From their ecstatic expressions, one would have supposed that, instead of viewing a thoroughbred racehorse, they were going to meet President Rutherford B. Hayes.

"I have plenty to do around here," she answered, noticing with mild concern the shyly curious glances Sarah and Micah kept sending each other when they thought no one was looking. They hadn't exchanged more than a few words, yet with amazing coincidence they always seemed to be in the same place at the same time. They had sat together during the noontime meal, just as they were sitting beside each other now in the buckboard.

At another time she might not have thought much about their obvious interest in each other, but their frequent glances looked distressingly similar to the looks of tender regard that Reverend Brown and Marabelle Brubaker had shared at the seashore. A wave of protectiveness surged within Prudence. At sixteen, Sarah was much too young to be exchanging such loving glances with a stranger. She made a mental note to speak with the girl about the matter.

The wagon pulled out with Richard driving it and Gladys beside him. It surprised Prudence that even their practical housekeeper had been caught up in the "horse madness" that seemed to have invaded Port Dodd.

Amid waves and happy shouts, Richard and his laughing passengers were soon out of sight. The noonday sun gave little evidence that a fierce rainstorm had passed overhead a few hours earlier. Since the garden was too wet to work and the house had been left in perfect order, Prudence had been less than truthful in saying that there was an abundance of things to occupy her time.

She looked toward the upstairs bedroom. Charlie and Davy's room. She was going to have to go up there sometime and pack Davy's meager possessions. Pain, hot and piercing, shafted through her. She couldn't face doing the task now.

She let her footsteps lead her where they would. It was a mild Texas summer day. Mockingbirds made a musical racket in the nearby pecan tree, and the recent rain had washed away the oppressive heat that had been building for the past few days.

She wouldn't lose touch with Davy completely, she assured herself. She would write to him, and she was certain he would write to her. While a great distance away, Arizona wasn't on the other side of the world. Perhaps she and the children would be able to visit. Such a trip would be both educational and an adventure.

When Prudence stopped walking, she found herself standing above the river that had made such a profound impression the first day they had arrived at Amos's farm. No longer shallow and muddy, the body of water had become a swollen tempest. Last night's rains had rendered what Sloan Coltrane had called a puddle of spit into a roaring river. The thunderous din made by the swirling, foaming water made it impossible to hear anything but its raging passage.

Awed by the sheer, naked power churning in front of her, she realized that had this been their day of arrival at the farm and had Davy wandered too close to the bank's edge, he would have fallen to certain death. And nothing she could have done would have saved him. She said a silent prayer to the Almighty that their close brush with disaster had been just that, a close brush. And while she addressed her Creator, she also said a special prayer for Micah and Davy's safety on their journey to their new home.

"And, dear Lord," she added softly, "please forgive me for my selfishness in not wanting to let Davy go." She squeezed her eyes shut. "It's so hard to lose a child. Even though it's only been four months, I've grown to think of him as mine.''

Her words trailed off. She rubbed her eyes; they were hot and burning. She sighed. Inexorably the pain within her chest began to lessen. It was as if she heard an inner voice, whispering that it had been natural for her to love Davy, but now it was time to let him go. Even though she wasn't ready. Even though it hurt unbearably. He belonged with his brother.

Gradually a feeling of peace unfurled within her, and she continued to stare into the thick, dirty river that swept past her. The longer she looked at it, the more the brown water resembled the bitter drink Sloan had served her—his powerful version of Texas coffee. She could probably dip a cup into the raging river and not discern the difference between it and Sloan's customary thick brew.

"So this is where you're hiding out."

Prudence yelped in surprise at the nearness of the deep-voiced observation. Her hand shot to her heart, and she jumped back.

"Careful!" Powerful hands jerked her around, toward a brick-hard chest. "Today's not the day to take a tumble into the Bartel."

Sloan!

She closed her eyes and allowed herself to be pressed tightly against him. It felt so good to be held, so good to feel his strong arms wrapped around her. The scent of him was frankly male, the feel of him reassuringly hard. How was it that his simple hug should have such a powerful impact upon her emotions?

His embrace lightened. She had no choice but to accept the separation. He took her hand and put a greater distance between them and the raging river.

"You weren't thinking of jumping, were you?"

"Of course not."

They reached his horse. She realized the deafening roar of the water had blunted the sounds of his arrival.

He tipped the brim of his hat and pinned her with a concerned gaze. She guessed he found out that Davy was leaving. The children had probably trumpeted the news of his departure the moment they'd shown up at Sloan's place. They did so love to impart every bit of knowledge they had.

A new thought struck her. Why wasn't Sloan with the children, showing off his precious horses?

"Why are you here?" she asked, forcing a light tone to the question.

"George and Junella are giving the kids a tour of the stables." His expression remained sober. "They introduced me to Micah."

"A fine young man, wouldn't you agree?" she mused woodenly.

"He seems pleasant enough," Sloan answered neutrally.

"Davy's ecstatic about living with him." *Was that brittle voice hers?*

"How are you handling it?"

"What do you mean?"

"I know you well enough to realize you love each and every one of your wounded critters. It's got to hurt like hell to lose one of them."

For once it didn't offend her that he referred to the children as critters, perhaps because she detected a trace of affection in his deep voice. She lowered her lashes, not wanting him to see how upset she was by Davy's leaving. She didn't like revealing her weaknesses to anyone, least of all Sloan.

"I want what's best for them," she said steadily. "It's important for Davy to be with a brother who loves him."

"Even if his going rips your heart out?"

Prudence raised her lashes. "That's right."

"You're one tough lady, aren't you, Prudence Abercrombie?"

"When there's no other choice."

"So you're not going to cry and make a scene or force Davy to choose between you and his brother?"

The question startled her. She'd briefly considered doing just that. Then, ashamed of herself, she'd forced the unworthy thought from her. Her stomach fluttered. That Sloan knew her so well made her feel dangerously exposed.

"I told you I want what's best for Davy. A scene like that would have caused him pain."

"What about your pain?"

Sloan's silvery eyes reflected a gentleness that made her mouth go dry. She truly hadn't thought him capable of gentleness.

"You said it yourself, I'm one tough lady."

"And the children really aren't yours to keep, are they?" he pressed, his tone hardening, his gaze narrowing.

Had she really thought him gentle? She pressed a hand to her temple. The sun must have scrambled her senses.

"They're mine to love and care for," she answered simply.

"And then to let go when someone comes along who wants them?"

"And, when loving people want to provide a home for them, to give them up," she said hollowly.

"How many times has that happened over the years? How many times has a family stepped forward to claim one of the children?"

Why was he making this so hard for her?

"After the fire—"

"I'm not talking about the children your mother and aunts offered temporary shelter to after the fire. I'm talking about the children who've come to you since then, the ones who were abandoned."

"Never," she answered tersely. "They've lived with us until they reached adulthood and had the opportunity to get more schooling or find employment."

"Then this is a new experience for you?"

She nodded jerkily.

"Such a tough lady," he repeated softly. He raised a hand and, with a gloved fingertip, traced a path down her cheek. "You've been crying."

Had she? She touched her other cheek and was surprised to feel the wetness. "It's not a crime to shed a few tears."

"I didn't say it was."

The sun was to the back of his head. Nearby a bee droned. The river proceeded at a dull roar. Without understanding why, she found herself trying to memorize everything about their surroundings. The way the soft dirt felt beneath the soles of her walking boots. The way the sunlight broke and splintered around Sloan's hat, bathing his lean face in a shadowy haze. The way the recent rain gave everything a fresh smell.

She cleared her throat. How long could they go on staring at each other and not conversing? Surely, if she put her mind to it, she could think of something relevant to say.

"Ah..."

"Yes, Prudence?"

Her eyes narrowed. It would help immensely if he would contribute something.

"I imagine the children are enjoying the opportunity to see your thoroughbreds."

There, that was a perfectly acceptable remark to make. Maybe now her heart would stop pounding so erratically and she would be able to breathe more normally. Maybe now her glance wouldn't keep sliding to Sloan's mouth. Maybe now—

"You could have come with them and seen for yourself."

"I don't get along with horses," she said, fascinated by the way his lips shaped his words.

"Why not?"

"I suppose because they're big smelly beasts and have minds of their own."

*Rather like men*...

Sloan's lips curved around his white teeth. Good grief, had he read her mind?

"You only think that because you don't know how to ride. You're probably afraid of them. A horse can sense when a rider is afraid. They won't obey anyone who's skittish around them."

Prudence tried to concentrate on Sloan's explanation, but during the middle of it, his hand had come to rest lightly upon her shoulder.

"What are you doing?" she asked, her gaze trapped by his.

"Talking about horses."

"I mean with your hand." Her cheeks heated. "What are you doing with your hand?"

"Touching you."

She was finding it difficult to get sufficient air. "Why?"

His fingers contracted. "Because I can't seem *not* to touch you."

"That's not an acceptable answer," she pointed out. "A person can't go around doing something so personal to someone else unless...unless..."

Unless *what?* her brain demanded.

"Touching your shoulder isn't so personal," he observed, his tone frustratingly casual. "Now, say my hand moved to your breast, and I began to fondle you there.... Well then, you might have cause to complain."

She swayed, wondering what the chances were she might faint. Her glance darted to her shoulder where his strong hand had taken up residence. She stared at his cowhide gloves. They were brown and stained with the hard usage they'd been put through. The bizarre urge rose up inside her to turn her head and rub her cheek against the worn leather. She swallowed. Or tried to. There didn't seem to be enough moisture in her mouth to do that or to speak.

"You have such beautiful breasts," he continued softly. "Soft and white and pink. I laid awake last night, thinking about them, remembering how they tasted. Sweet, they were incredibly sweet, just like you."

This had gone on long enough. She was exactly where she'd been last night. Alone with Sloan Coltrane. And she'd promised herself that wasn't going to happen again. Only she hadn't been thinking about the passion they'd shared when he'd joined her. Her thoughts had been full of Davy and her anguish at his leaving. Her preoccupation had allowed Sloan to sneak past her defenses.

"You think too much about my...chest."

His laugh was low and wicked. "Believe me, it's an entirely pleasurable experience." He shifted his stance so that he stood even closer to her. "Your...chest is one of nature's more inspiring creations."

"Now you're being foolish."

"Tell me the truth," he said, his tone coaxing. "Haven't you had a few thoughts about me?"

"You're a fine figure of a man," she snapped. "Is that what you wanted to hear?"

"Not exactly."

"Did you want me to praise your chest?"

He brushed his hand across his mouth. "Some women have."

"Did they call it an 'inspiring creation of nature'?" she asked sarcastically, incensed that he would mention the other women he'd been with to her.

Unholy amusement lit his silver eyes. "Actually, they reserved those words for another part of my anatomy."

"Pray tell, it wasn't your brain!"

"Try lower."

Her mind went blank. Unfortunately, only for a half second. Then a blast of hot embarrassment singed her skin, all the way from the soles of her feet to her scalp.

"I asked you not to talk that way around me. It—It's disrespectful."

His smile never wavered. "Honey, that's not true."

"Don't call me 'honey.'"

"Well now, there's 'sweetheart' and 'darlin','' but I've always been partial to *honey*."

"Remove your hand from my shoulder." It was a command, pure and simple.

His eyes glinted with sudden purpose. "All right."

She was expelling a sigh of relief when the burning trail of his caress meandered lazily to her right breast. The sigh became hopelessly trapped in her throat.

"As I was saying," he drawled, his voice impossibly low and gritty, "I've always been partial to sweet-tasting honey."

Her stomach rolled over. She felt a clenching spasm deep inside her. His fingers brushed lightly against the front of her dress. She knew the moment he found her nipple because it had grown hard and sensitive, shooting tingling tremors through her.

"Why are you doing this?" she asked hoarsely.

His head lowered until the sun ceased to exist. "Because you need shaking up, honey. It's not healthy holding everything in the way you do. You've got to let loose once in a while."

"You have no right to—"

His lips brushed hers. "I have every right."

She started to move her head in denial, but he deepened the pressure. His mouth slanted over hers. Darkness descended. Tears stung the back of her eyes as she leaned into him, her hands rising to rest upon his shoulders. Oh, how she hated her weakness toward him, hated how it reduced her resistance to nothing. Yet, even feeling as she did, she knew no force on earth could keep her from yielding to him, to the beckoning male heat that enfolded her.

His lips persuaded, his tongue courted. She softened against the relentless assault upon her senses. Gently, he eased the pressure of his mouth and breathed soft kisses against her cheeks and forehead.

"I have the right to do this," he told her, his voice excitingly rough, "because we both need it so bad."

She stroked the thick hair that lay at the nape of his neck. "Needing...it," she began slowly, "isn't enough. There has to be..."

Her protest dwindled. She'd been about to tell him there had to be love. She refused, however, to break the promise she'd made to herself that she wouldn't speak that word to him again.

"I know," he said, his lips still trailing kisses over her face. "There has to be respect."

"Yes," she agreed weakly, wondering how she could shut off the dizzying sensations he continued to send soaring through her.

He stepped back. "Let's go."

*Go?*

Where? To the nearest bed?

"I'm not going anywhere with you."

It was time he learned she was not a woman of easy virtue. The very idea that she would lie with Sloan Coltrane in the middle of the day to appease the earthy appetites he'd aroused within her was... She blinked. Actually, it was exceedingly tempting.

He took her hand and pulled her resisting feet toward his horse. "It's time you learned to ride. You won't be a real Texan until you do."

"Sloan, this may come as a shock, but becoming a real Texan hasn't been one of my foremost yearnings."

"You can't know if you like something unless you try it first."

"Are we talking about riding?"

She had meant to think that question, not grumble it aloud. Another blush swept over her. She began to feel as if some internal furnace was running amuck inside her.

Naturally Sloan stopped when he heard her question. She refused to look at him and stared at his horse instead. His overly large horse.

"*Now* we're talking about riding. You'll be the first to know when the subject changes."

"How very kind of you to keep me posted," she stated coolly, wondering why Lucky's jaws were so huge when they merely had to graze upon grass and munch meals of hay. One would assume by the animal's dimensions that he ought to have been a meat-eater. It didn't soothe her nerves that the beast was returning her intense regard. She had the unsettling feeling he was taking her measure.

Sloan laughed. His amusement at her expense nettled her. She was fully prepared to tell him off, but she didn't dare look away from Lucky's hostile glare. Yes, she thought, the horse was definitely glaring at her. Maybe he held her responsible for almost being swallowed up in that twister, or perhaps he was still irritated about his descent into the river on her behalf. Who knew what a horse thought or what type of ill will he might harbor?

"Uh, Sloan, do you think Lucky remembers me?"

"What?"

"Lucky, your horse," she prompted impatiently. "Do you think he remembers me?"

"I'm not sure I know what you mean."

"Good grief, isn't it obvious? The few times I've been around him I've caused him nothing but trouble. First there was that business with the river. Twice, if you count chasing down Davy's crutch. Then there was the time you rode out at night to find me. Have you ever considered that horses don't like being out after dark?"

"I can't say that I have."

"And what about when you saved me from the twister? Poor Lucky was left on his own that whole horrible time. Out in the rain. Probably scared out of his wits. You can't say that was a pleasant experience for him."

"Prudence, have you been nipping something with more wallop to it than that tea of yours?"

"Of course not!"

"Then you're teasing me, paying me back for what happened a couple of minutes ago."

"If you're referring to that kiss..." She thought she saw Lucky glower at her. She retreated a step. "This has nothing to do with that. It has to do with your horse—I don't think he likes me, and I don't think it's a good idea for me to try to ride him."

"As long as you're calm around him, he'll be fine," Sloan advised with what she detected as strained patience.

"But I'm sure he remembers—"

"Prudence, he's a damned horse, not a person. His brain doesn't work like ours."

"You said yourself that horses like to win races. That must mean that they *do* think like us, or else it wouldn't matter to them if they came in dead last."

"I give up."

Her spirits soared, and her gaze flicked to his. "You do?"

"Yep. There's no reasoning with you, woman. Not when you get like this."

Before she could thank him for changing his mind, his hands were around her waist and he was swinging her upon the saddle.

"Wait!"

"I've waited long enough," he said, mounting behind her. "We've got ourselves a couple of hours without the children underfoot, and we're going to put that time to good use. Giddyap!"

# Chapter Fourteen

"I don't see how I'm supposed to learn to ride with you and Lucky doing all the work," Prudence complained in her well-bred voice.

Sloan smiled against the crown of her head. He couldn't explain exactly why she made him feel so good, but there was no getting around that the more she opened herself up to him, the happier he was. Even when she was complaining.

"Relax, we're almost there."

"And where's there?" she demanded.

"Somewhere you can take a spill and not get hurt," he told her patiently.

There was a moment of silence. He figured she was digesting his statement. More than likely she didn't approve of his vague explanation.

"You must not be a very good teacher, if you expect me to fall off," she said petulantly.

"I don't expect you to fall off." He shifted her position so her back rested more fully against his chest. "I just don't like to take chances."

"Then you've selected the wrong profession—horse racing."

Sloan sighed. The woman really was a handful. "You're forgetting that I own the track. Either way I win."

"You've got an answer for everything."

"Not everything," he muttered. He was still resisting the strong feelings she aroused within him. Damn, for years he'd dreamed and planned how he was going to use his freedom when he finally attained it, and now this female had made the freedom he'd yearned for seem empty and meaningless. Not only that, she'd made him yearn for something else. Something more precious than smoking his cheroots, playing his poker, drinking his whiskey, racing his horses and cavorting with a variety of pretty women. She'd made him yearn for her.

Hell, she'd made him burn for her.

"We're here," he said when they crested the last hill between them and the Gulf of Mexico.

Prudence shaded her eyes. "This is where you're going to teach me to ride?"

He eased himself off Lucky and reached for her. "After we make a few adjustments."

She looked down at him from atop the horse with obvious misgivings. "What kind of adjustments?"

Sloan plucked her from his saddle. "Have I ever mentioned how tired I am of seeing you in black?"

Her booted feet sank into the sand. She gazed at him with a bewildered look in her green eyes. Gulls circled overhead. Their discordant screeching blended with the salty breeze that swirled around them. He felt a curious fullness in his chest and sensed that this moment would be forever seared in his brain. She appeared so feminine. Clearly filled with uncertainty, but oddly trusting, also. No longer was he able to resist her allure.

"On more than one occasion, you've told me you don't like my clothes," she answered. Several tendrils of reddish hair blew across her soft lips. She combed back the strands with her fingers. "Marabelle Brubaker donated several bolts of colorful material to us. There's bound to be enough for me to make a new dress."

Her cheeks grew flushed, as if she were uneasy about the frivolity of having a new gown.

"Is any of the material black?"

She shook her head.

He wanted to kiss her, but refrained. He knew if he did, there would be no stopping before he fully possessed her. He looked away from her sparkling green eyes. He'd chosen this secluded cove for more than just teaching her to ride Lucky.

"You're beautiful in white," he said softly, watching those pink cheeks blossom into a deeper shade of red.

"There's one bolt of white muslin."

"But then you'd look beautiful in yellow or pink or blue or green," he continued huskily.

She lowered her head. "Shouldn't we be getting on with this?"

He impressed himself by not groaning aloud. "There's no one around for miles, honey."

"That's good. I don't relish the thought of having an audience if I am thrown."

"Lucky isn't going to throw you," he said, trying his damnedest not to become impatient. "I own this stretch of land and I can guarantee that no one's going to come along and disturb us."

"I see."

Did she? he wondered. "So I'm thinking you could slip out of that dress of yours and—"

Her head snapped up. "Sloan Coltrane!"

He ran his fingertip across her top button. It was shiny and as black as her dress. "I'm not suggesting anything improper. Just think how . . . relaxing it would feel to ride

Lucky across the sand without that heavy, long-sleeved dress. You'd still be covered.''

"Barely!''

"I've seen you in your underwear, Prudence. And less. Nothing bad happened. For once in your life, wouldn't you like to feel free? Wouldn't you like to have the wind and the sunshine all around you? Wouldn't you like to just . . . be?''

Her face was all eyes now, and those eyes were beginning to simmer with green fire.

"Why are you doing this?'' Her voice was a thick whisper.

"I can't think about anything else but you, Prudence. You're like a . . .'' He'd been about to say burr beneath his skin, but sensed she might not like that comparison. "You're like that ocean over there.''

"Wet and salty?'' she asked, her tone ironic.

She was obviously trying to put him in his place. Unfortunately in her innocence she didn't realize that wet and salty wasn't a wholly inaccurate picture of how he wanted her. Damp and ready inside, her skin slick with perspiration caused by uncontrollable excitement.

"I want you.''

He hadn't meant to say it, to announce it, in such blunt terms. He'd meant to . . . ease her into loving him. He'd meant to lead her down the garden path, until the cautious, logical side of her mind was no longer working. He'd meant to make her want him as much as he wanted her.

He should have known better. Prudence wasn't the kind of female to allow herself to be blindly led where she hadn't already been. She wasn't a woman to be controlled by her passions. If he was going to get anywhere with her, he was going to have to mentally seduce her first. A daunting enterprise for even the most stout-hearted male.

"You want me for the afternoon?"

Her question struck him in the gut like a shot of warm whiskey on an empty stomach. In that moment, he knew he wanted her for more than an afternoon. He also knew the only way to have and keep Prudence Abercrombie was to marry her. It came as a shock when he realized just how much he did want to keep her. In fact, the more he reflected upon the matter, the more he became convinced he wouldn't let her go. If marriage was what it took to make her a permanent part of his life, then marriage it would be.

"Are you proposing matrimony to me?" he asked, more than ready to stake his claim.

"Lord, you're arrogant!"

He had his work cut out for him.

"Because if you are asking," he continued doggedly, "my answer might surprise you."

She went still, her expression sobering as she contemplated him. "I never know what to expect from you."

"Life wasn't meant to be boring." He gently slipped her top button from its mooring, studying her intently to see how she reacted. He was gratified by the shudder that rippled through her. It helped to know that he wasn't the only one struggling for control. "Sometimes a person has to break out of her rut and try something new."

His hand dropped to the second button. Her palm came up, and, with trembling fingers, she forestalled further trespass. "But this isn't new for you."

He was so hard he hurt. "Yes, it is."

"You don't have to lie to me," she protested gently. "According to your brother, you've been with dozens of women. You probably can't remember all their names."

"I never taught any of them to ride," he told her simply.

"Oh, well, then I am honored."

"I never asked any of them to become my wife."

From the way she jerked, he could tell he'd truly shocked her. He held his breath, waiting to hear what she would say. It didn't matter, of course. Even if she told him no, he'd find a way to change her mind. She was right. He was arrogant. And stubborn. And ruthless when it came to getting what he wanted. The last came as a revelation to him. He'd never thought of himself as ruthless before. But in this moment of truth, he knew he'd break both the laws of God and man to have this woman.

He was almost tempted to laugh at himself—if the situation with her wasn't so precarious. She hated gamblers in general and horse racing in particular. Both meant the world to him. Laugh? Hell, he should be on the verge of tears. This woman was going to make his life one crisis after another, what with her penchant for adopting stray children and her inclination to follow a most straight and narrow path. But he wasn't a man given to tears, and the moon wasn't out for him to howl at it, so he was just going to have to hunker down and get the independent and indomitable Miss Prudence Abercrombie to see things his way.

"Well, aren't you going to say something?" he pressed. The sooner she started making her objections, the sooner he could level them.

She shook her head solemnly.

"Why not?"

"I—I'm not sure what it is I want to say."

He was about to tell her that it didn't matter what she said when the fingertips that rested lightly against the back of his hand began to stroke him. A hot tremor squeezed his groin.

While he stood almost paralyzed with desire, she stepped back. His protest lodged in his thickened throat as he watched her shaking hands unfasten the second button.

"What are you doing?" He didn't know how he got the question unstuck from his throat.

"I'm going to ride across the sand," she answered, her gaze sliding from his. "Without my black dress."

Absently Sloan realized that they hadn't settled the fact that she would become his bride. Maybe this was her way of saying yes. As the thinking side of his brain closed down, further rational thought eluded him. He'd already reached the point where buzzing pricks of desire and the driving need for release obliterated everything else. It stunned him that he could be brought to this level of excitement merely by words. But they were her words, spoken in her bewitching voice.

Sloan watched in aching silence as Prudence shed the unbecoming black garment. Dazzling sunlight transformed her plain chemise and pantaloons to a startling shade of white. He didn't suppose he'd ever get his tongue pried from the roof of his mouth. With the sea and surf pounding in his ears, he wondered if it was possible to have a climax just by looking at her. Hell, he hoped not. The disappointment would kill him.

As his gaze caressed the creamy swells of her bosom, he guessed there were worse ways to go. It was that corset of hers that caused him to go weak in the knees. It made her waist look incredibly small, while accenting the feminine flare of her hips. The shadowed cleft between her thighs proved a subtle magnet to his appreciative gaze. His heart thundered in his chest as he thought about the soft heat waiting for him beyond the downy barrier.

"You're making me very uncomfortable by staring at me," she said in an aggrieved tone. "I thought I was going to be riding Lucky."

*Instead of me?* Sloan cleared his throat. "Honey, there isn't a man alive who wouldn't look his fill at you, given this opportunity."

She crossed her arms across her breasts, which didn't disturb his captivating view one bit. "Have you looked your fill?"

He choked back a strangled laugh. She had to be kidding. "Are you that anxious to learn how to ride?"

"Now that I've gone this far, I might as well go all the way," she answered, approaching his horse.

*Lord, he hoped so.* Her backside swayed provocatively as she crossed the sand and moved closer to Lucky. As far as he could see, there were only two things amiss with her appearance. Her glorious reddish hair was tightly bound instead of falling loose around her shoulders, and she was still wearing her proper, little black boots. He sighed. One thing at a time, he told himself. At least he'd gotten her out of that godawful dress.

"Here, let me give you a leg up."

Prudence felt Sloan move close behind her. One minute she was standing beside Lucky, and the next she was in the saddle. *High* in the saddle. Goodness, Sloan's horse seemed farther away from the ground without him on it with her.

"I'll adjust the stirrups for you."

Prudence tilted her face to the sun and closed her eyes. A salty breeze whispered across her face. Gulls and waves made a semiconstant racket in her ears. Her skin, already warmed by her shameless behavior, was heated even hotter by the afternoon sun. Sloan's hands moved efficiently and methodically across her feet and the stirrups as he adjusted things to suit her.

*What are you doing, Prudence Britannia Abercrombie?* Something reckless and dangerous, she answered herself honestly. Just once, she told herself. *Just once I'm going to do something wild and free.*

Tomorrow she'd go back to being the careful, cautious Prudence that was her real self.

"The important thing to remember is to use your knees to support your weight," Sloan instructed her. "Lucky has a good mouth, so you don't have to pull on the reins to control him. He likes to run, though, so you need to let him know you're in charge."

"How do I do that?" she asked, trepidation growing inside her.

"Just hold the reins firmly. If he starts to turn to the right or the left and you don't want him to, use those knees of yours to tell him what you do want—the reins, too. If he starts to go too fast, don't be afraid to pull back on them. He's a good horse—he'll take your commands."

"All right," she said dubiously. It seemed unlikely that an animal so much bigger than she would obey her. "As soon as I say 'giddyap' he'll go, right? Just like with our team."

At her use of the command word, Lucky took a step forward, then stopped.

"Just like with the team," Sloan concurred. "Remember to say it in a firm voice and lean forward, giving a little shake on the reins."

She closed her eyes and took a deep breath. This was it.

"Open your eyes, Prudence."

Her eyelids jerked up. "They're open!"

"Good, I wouldn't want you to ride into the ocean."

She gave Sloan a brief glare, swallowed and leaned forward. "Giddyap!"

Lucky loped forward. Prudence squeaked and held on to the saddle horn with one hand. Her bottom bounced up and down against the saddle, making thumping sounds that vibrated through her entire body. She didn't recall Sloan thumping when he rode.

Sloan called something from behind her, but the wind and the surf carried what he said out to sea. Lucky continued to lope across the sound, drifting closer to the sea-dampened shoreline. She concentrated on using her knees, putting some of her weight on the stirrups, which spared her bottom further jarring. It was somewhat frightening to feel Lucky's powerful frame moving beneath her, but it was also invigorating. The sense of speed and freedom she experienced sent a wave of euphoria sweeping through her. Why, it was as if she'd saddled the wind!

They sped along at a brisk pace for several hundred yards before Prudence thought about how she was going to stop the spirited beast and turn around. The command word was *whoa,* she knew that, of course, from driving the team. And she knew she needed to pull back on the reins. It was just the idea of being alone with the immense animal that caused her heart to race. At least with the team, she had a whip and a hand brake. With Lucky, all she had was the reins and her knees.

"Whoa!"

It astonished and delighted her when Lucky obediently came to a stop. Using the reins and her knees, she guided him to turn the way they'd come. Like a perfect gentleman, he obeyed her silent commands. Growing more confident by the minute, she leaned forward and issued another giddyap.

Lucky took her at her word and surged forward. They were racing with the wind and the salty sea spray misting over them. It was a completely magical experience. She'd gone past flying—she was soaring.

At first Sloan was a dot on the horizon. But with each galloping lunge across the sand, he loomed larger. When she was just a few feet away from him, she drew in Lucky with what she silently thought was perfect control. Flushed with excitement, she waited for Sloan to congratulate her. She couldn't have been any more thrilled than if she'd won a race with one of Sloan's costly thoroughbreds.

"Well? Aren't you going to say something?" she finally demanded when Sloan remained silent.

"Get down from the horse."

Her spirits sank. Sloan didn't seem at all impressed by her unexpected confidence and skill. Her eyes narrowed. Maybe he needed another demonstration. Or spectacles, if he hadn't noticed what an outstanding job she'd done.

She tossed back her head. "I'm not ready to get down. I want to ride some more. You were right, it feels wonderful not to be encumbered by my dress."

"Prudence—"

She never gave him a chance to say whatever it was he wanted to say. Instead, she dug her heels into Lucky's sides. He responded immediately, and they were off again. This time heading south instead of north.

"Damn you, Prudence—"

Again the rest of his words were swallowed up by the dull roar of the sea. But this time she wasn't able to lose herself in the joy of the ride. It hurt that Sloan didn't share her excitement. She rode south for several minutes before stopping. She really had no choice but to return Sloan's horse to him. It wasn't as if she could go anywhere in her chemise and pantaloons. Dispirited, she turned Lucky around. Why were men such unpredictable creatures? It was a pity that they couldn't be trained like their horses to take simple commands.

When Sloan came into view the second time, he was standing with his hands on his hips. Every lean, angular line of his body radiated anger. She sat up straighter. Well, she was angry, too. His mean attitude had spoiled a most remarkable afternoon.

This time when she drew alongside of him, she said nothing. Instead, she swung herself down from the saddle. Or at any rate, she attempted to. Unfortunately, her lowered foot didn't quite touch the ground. She was stuck midway between the horse and sandy shore when Lucky took a step forward.

"Oh! Hold still, you infernal beast."

Strong hands closed around her waist. "Are you referring to me or my horse?"

She decided to let Sloan assist her from her precarious position before answering. When both of her feet rested upon the sandy terrain, she turned sharply.

"Get out of my way," she ordered through gritted teeth, not in the mood to be polite. Sloan's unpredictable manner had her ready to push him out of her path if he didn't step aside.

"I'm not going anywhere," he growled at her. "Lady, you haven't got the sense the Almighty gave a flea."

His insult was the final straw. She brought both of her hands up to his chest and shoved. He took a surprised step backward. "What in blazes is the matter with you?"

"Not a thing," she informed him. "I just refuse to stand here and let you badger me."

He rubbed his chest, his silver eyes gleaming. "I don't know what's stuck in your craw, but—"

"My *craw* is my own business," she snapped. "Now step aside. I want to go home."

"You're staying put until we get this settled."

"There's nothing to settle."

His lips formed a shockingly savage smile. "That's where you're wrong. I can think of two or three things that need settling."

Her stomach quivered. There was something downright alarming about Sloan when he was this irate. Though for the life of her, she couldn't imagine what she'd done to upset him.

"Say what you have to say, then," she said to him coolly while looking around for her discarded dress. She really couldn't go anywhere until she was again properly covered.

"First off," he began, his voice sharp with obvious irritation, "you had no business riding Lucky hell-bent for leather, not when you were just learning how to ride."

Sloan's complaint caught her off guard. "Isn't it good for him to go fast?"

Sloan's blunt oath made her cheeks burn. "I'm not talking about what's best for him. I'm talking about what's best for you and your fool neck."

She darted a glance to her left. Where was that wretched dress? One would think the black material would contrast starkly against the sun-bleached sand. "Rest assured that my 'fool' neck is just fine."

"Prudence, what are you looking for?"

The exasperation and disgust in his voice scraped her nerves. After all, he had nothing to be exasperated or disgusted about. Whereas she had every reason to be furious. Hadn't he a short while earlier all but proposed to her? And now he was being as uncivil as a man could get. It was fortunate she hadn't taken his talk of marriage seriously. Surreptitiously, she brushed her eyes. The brilliant sunlight was beginning to make them tear.

"I'm looking for my dress," she told him, trying again to move past him.

His hand came out with rapid lightning speed and curled around her arm. "What for?"

"I might have the intelligence of a flea, but I rather like having my clothes on when I'm traipsing about."

"But you're not," he said with maddening composure.

His purposeful expression added to her already overwrought nerves. "Not what?"

"Traipsing about. You're here with me, and I'm just getting started."

*Don't ask,* some self-protective inner mechanism advised. "Doing what?"

He drew her to him. "Taming you, honey."

She'd had to ask.

His words set loose a white-hot ribbon of fury. And excited curiosity. She considered the latter sensation a deplorable lack of character and sought to suppress it.

"You're overlooking one thing," she said, striving to act as if they were having the most ordinary of conversations. She sensed it was crucial to handle Sloan in a civilized manner, even if she wasn't the least bit certain he could be counted upon to act civilized.

"What am I overlooking?" he drawled lazily as his other hand reached out to tamper with her hair.

"I don't need taming." She smiled confidently at him, willing him to bend to her superior reasoning.

"Sure you do. In the worst way. And I've decided I'm the man to do it."

She felt her smile falter around the edges as one hairpin and then another was slowly extracted from her braided twist.

"You have the most beautiful hair," he said. "It reminds me of a Texas sunset. All red and fiery. Like the sky's going to go up in flames."

Her scalp tingled beneath his ministrations. She tried to collect her thoughts, but they hovered elusively beyond her grasp. "Sloan . . ."

"Hmm?"

He had her hair in his hands and was spreading it across her shoulders. She couldn't remember what she'd been about to say.

The background din of the sea and the squawking gulls faded. Sloan stood with the sun to his back, and she became lost in the shadow of his lowering head.

His kiss was bold.

His hands possessive.

His body . . . everywhere.

Something inside her, a barrier that had been erected to withstand the trespass of all men, dissolved under *this* man's ardor. Dimly she realized he had lowered her to the dampened shoreline. Then his dark murmurings, his thickened words, wove a spell so complete that her surroundings disappeared from consciousness.

"You're so soft, so beautiful. Kiss me back. Yes, that's it. Harder, honey."

Soon her skin, all of it, was exposed to the sun and to Sloan. Magically his clothes, too, ceased to be a constraint between them. Her world shrank to that of texture and sensation. His chest—hair-roughed, firmly muscled, rubbing against her bared breasts. His scent—rawly masculine, teasing her to new heights. His hands—clever, persuasive, exploring her quivering flesh. His mouth—burning, relentless, setting her skin ablaze. His legs—powerful, shifting, parting her legs for his ultimate possession. His manhood, more than she had imagined it would be, seeking her most private place, awakening and stirring wanton sensations that tugged and pulled at her feminine core.

"Tell me you want this," he groaned hoarsely as he rose above her, poised to enter.

Her palms caressed his straining arms. His face looked as if it was etched in pain, not pleasure. But even as the inner voices that she'd repressed began to call her back from this dangerous precipice, Prudence knew there was no turning back. She might regret this act later, but nowhere within her was the will to resist giving herself to Sloan.

"I want this," she whispered brokenly. "I want you."

With a victorious groan he eased himself inside her, slowly filling her until he was stopped by her virgin's barrier.

"I know it's going to hurt," he told her, "but there's no other way."

She braced herself for the pain she'd overheard other women refer to in hushed tones. But as Sloan increased his pressure against her, he used his fingers to massage and stroke her. In the final seconds, there was pain, but it was a fleeting memory in the face of his intimate caress.

"Are you okay?"

The concern reflected in his eyes made her melt. She touched his perspiring brow. "I'm fine."

He frowned. "I want you better than fine. I want you out of your mind with pleasure."

Slowly he withdrew from her, then reentered. He left a trail of falling stars and exploding comets.

"Oh!"

"It feels good, doesn't it?" he asked, closing his eyes to savor the sensation.

She couldn't resist.

"Open your eyes, Sloan."

He did so immediately, and she was pinned by twin silver suns. "Thanks for reminding me, darling. I don't want to miss a minute of this or you."

She smiled uncertainly. "I don't feel as if I'm helping very much. It's like when I was riding Lucky and he was doing all the work."

Sloan made a peculiar sound deep in his throat. Not a growl, exactly, but similar. "Honey, I want to make this last. Any more help from you and I'll most likely embarrass myself."

"Embarrass yourself, how?"

He made another strangled sound. "Believe me, you don't want to know."

He bent down and kissed her deeply. Her senses swam, then floundered. She was in water every bit as wild and dangerous as the swollen river they'd stood beside earlier.

His fingers still moved with tender purpose at the juncture of her thighs. There was a strange tingling, a dull pulsing that made her shift restlessly beneath him.

"That's it, sweetheart. Let me make it happen for you."

"M-make what happen?"

He laughed softly. The sound seemed to trigger an alien inner convulsion within her.

*"This."*

His deep, husky voice sent her over the edge. And the edge was higher and sharper than anything she had ever imagined. It was as if the cells in her body united for one dazzling explosion. She shuddered. She cried out.

She closed her eyes.

Sloan's shout was brief and triumphant.

He was holding her tightly to him, as if he never intended to let her go. But she knew that was a mistaken notion on her part. Even as her body experienced the greatest pleasure she'd ever known, Prudence prepared herself for what was going to happen next.

Sloan was going to return to his racetrack and forget about her and this remarkable interlude, despite his words of marriage. For she knew he'd only spoken them to bring about her surrender. Sloan was no more interested in marrying than he was in giving up racing and adopting five orphans.

Even as she reeled from the pain that was beginning to spiral through her, she had to accept the cold, hard fact that she was probably the last woman on earth Sloan Coltrane would want to marry. She was, after all, the spinster he'd called her on the first day they'd met. She allowed her fingertips to blaze a trail through his thick, sweat-dampened hair. She'd given herself to him, knowing this, knowing they had no future together.

She'd decided it would be her one reckless act. And the memory of it would have to last her a lifetime, because she would not allow herself to become a casual plaything for any man. Not even the one she feared she'd lost her heart to.

# Chapter Fifteen

"I suppose we should be getting back," she said, resigned to their inevitable parting.

"Not yet."

There was a smoky intensity to his gaze that had her heart racing again. "It's getting late. The children will—"

"It would take a keg of blasting powder to get those kids to voluntarily leave the track." He placed a proprietary kiss on her shoulder. "Besides, before I left, I heard Junella invite everyone to stay for supper."

Prudence tried to steel herself against the skittering dance of tingles his kiss sent rippling across her flesh. She wasn't wholly successful. Sloan had withdrawn from inside her and rested upon one elbow, staring down at her with leisurely interest. All at once she felt terribly vulnerable. Good grief, she was outside in broad daylight without a stitch of clothing!

She dug her toes into the sand. It came as a total shock when she realized that, in the throes of his passionate assault, Sloan had managed to divest her of her shoes. Never would she have imagined she could have become so lost in a man's embrace.

"I would like to get dressed now." She attempted to make the request a lightly voiced one, though the sight of

Sloan's softly furred chest in all its male splendor stretched out so invitingly near made her tongue grow clumsy.

Concern filled his eyes. "Are you hurting, honey?"

She averted her gaze. "Not really."

"I tried to be careful."

"You—you were fine."

"But you're probably sore." He rose to a sitting position and frowned. "I guess I should apologize for not picking a better place for your first time."

"Uh, I'm as much at fault as you are."

Prudence knew her cheeks were flaming. Nothing in her life had prepared her for casual conversation with a man she'd just made love to. Nor did it help matters that the man was savagely naked.

His features clouding, Sloan uncurled to his feet. "'Fault'? What happened between us wasn't anyone's fault. It was something we chose to do." He extended his hand. "Come on, we'll rinse off this sand."

Reluctantly she accepted his hand and rose, wishing there was a convenient fig leaf with which to cover herself. It astonished her that Sloan didn't seem the least bit self-conscious about his nudity. Clearly, the man had the sensibility of a range steer. Well, perhaps *steer* was the wrong analogy.

"The sand doesn't bother me. I just want to get dressed."

"Not yet."

If he said that one more time, she was going to scream.

He tugged her hand and drew her to where the surf's foaming bubbles skipped across the sand. He didn't stop at the water's edge, but drew her beyond the first shallow line of breaking waves. Soon the shifting sea reached their waists. Partially covered by the buoyant water, Prudence felt herself begin to relax.

When Sloan pulled her yet farther into the sea, she appreciated the fact that her breasts were no longer exposed to his view. Considering that she possessed only the most rudimentary knowledge of swimming, she supposed her lack of fear could, in some part, be attributed to her confidence in her partner, and to her natural affinity to the gentle tide.

A satisfied grin slashed his features. "It's great, isn't it."

She wasn't prepared to go that far, but it did feel strangely invigorating to have the sea swirling across her bare skin.

Still holding on to her hand, he ducked his head beneath the water's restless surface and came up laughing. Prudence couldn't look away. His black hair was slicked to his scalp, casting his strongly sculpted features into bold prominence. His eyelashes were wet spikes. A primitive fire radiated from his eyes. Her stomach quivered. He reminded her of a fierce warrior from ancient times of old, the kind who strode through history conquering whole kingdoms. She knew that as long as she lived, she would remember this moment always. Remember this man always.

"You're too far away."

His observation ignited a dull throbbing within her. "I'm not—" she licked her salty lips "—that far away."

He exerted the necessary force to draw her through the water and bring her flush against him. The sudden impact of her breasts against his wet, hairy chest made her gasp. He moved farther from shore. The sea's restless jostling diminished.

"This is better, isn't it?"

She was grappling with the discovery that her feet no longer touched the sandy bottom. With Sloan's hand supporting her, however, it was surprisingly easy to stay afloat. Because of his height, she realized his feet were still firmly planted upon the ocean floor. She was just accustoming herself to her watery environment when he reached out with his other hand and cupped her bottom, drawing her even closer to him. Of their own accord, her legs encircled his waist.

"Ah, Sloan. If you're planning to... I mean, if you think it's possible to..."

She cursed her inability to speak a coherent sentence.

"Rise up a little and give me your mouth, honey."

Ultimately, she gave him much more than her mouth.

This time when her senses calmed and she sought to return to earth, there was no solid ground to cling to. Just Sloan and the sea, a tempestuous combination of fire and water, of hot licking flames that set her insides ablaze while cocooning her in a cool, turbulent world of blue.

She clung to him.

She wept.

She died a little.

And she soared far and high, to a place that flooded her with exquisite, unspeakable shards of exploding pleasure.

"Hold on." The groaned command came from Sloan as they were caught in the surf and thoroughly tumbled for the brief but bumpy journey to shore.

They were both gasping for air when the tide deposited them onto the damp shoreline. Sloan lay on his back with her sprawled upon his chest. It was a most unseemly position. She looked into his relaxed features and tried to memorize every line and angle of his strong-boned face. She wanted to lean forward and kiss him. But if she did that, if she surrendered to the deep yearning within her, she was afraid she wouldn't be able to survive his abandonment. It was better to hold at least a portion of herself separate.

"What are you thinking?"

His question jarred her. The last thing she wanted was to reveal how much he had come to mean to her. He might think she was asking for more than he was willing to give. He might think she was going to hold him to his impulsive offer of marriage. He might think... she loved him.

"It's getting late."

The familiar refrain came easily to her lips.

"You're not going to be happy until you get your clothes back on, are you?"

There was no condemnation in his statement, just a rueful acceptance of her feelings.

"I will be the first to admit that I'm not comfortable with public nudity."

"How about private nudity?"

She slipped from his embrace and sat as primly as she could upon the damp sand. "You really are incorrigible."

"With your accent, you make me sound like something that needs to be dragged outside and buried."

She drew her knees to her chest. "That's what incorrigible is supposed to mean."

"I like the Texas version better."

He'd pricked her curiosity. "And what is that?"

He rose and stretched. "Inventive, honey. We like to think of ourselves as inventive and resourceful."

He certainly was that! And immodest and blunt and bold and... alarmingly irresistible.

She watched him walk around the cove, retrieving pieces of clothing and shaking out the sand. She was vastly relieved when she saw him locate her black dress. She'd been afraid she would have to return to the farmhouse without it.

In a surprisingly short time, she and Sloan were dressed, though their clothes were suspiciously rumpled. And, despite Sloan's thorough shaking, particles of sand chafed her skin.

He mounted Lucky and pulled her in front of him. His arms encircled her with devastating familiarity. She bit her lip against voicing her disapproval of his presumption. Instinct warned that she would be better off to avoid any confrontation with this man until she was back again on her own property.

A light breeze blew her unrestrained hair across her face. She supposed it was foolish to regret the loss of her hairpins when she'd lost something far more precious. Her virginity. She wondered when the shame would settle in. Right now her emotions ran a wild gambit between bemusement, fatigue and . . . awe.

"How are you feeling?"

It took a moment for her to realize the question was his and not a product of her overwrought mental processes.

"I'm a little tired." That much was true.

He squeezed her. "Was the second time too much for you?"

"Must we rehash this?" She winced at the sharpness of her tone. "I'm sorry, I didn't mean to snap at you. It's just that I'm not used to discussing such personal things."

"You'll get used to it," he assured her with infuriating male confidence.

She pressed her lips together to forestall correcting him. No matter what he did or said, she refused to get into a disagreement with him. Her feelings were too close to the surface. She knew she would embarrass herself by doing something utterly mortifying. Like bursting into tears.

"A hot bath will take away any aches and pains you might be feeling," he advised, clearly oblivious to her deepening melancholy state.

"I'll keep that in mind."

"I'd like to be the one to take care of you."

"I'm an adult," she reminded him. "I hardly need someone to help me bathe."

"Your being an adult would be what made bathing you so...interesting."

The man was insatiable.

A mental image of herself immersed in a tub filled with hot, steamy water with Sloan looking on invaded her thoughts. She felt herself become warm and mushy inside and scowled. Surely her head was composed entirely of mush for allowing Sloan to seduce her with words.

"You're awfully quiet."

He didn't know how fortunate he was that she was keeping her thoughts to herself.

"I just don't feel like talking."

He drew Lucky to a stop. "You're not regretting what happened, are you?"

At this rate, she was never going to get home! Impatiently she surveyed their surroundings to determine how much farther it was to the farmhouse. With a start, she discovered they were headed in the wrong direction.

"Where are you taking me?"

"To supper," he answered with infuriating matter-of-factness.

"But I want to go *home*."

She cringed at the definite whine she detected in the request. She was a grown woman. She did not whine.

"I thought you'd like to eat supper with the children," he said. "Though on second thought the idea of being alone with you at Amos's farm is damned enticing. I could give you that bath and we could—"

"You're right," she interrupted hastily. "I would like to eat with the children. I'm starving."

"Prudence, there's something you should know."

"What's that?"

She braced herself for anything. With a man as unpredictable as Sloan Coltrane, she had no idea what he might say or do. She hated admitting it, but that was part of his appeal. He did have a way of keeping her on her toes. She could visualize no other man on this planet who could have lured her into making love outside. In broad daylight. That, however, was what also made him so dangerous. He brought out the very weakest element of her character, fanning her heretofore undiscovered propensity for wanton abandonment.

"I've only got so much patience."

*That* was what he wanted to tell her?

"Patience is a virtue that lifts the spirit and refines the soul," she recited.

She'd once embroidered the simple platitude upon a throw pillow and felt it fitting for Sloan's edification. By working very hard, he could probably overcome a majority of his vices. If he lived to be a hundred.

He whistled. "That's amazing."

"What is?"

"You used patience, virtue, spirit and soul in one sentence. I bet even Reverend Brown doesn't do that on a regular basis."

It required no effort on her part to detect the amused derision that laced his husky observation. They rode in silence for several minutes. Lucky's plodding hooves and the creak of saddle leather were the only sounds to accompany her tortured thoughts. No matter how hard she tried not to, she kept seeing herself and Sloan together on the sand. She had given herself to a man without any thought to her future.

Why, she was a fallen woman.

That sobering realization struck Prudence as Sloan's horse crested the hill overlooking his property. The large racing track, the horse barn and several other buildings came into view. A tangible display of Sloan's moral decadence.

As they descended the gravelly slope, she noticed Reverend Brown's buggy was present. Oh dear, the last thing she needed was to come face-to-face with a servant of the ministry. Would he be able to tell by looking at her what she'd done? Her hands went to her hair, and she tried to organize it into something resembling an acceptable style. What had she been thinking to allow Sloan to bring her directly here without taking the opportunity to freshen up?

Abruptly, she remembered what she'd been thinking. That under no circumstances did she wish to be alone with Sloan at the house. She didn't trust him, and she didn't trust herself not to…not to be caught up in another round of reckless lovemaking. Good grief, with his sensual appetites and her woeful lack of resistance they might end up coupling on the kitchen floor!

"Looks like we've got some extra company," Sloan observed. He felt Prudence stiffen in his arms and realized she was trying to do something with her hair. Subdue it into a prissy little bun, most likely. "I'll take you to the shack so you can set yourself to rights."

Her fingers stilled their frantic combing efforts. "Uh, I'd appreciate that."

"It's the least I can do," he said softly.

He waited for her to acknowledge his remark, but she remained silent. Something was bothering her; he'd sensed her withdrawal the moment they'd finishing making love. It was to be expected, he thought. She was a lady. It was going to take some getting used to on her part to accept what had happened between them. He'd neglected the courtship phase of their relationship and had rushed the honeymoon a bit. The thing was, he hadn't been able to tamp down his hot-blooded eagerness to possess her.

He'd wanted her in the worst way. And he'd taken her in the worst way. He probably deserved to be shot, but the truth was he was feeling pretty good. Which said little for his character. He rubbed his jaw against Prudence's silky hair and decided that having a sterling character was all right, so long as it didn't interfere with a man's fundamental need to claim the woman he'd decided to make his wife.

When they reached the shack, he helped her down from his horse, making a point of being gentle with her. She had a fragile air about her that prompted such consideration. He shook his head in bemusement. Until this very moment, he hadn't even realized he possessed a streak of tenderness. Maybe it and the softer feelings squeezing his chest came from the petite woman at his side and the knowledge that, for the rest of his life, he would always put her safety ahead of his own.

He shoved open the rough wood door. "There's water in the pitcher over there on the stand. There's a comb and a washcloth, too. I'll leave you to your privacy."

He tacked on the last statement to earn a smile. He settled for the flash of appreciation that briefly lit her green eyes.

"I won't be long," she said quietly, closing the door in his face.

Sloan's gaze narrowed. He found he didn't like the idea of a door between them. He hoped Prudence realized that theirs was to be a short engagement.

He turned from the shack and led Lucky to his stall. As far as he was concerned, the Reverend could marry them here and now.

Sloan remembered his sisters' and Jeremy's weddings. All of them had been fancy affairs, involving area residents for miles around. Even though Kate's marriage to Dan had been on a more modest scale, it had taken weeks to plan. Did Prudence expect some kind of fancy doings for her wedding?

When he returned sometime later to the shack, his mood had darkened. She was probably like any other woman and considered a wedding a major social event. He took some consolation from the fact that she would be wearing a pretty new dress for the occasion. White satin, he figured. After the wedding, he'd make certain he burned every black dress she owned.

He knocked on the door, wondering if she appreciated how considerate he was being by not simply barging in. It was his place, after all.

Instead of inviting him inside, Prudence met him on the threshold. Her face was washed, her hair tamed into a braid that hung down the middle of her back. Her dress had been brushed free of sand, and she looked entirely presentable. Except maybe for her kiss-swollen lips and sunburned cheeks. And eyes that still had a dazed look that caused his chest to tighten. She looked so sweetly vulnerable. He found himself anticipating the adventure of caring for her.

For a lifetime.

And sleeping with her small body curved next to his—after hours of slow, sensuous lovemaking. For a lifetime.

"Your time is up."

She cocked her head. "You make it sound as if I've been primping for hours. It's only been a few minutes."

He'd meant her days of being single were at an end, but felt no need to clarify the point. "I've got something I want to show you."

Her sun-kissed cheeks blossomed with additional color. "I've already seen it."

A full second passed while Sloan let Prudence's risqué remark sink in. She never ceased to surprise him. And every surprise made him want her more.

"I wasn't referring to my..." He searched his mind for a term that wouldn't offend her. She was, after all, a lady. His task wasn't made easier by the fact that he was a bluntly spoken man. "My male member."

He felt utterly ridiculous babbling such a foolish term, but thought if he said "pecker," Prudence would promptly faint dead away. And when she revived, she probably wouldn't be inclined to follow through on marrying him. He figured that, for the next few weeks at least, he was going to have to be on his best behavior. Until he got her safely hitched to him. Then he'd slowly ease her into accepting what a real man was like.

"I'm glad you understand," she said stiffly. "I didn't agree to come with you so that we could...could..."

His lips twitched. "Could what, honey?"

He could tell he was making her nervous. For some obscure reason that knowledge was immensely satisfying. And she *was* nervous. He'd noticed her habit of reverting to more formal speech when she was caught off balance. And her English accent was stronger than ever. A dead giveaway that her nerves were getting the best of her.

Her green eyes shimmered angrily. "Could continue doing what it was we were doing at the beach."

"You mean me teaching you how to ride?" he asked with feigned innocence.

"You know what I mean!"

He had to fight the impulse to draw her into his arms. "I'm not an animal, Prudence. I know you're going to need a day or two before you're ready for me to be inside you again." He stepped forward and ran a fingertip across her flushed cheek. "But there's some other things we could do together, things we could do to each other, that would make us both very happy."

"I'm not one of your easy women," she said quietly.

"You're right about that, honey. There's nothing easy about you."

"Sloan..." she began haltingly. "What happened between us..." Her gaze slid from his. She cleared her throat. "Well, you must realize that it was a one-time occurrence."

She couldn't be serious. "You're wrong."

"Uh, I was hoping to have this discussion later, but I suppose there's no point in delaying it."

He quashed the initial flash of dread her words sparked, assuring himself there was no way he was going to let Prudence slip through his fingers. He'd had her once. Hell, he'd had her twice, and he intended to keep on having her.

Today had been the beginning, not the end of their time together. Now all he had to do was convince her of that. He strove for patience. Surely, he could be sympathetic and understanding of her misgivings. She'd only lost her virginity a short time ago. She was probably scared and ashamed and . . . He scowled, realizing there was no way he would know what was bothering his skittish bride-to-be unless she told him.

"You're right, Prudence. There's no point in putting off this discussion." He took her arm. "Let's go inside and settle this."

"No!"

Her high-pitched protest pushed him over an invisible edge.

"You wanted to talk," he reminded her curtly. "We have to do it somewhere."

"Uh, why don't we go for a walk?" She looked at him entreatingly. "We can converse as we stroll around the grounds."

"We'll probably be interrupted before we go ten feet," he felt obliged to point out. "The kids are around here somewhere."

"It won't take me long to say what I have to say."

"Fine. We'll walk." He'd wanted to show off the thoroughbreds George had brought with him by train. This would give him the chance to do so. As well as letting her know in no uncertain terms that she now belonged to him. Her days of spinsterhood were finished. He ground his teeth. Any other woman of her years would be thanking him for his offer of marriage.

"I suppose the first thing I should tell you," she said, breaking the tense silence that had sprung up between them, "is that I don't hold you responsible for what happened."

"So you've said."

"I realize that had I asked you to stop, you would have honored my request."

He tossed her a look of stupefied amazement. If she thought that, the woman had no sense at all. If someone had pointed a cocked gun to his head and demanded he release her, he wouldn't have been able to stop himself from sheathing himself inside her wet, trembling channel.

"I think you have a high opinion of my willpower," he confined himself to saying.

"You were very careful with me," she went on softly. "I may not have much experience in such things, but I was keenly aware of your strength and, had you been heedless of my welfare, you could have hurt me."

Her words proved strangely humbling. "I will never hurt you, Prudence."

She brushed at her eyes with her free hand. The gesture tugged at Sloan's heartstrings. He hated the thought that she was near tears. But until she told him what was troubling her, there was nothing he could do to comfort her. He stopped walking and studied her bent head. Indisputably, life had been less complicated when he'd bought and paid for his female companionship.

"I want you to know that I don't expect you to marry me."

"*What?*"

"I understand that you only asked me because... Well, because you wanted to... to lie with me."

For the first time during their incredible conversation, Sloan felt his temper begin to simmer. "You think I lied to you about wanting to marry you?"

She raised her red-rimmed eyes. "I'm not upset with you. I was quite carried away myself by... by the feelings of ardor you stirred within me. Because of your many past experiences, you knew how wonderful everything was going to be. It's understandable that you would say or do what was necessary to... to enjoy another carnal interlude."

Sloan didn't know which of what she said enraged him the most. He decided to dive in at the beginning. "I haven't had that many experiences. You make it sound like I've been with a hundred women."

"The exact number isn't important."

"The hell it isn't!" Frustration gnawed at his gut. "I'm not some potentate with a harem of women at my beck and call."

"I didn't mean to imply—"

"And another thing, where do you get off saying that I'd lie to you in order to get you on your back beneath me?"

"There's no need to be crude."

He jabbed a forefinger beneath her startled gaze to punctuate his remarks. "I don't have to lie to get a woman to make love to me."

"But—"

"I asked you to marry me because I want you to become my wife."

"Surely you can see that's quite impossible."

A red haze filmed his vision. "Lady, we just proved it was possible. And highly enjoyable!"

"But that was lust. It had nothing to do with..."

"With what?"

"With love," she whispered brokenly.

Sloan felt as if he'd been struck. Prudence didn't love him. She'd surrendered her virginity but not her heart. He took the blow in silence. It didn't matter if she loved him. He'd take her any way he could get her.

"Nevertheless," he said harshly, "I asked you and you accepted. We will be married."

"I did not accept!"

"The hell you didn't," he grated out. "You accepted when you parted your soft thighs to let me inside. You accepted with every little sigh and moan you breathed into my ear. You accepted with the scratches you put on my back."

"You can't make me marry you."

"I don't see where you have any choice," he returned levelly, ignoring the childish rebuke. "Not as long as you want to keep those children you've taken in."

Her face paled. "What are you saying?"

The shocked horror in her voice made him ashamed, but he'd gone too far to back down. "Do you think the good townspeople of Port Dodd are going to want a woman of questionable morals looking after that innocent flock of lost sheep?"

She stared deeply into his eyes, and Sloan felt lower than the mangiest polecat.

"I'm not afraid of you, Sloan Coltrane." She stunned him by reaching up and touching his cheek. "You're too honorable to do something so evil."

"An honorable man wouldn't lie to a woman to get her to sleep with him," he pointed out roughly.

"I can see that now," she said, her eyes dewing with moistness. "I was wrong to doubt your sincerity."

"I accept your apology. We'll be married as soon as—"

She shook her head.

Sloan was ready to throttle her.

"I won't become your wife."

"If you say that one more time, I swear I'm not going to be responsible for my actions."

He glared at her with what he hoped was sufficient menace to cow her into accepting the inevitable—his word as law.

"It must be obvious to you that we don't suit each other."

"I've never been with a woman who suited me more," he countered grimly. "In fact, if we suited each other any better, we would have drowned out there today."

"I keep telling you that was lust, not love. Perhaps it's because you're a man that you cannot distinguish the difference between the two."

He marveled at the variety of ways she chose to insult him. He might not have come right out and said it, but... Well, what he felt toward her seemed as if it could be love. He just didn't feel comfortable saying the words out loud, especially when she kept saying she didn't want to marry him.

"There's a lot to be said for lust," he suggested, trying to find his way out of the box canyon she'd backed him into. "It can make the nights less lonely and the days more interesting."

"I've heard it doesn't last," she observed with maddening calm. "It's like that twister that came charging through the area last month. Ferocious and overwhelming, but soon gone."

How was he supposed to answer that? He wasn't ready to put his raw feelings about her into words, not before she admitted that she cared for him. He squared his shoulders. If lust was all he had going for him, he'd damned well make the most of it.

"What's between us won't be shortly gone, Prudence."

"How can you be sure? It would be dreadful for you to be saddled with a wife you didn't love *and* a houseful of growing children, when all you really wanted is to race your purebred horses."

He pulled her hand, the one with which she'd caressed his cheek, to his lips and kissed her fingers one by one. "I still intend to race my horses," he explained quietly. Anger and threats hadn't moved her. Perhaps a little calculated tenderness might do the trick. "Horse racing has nothing do with what happens between us."

"I don't feel it's a suitable..." She broke off and swallowed.

Sloan gathered her closer. "A suitable what?"

"Environment for the children. All that gambling."

He lowered his head and brushed his lips against hers. "We'll work that out."

She sighed and opened her mouth more fully to his deliberate invasion. Moments passed as he tasted and played with the sweetness that was Prudence Abercrombie.

"The thing you've been overlooking," he breathed against her throat, "is that we're going to keep wanting each other. When you lie in bed at night, you're going to remember what it was like between us today, and you're going to be wanting me there beside you. Your hunger is going to keep growing and growing. Your skin is going to burn for my touch." He rubbed his palm against her breasts, then let his hand drift lower. "And here, you're going to be aching to feel me inside you. You can't go back to what you were, honey."

"But I—I must."

He contracted his fingers against her mound, and she shuddered against him. "And every night, when I'm in my bed, I'm going to be remembering and wanting you. There's no way we're going to be able to stay away from each other. The hunger and desire is going to keep building and building until we won't be able to stand it."

Sloan looked over his shoulder to make sure they were alone. Damn, he wished they were inside the shack instead of standing on the south side of the barn. The hunger he'd tried to arouse in Prudence was all but eating him alive. He sucked in a ragged breath. His hand stilled its movement against her skirts.

But when he tried to pull away, her palm closed over his fingers.

"Please," she whispered. "Don't...stop."

He smothered a groan and looked over his shoulder again. There was no sign of another soul. Everyone was probably at the supper table.

With a silent oath at his own stupidity, Sloan swept Prudence into his arms and carried her into the barn. There was no way he was going to leave her hurting for release, even if it meant he suffered the pains of the damned. He lowered her to an empty stall filled with fresh straw and came down beside her, easing his hand beneath her skirts.

"I'm with you, honey. I won't stop."

For the next few minutes, he kissed and petted her. She squirmed and moaned beneath his ministrations. Then a broken cry escaped her lips. He could feel her wet, trembling climax against his fingertips and bent his head against her throat to keep from tearing off his clothes and finding his own release inside her. Maybe he didn't have the words to tell her how much she meant to him, but he could show her by controlling the desire pounding through him.

After a few shuddering seconds, she went completely still. Reluctantly, he withdrew his fingers from beneath her skirts. She remained with her face buried against his shoulder. More time passed. She didn't move. She didn't speak. She didn't even seem to be breathing.

"Prudence?"

"Don't," she said dully.

"Don't what?"

"Don't talk to me."

"For how long?"

"Forever."

He stroked the lush hair that had escaped her make-shift braid. "Honey, that's a little longer than I could stand."

She pulled away from him and sat up. Her gaze seemed to be lodged somewhere above his right shoulder. "I'm so ashamed."

"There's no reason to be."

"Actually, I'm ashamed, embarrassed, mortified, humiliated and—"

"I get the idea," he cut in, before she could add to the seemingly endless list. "And I'm telling you that whatever happens between us is all right."

"*All right!* How can you say that?"

He'd reached the outer limits of his patience, he realized abruptly. There was simply no reasonable course to take with a woman who was emotionally overwrought.

"It's a waste of energy for you to try to fight what's between us, Prudence." He paused to collect his thoughts, but the sight of her with straw stuck to her hair and her eyes dominating her sunburned face made logical thinking an impossible goal. "It's a waste of energy for you to feel guilty, especially when it feels so damned good and it's going to keep happening between us. Again and again."

"But—"

"And as long as we keep doing it, we run the risk of people finding out about us. When they do, all hell's going to break loose. Marry me and all your problems will be solved."

Even to his own ears, his words sounded less than romantic. It struck him that was probably why Prudence was balking at the inevitable. He hadn't used any flowery or pretty words. Stunned by the simplicity of what he had to do to persuade Prudence to marry him, Sloan immediately set about to woo the reluctant maiden.

"What I meant to say—"

The sound of approaching voices stopped Sloan from proceeding. Damned, it sounded as if all of Port Dodd were about to enter the barn.

Sloan jumped to his feet and pulled Prudence to hers. Frantically, he brushed at the straw that was decorating them both in great profusion.

"What are we going to do?" Prudence demanded as she went about trying to straighten her state of dishabille.

"Brazen it out," he informed her, hating the thought of her being publicly branded a loose woman. It didn't matter to him. But he knew it mattered to her. "I've been wanting to show you my thoroughbreds, and that's exactly what we've been doing."

The doors opened. Shafts of afternoon sunlight invaded the barn. Sloan made sure that he was standing several feet from Prudence when they were converged upon by the horde of voices.

"You've got to see Warlord" came Charlie's excited cry. "He's got to be the fastest horse in the whole world."

"How do you know? You've never seen him run," Davy protested.

"You can tell by looking at his legs, right Mr. Curtis?"

"You can tell a lot by a horse's legs," George said agreeably.

"I like Lord Triumph the best," Janey confided. "The white star on his forehead is pretty."

"Horses aren't pretty," Charlie scoffed.

"Lord Triumph is," Janey maintained stubbornly. "Isn't he, Miss Marabelle?"

Reverend Brown stepped forward and, smiling widely, scooped the little girl into his arms. "I agree with Charlie. Horses aren't pretty, but little girls like you and Charlotte sure are."

Janey squealed with delight while Marabelle Brubaker looked on with radiant satisfaction.

Those entering the barn, coming as they were from bright sunlight to the shadowed interior, hadn't yet noticed Sloan or Prudence. In a timeless moment that sometimes happens in a person's life, Sloan was able to see in perfect clarity what the future held for Prudence's charges.

Reverend Brown and Marabelle Brubaker were clearly in love with each other. Just as clear was the fact that both of them loved and wanted little Janey. George was holding Charlie's hand, while Junella was grasping Charlotte's pudgy palm. The foursome already looked as if they were a family. Davy stood close to the young man who was his older brother. And next to them, Sarah's blue eyes were filled with innocent adoration as she stared at Davy's brother. Then there was Richard, the last to enter the barn. He cast several suspicious glances as he surveyed his unfamiliar surroundings. Always the loner, the outsider, Sloan wondered how long he would remain with Prudence before he disappeared into the night.

And then she would be alone.

Without the children who meant everything to her.

And just as Sloan knew what was coming, he was convinced Prudence must sense the same future for herself. Unless she refused to surrender the children to the people who wanted to adopt them. And she'd already proved with Davy that it was impossible for her to put her wishes ahead of those of her charges.

His gaze went to her. She stood with her arms wrapped around herself, a haunted look of anguish gripping her delicate features.

She knew.

# Chapter Sixteen

"Miss Prudence! Mr. Coltrane! We didn't know you were here," Charlie said excitedly after practically running into them.

"We've been waiting for you to join us so we could all see the horses together," Sloan said with a naturalness that could have convinced even Prudence that there was nothing amiss with them being found together in the barn.

She put a hand to her throbbing temple, steeling herself against the desperate longing with which Junella gazed upon Charlie and Charlotte. Just as she tried to ignore the spontaneous warmth lighting both Marabelle's and the Reverend's faces as they fussed over Janey.

Nor did she want to acknowledge that Davy and his brother had already become an inseparable twosome, and that Sarah had surrendered her young heart to Micah. Prudence's gaze went to Richard. He was haunted by demons from his secret past; she had no idea how long he would remain under her care.

She reeled at the realization that in scant seconds her entire world could be shattered, her entire purpose for living could be taken from her. As if reading her tortured thoughts, Sloan's arm came around her shoulders, and he anchored her to his side.

"Prudence," Marabelle said cheerfully, stepping forward. "I'm so glad you changed your mind about seeing Sloan's thoroughbreds. I think Janey's right. They are beautiful. Come and see if you don't agree."

Prudence summoned every ounce of composure she possessed.

"I've heard a lot about them." Did the words sound as stilted to the others as they did to herself?

"They're right this way, ladies," George announced. "Two of the grandest three-year-olds you've ever set eyes upon. They're going to win a passel of races for us. And other horse owners for miles around are going to bring their thoroughbreds to try to beat them. Warlord and Lord Triumph are going to make Sloan's racetrack a success, just you wait and see."

As Prudence stared at the magnificent beasts their owner had imported to Port Dodd, she finally realized what all the fuss was about. The purebreds were astonishingly formed, or "configured," as George kept saying in a barrage of admiration that flowed through the dimly lit barn like a gusting Texas wind.

The children, too, were taken with the horses. Eager voices rose and fell with equal fervor as they praised the animals' merits. The Reverend, Marabelle and Junella contributed their glowing comments about the regal beasts. Even Gladys, the last to join the group, added her favorable impressions about Warlord and Lord Triumph.

Only she and Sloan remained silent. Briefly she wondered what he was thinking behind his enigmatically composed features. Then her thoughts turned to the children, and what her life would be like if she lost them. She didn't know how she could stand to live in Amos's farmhouse alone.

The throbbing in her head built to an unbearable crescendo. She tried to ease away from the throng of talking people. Sloan's grip tightened around her shoulders.

"I need some air," she said, feeling as if she was going to faint.

"I'll carry you."

"No!"

Naturally her protest fell upon deaf ears.

Sloan had her in his arms and was striding toward the barn's entrance before she could say another word to stop him.

"What's wrong with Miss Prudence?" Davy asked.

"She just needs some air," Sloan answered with habitual matter-of-factness.

"How come?" Janey inquired, her young voice clearly worried. "Isn't barn air okay?"

"The horses seem to like it," Charlie pointed out.

"Miss Prudence isn't a horse," Charlotte evidently felt compelled to remind everyone. "Maybe horse air and people air are different."

"I like horse air," Charlie said defensively. "It smells good."

And so it was that even though she was on the verge of tears, Prudence found herself smiling. There was nothing in the world like listening to the children as they sorted through their creative perceptions about life.

"Bring her to the house," Junella instructed in a nononsense tone that sounded similar to Gladys's when the housekeeper was dispensing orders. "Good grief, Sloan, what have you done to the woman? Her skin is as cooked as a cherry pie."

"I was teaching her to ride," Sloan answered. His voice seemed surprisingly far away. "We must have been in the sun too long."

"Well, I should say so," Gladys said, getting her two cents in. "What she needs is a vinegar sponge bath. That will cool her off."

"Isn't vinegar what we dip our cucumbers in?" Charlie asked, his tone speculative.

"And beets," Davy added. "That's what makes them pickled."

"Does that mean they're going to pickle Miss Prudence?"

"I want to watch," Janey said. "I've never seen a pickled person before."

Hers was the last comment Prudence heard as Sloan carried her through Junella's front door.

"I'm fine now, really. I was just feeling a little lightheaded."

"Gladys is right." Sloan's silvery eyes regarded her with deep intensity. "I kept you in the sun too long. I should have known better—I've seen what happens to a man on the range when he gets heatstroke."

"I'm not going to die," Prudence felt obliged to reassure him.

"You've got that right," he muttered, following the black woman into a bedroom. After laying Prudence on the patchwork quilt, his fingers went to work on her buttons. "Bring some wet cloths so we can cool her skin," he ordered over his shoulder to the room at large. "Bring a glass of water, too. We need to get some liquids in her."

Alarmed by Sloan's take-charge manner, Prudence slapped ineffectually at his hands. "What do you think you're doing?"

His gaze trapped hers. "Making sure my carelessness causes no further damage."

*His* carelessness! She swallowed back a nervous laugh. It had been her carelessness, her recklessness, her... wantonness that had precipitated them spending the afternoon outdoors beneath the blazing Texas sun. There certainly was no call for Sloan to assume responsibility for her abandoned behavior. Nor was there any call for him to feel guilty about her sun-broiled condition.

Besides, the most pressing danger, as she saw it, was that Sloan's familiar manner was going to make it obvious to the adults present that she and he had...had become more than acquaintances. He was behaving with a degree of possessiveness toward her that, while secretly gratifying, was publicly embarrassing.

"Sloan, please. I'm sure that Gladys, Junella and Marabelle are fully capable of assisting me."

His gaze hardened, and she feared she was going to have to engage in a wrestling match to keep him from divesting her of her clothing. His lips parted. She held her breath, waiting to hear what he would say next. She sensed that the others who'd crowded into the chamber shared her curiosity.

"You will marry me."

There was a predictable collective gasp. Despite her overheated state, goose bumps played leapfrog across her skin. "Sloan, this is hardly the place or time to—"

He bent over her. His lips teased her own apart and his tongue leisurely claimed her. She closed her eyes to savor the splendid invasion. When he raised his head, she swore she could see tiny sparks shimmering in his eyes.

"I'll leave you in your friends' capable hands."

Sloan was gone before she could tell him that she had no intention of marrying him. Which was just as well, she supposed, since she lacked any enthusiasm for the endeavor. The men present left the room when Sloan did. Gladys had to shoo the children out to provide a measure of privacy.

Within a few minutes, Prudence's dress had been slipped off and she was covered in cool, wet cloths. It was mortifying to realize that every inch of the skin beneath her chemise and drawers was vividly pink. There could be no doubt in anyone's mind that she'd been outside in the altogether. With Sloan. Also highly discomfiting was the small bits of grainy sand that managed to find their way upon Junella's fresh-smelling sheets.

The women spoke in soothing tones of half sentences and vague words with indefinite meanings.

"There, dear..."

"This should feel better...."

"Don't drink too quickly...."

"We'll draw the shade...."

"Rest awhile...."

Throughout the ordeal of kindness, Prudence felt raw and exposed. Surely Gladys, Junella and Marabelle knew that she was a fallen woman. She snagged her bottom lip between her teeth. She didn't mean to fall asleep, but her eyelids became a heavy burden. With the smell of vinegar stinging her nostrils, she felt herself drifting, dozing...

Sometime later she awoke in the darkened room. Grateful she was alone, she slipped from the bed and walked across the braided rug to the window. Curious as to the time of day, she pushed back the shade and looked outside. Judging from the angle of the sun, she concluded she'd only slept for an hour or so.

With the strong scent of vinegar accompanying every movement, she redressed. For the third time that day. She dreaded facing the women who'd taken care of her, but knew there was little point in putting it off. She had enough respect for Gladys, Marabelle and Junella to hope they wouldn't gossip about her actions. Still, it bothered her that they might no longer wish to associate with her.

It was with definite trepidation that she stepped from the bedchamber into the hall. She came up short, unprepared for the sight of Sloan seated outside the room in a wood chair propped against the hallway wall.

"What are you doing out of bed?"

She raised her chin defensively, not at all pleased that he had the power to make her feel as if she needed to explain her actions. "As I'm fully recovered, there's no reason for me to remain in bed."

The legs of the chair came down hard on the floor as he rose. "You barely slept an hour."

"Sufficient time to be up and about."

A frown marred his rugged features. "Prudence, has anyone ever told you that you can be a real pain in the fanny?"

"Certainly not!"

"That's probably because the town matrons you associate with are too polite to tell you the truth."

It was ridiculous for his rude remark to make her feel the least bit weepy; nevertheless, the telltale pressure of tears began to build.

"That must be it," she said quietly, wondering if his sole purpose for waiting outside her door was to hurl snide comments at her.

"But when you're my wife, I'm going to expect you to become more reasonable."

"I hadn't realized that you had a hearing problem, Sloan." She shook her head with mock sorrow. "What a tragedy for someone not advanced in years."

"My hearing is just fine."

"But it can't be," she said, coating her words with magnified sympathy. "Or else you would have heard me when I said I wasn't going to marry you. Perhaps you ought to make an appointment with Dr. Sparks. He can prescribe a listening device that will help you. Of course, it probably will be a bit of a struggle to carry the cumbersome thing around, but then—"

"Maybe we ought to get *you* in to see him, then." Sloan edged closer. "Because you're the one who's evidently having trouble hearing."

*Why don't you tell him you will marry him? You want to. You love him. He's everything and more than you thought you would find in a man, in a lover, in a life mate.*

If she thought for one minute that he loved her, she realized that would have made all the difference. But she couldn't give herself to a man who merely wanted her because he enjoyed rutting with her. Not when he considered her a general nuisance in every other area of his life. Not when he called her a pain in the fanny!

"We don't have to resolve this now," she said, stalling for time. She wondered if in a month he would still be pressing for this union. He seemed a man of quixotic temperament. Perhaps the best way of dealing with him would be to simply delay giving him an answer. Eventually his bestial interest in her would wane.

"You're wrong, we need this settled. Now. In case it escaped your notice, there's five people who know that we were together under compromising circumstances for most of the afternoon."

"Well, they wouldn't have if you hadn't overreacted to my need for some fresh air. Really, Sloan, what possessed you to make such a ninny of yourself?"

A look of bemusement erased his frown. "You can't call a man a ninny."

"Why not? You called me a pain in the fanny." Hah! Let him argue himself out of that reprehensible act.

"This has got to be the damnedest courtship in history."

"You haven't courted me," she pointed out, miffed that he didn't seem to realize how much he'd affronted her.

"That's true," he admitted, a new husky quality entering his tone. "But as I recollect on the matter, I guess you aren't the kind of woman who invites a romantic courtship. A man would be better off with a whip or a gun."

"That's a despicable thing to say!"

"That would be just to get your attention," he continued. "The truth sometimes hurts, Prudence. But the truth is that you aren't the kind of woman a man can woo. He needs to tame you instead."

"With a whip or a gun?" she sputtered, outraged at his misconceptions about her.

"A lesser man might have to resort to those kinds of weapons," he conceded so agreeably that she wanted to slap the superior expression from his face.

"But, of course, you don't consider yourself a lesser man."

He leaned toward her. "I've found a better way to subdue you."

Her hand came up hard against his chest. "Don't you dare try and resolve this argument with a kiss."

"Why not? It's worked before."

"How can you joke about this?" she demanded furiously. "We're talking about the most solemn and holy relationship that can exist between a man and a woman."

"Honey, you're not listening. I want to make an honest woman of you. I'm looking forward to singing hosannas with you for the next sixty or so years."

*You don't love me!*

She almost blurted the words aloud, but she couldn't bear it if he laughed at her. And in his present unpredictable mood, he probably would do just that. A woman could only take so much, and Prudence was beyond the point of taking any more of Sloan's rough-and-tumble brand of humor.

"I don't see what the problem is," he continued with equanimity. "You're more than willing to adopt any wounded stray that comes along. Why not think of me as one of your lost sheep?"

The task of imagining Sloan as an abandoned or lost child was simply beyond Prudence. He was the most capable, self-sufficient person she'd ever met. But his mention of the children brought an emptiness to her heart. She knew that she was going to lose them. Maybe not today. Maybe not all at once, but she'd seen clearly those who would take her babies from her and provide them with loving, complete homes. Something she hadn't been able to accomplish.

"It's going to be all right, honey."

"What is?" she asked, shaken by the certainty Sloan had been able to read her thoughts.

"Everything. The children. You. Me. We're going to be just fine."

He brushed away the hand she'd tried to use to keep him from pulling her into his arms. Even though his embrace was the last thing she'd told herself she wanted, she found it strangely comforting.

The contradiction of what she felt and what she wanted to feel frightened her. Why couldn't she hold herself apart from this man? What was it about him that made her so susceptible to him? As she rested her cheek against his solid chest, she wondered if her vulnerability was some kind of family disorder she'd inherited from her mother and aunts. Each of them had surrendered their hearts late in life.

"I'm going to lose the children," she finally admitted against the fabric of his cotton shirt.

"Yes."

Hot tears scalded her eyes, and she shuddered. "How can you say that everything's going to be all right, then?"

His wide palms rubbed her back. "Because it always is. I don't know why or how, but as I've gotten older I've learned that everything happens for a reason. It just sometimes takes a while to find out what that reason is."

"That doesn't stop the hurting. And, oh, Sloan, I can't tell you how much it hurts to know I'm going to lose them."

"Yeah, it hurts, honey. There's no denying that. I remember when my father died. God, I'd thought my guts had been ripped out and strung over barbed wire. As time passed, I had to take his place at the ranch. Because of that, I learned a lot of things I never would have learned. The experience forced me to become who I am."

"You're wonderful." Her defenses were so riddled she couldn't prevent herself from admitting that aloud. She was sure she would regret the remark later.

"Lord, you really are upset," he said, and she heard the amusement in his voice.

"Obviously." She prepared herself for the moment he would release her from his embrace. She needed to be strong.

"I know you love those kids," he went on to say, giving her a squeeze. "If it weren't for you, God knows what would have happened to them. You kept them safe. You provided food and shelter. You gave them a home. You loved them."

"I—I still do."

"You've been their caretaker when there was no one else there for them."

"George and Junella are going to want to adopt the twins." It was a tentative statement of fact that became real when she said it.

"I know, honey."

"Reverend Brown and Marabelle are going to marry." She paused and drew a deep breath. "Both of them seem to love Janey very dearly."

"They've already adopted her in their hearts."

"Davy's going off with his brother. And Sarah...I'm going to have to talk to her. She's looking at Micah Bowcutt with stars in her eyes."

"He seems like a responsible young man. He had enough character and integrity to come looking for his younger brother."

"She's too young to be thinking about . . . love."

"You can try to tell her that when you talk to her, but it's been my experience that when somebody makes up their mind to marry someone, it's damn near impossible to get them to change it."

Prudence extricated herself from Sloan's arms. "We are talking about Sarah, right?"

He smiled at her with sufficient gentleness to make her stomach roll over. "Of all the things I've come to appreciate about you, your bravery has been at the forefront."

"My bravery?"

He nodded. "So that's why it comes as a surprise to me that you're afraid to get married."

"It's not that I'm afraid," she objected immediately. "It's a matter of proceeding cautiously so a mistake isn't made."

"You're overlooking something."

She didn't trust the predatory look in his eyes. "What's that?"

"I'm not a cautious man. When you get right down to it, I guess you could call me reckless."

Wasn't that what she'd thought from the first time she'd conversed with him. A reckless man!

"Be that as it may, I have no intention of being rushed into becoming anyone's wife."

"Not anyone's wife," he chided. "*My* wife."

The delicate muscles in her womb clenched. "I am not sure of the durability of your feelings, Sloan. Especially since I heartily concur with your assessment of yourself as being entirely too reckless. Why, you could wake up a month after we'd become man and wife and decide you want your precious freedom again."

"Is that what you're afraid of, that I'm going to change my mind?"

"I'm not afraid of anything," she protested. "I just want to make certain whatever it is you feel for me isn't going to evaporate one of these hot Texas mornings."

"'Whatever it is I feel for you'?"

A dangerous edge crept into his tone.

"Lust, carnal desire, amusement..." She gestured with her hand. "Only you can say what's driving you."

His eyes smoldered. "Right now it's anger, pure and simple."

"You certainly have no reason to be angry with me," she sniffed. "I'm being excessively reasonable about the entire affair."

"If you become any more reasonable, I'm going to—"

"Miss Prudence, you're up!"

Janey's excited voice rang through George and Junella's hallway.

Prudence jumped back from Sloan, as if being discovered with him in the hallway could further compromise her reputation. Talk about closing the barn door *after* the horse had bolted.

Janey dashed to Prudence. "Reverend Brown and Miss Marabelle took me for a buggy ride!"

A sharp-edged lump formed in Prudence's throat. "That's wonderful, Janey."

"They said they would take me for a ride any time I wanted," the girl boasted with giddy enthusiasm. "They like me."

Prudence knelt so that she was eye level with the girl. "Well, of course they do. You're a very special young lady."

"For a cyclops."

"Janey! Whoever called you that was very cruel. You mustn't listen to such things."

The little girl shrugged. "It was somebody at school. Davy bonked him with his crutch. I don't mind, Miss

Prudence. Most folks are real nice about me only having one good eye."

"Oh, Janey." Prudence hugged the sweet child to her. How was she ever going to let her go if Marabelle and the Reverend wanted to adopt her?

The answer came with the realization that she herself had set the stage for letting the children go. Janey had called her Miss Prudence.

*Miss Prudence...*

The name carried with it its own distancing barrier. "Miss Prudence" was, as Sloan had said earlier, the caretaker of children who'd lost their homes and needed temporary shelter.

Not one of those children had ever called her mother.

She gave Janey a final hug and straightened. A caretaker was a very nice thing to have in a pinch, but given a choice any child would most certainly choose to have a mother instead.

"Are you crying, Miss Prudence?"

Janey's worried voice cut through Prudence's settling thoughts. She smiled at the child. "Probably."

"Is it because you stink?" the girl inquired gravely.

Prudence blinked. "I beg your pardon?"

"That vinegar smells just awful. I thought maybe it was making your eyes water."

Prudence discovered it was possible to smile in the midst of heartbreak.

# Chapter Seventeen

"**Y**ou wanted to see me, Miss Prudence?" Sarah asked as she entered the parlor.

Prudence set aside her embroidery hoop. "Yes, dear."

The young woman crossed the room and stood uncertainly before her. "Is something wrong?"

*My world's falling apart around me, and for the past two days all I've managed to think about is Sloan Coltrane and his proposal of marriage.*

"I'm not sure, but I felt that we should talk. Please sit down."

Sarah did so with an alacrity that revealed how nervous she was. Prudence had been nine when Sarah had arrived at Draper House as a toddler. Loud noises had been particularly frightening to the girl. She'd learned to talk at a relatively late age—five. She'd had a stutter that she'd only recently seemed able to control. She was Sarah the quiet one, Sarah the book reader, Sarah with the poignant gaze.

"Are you happy here, Sarah?"

"V-very much so."

"It seems that I've come to count very heavily on your help with the younger children without realizing I was doing so. You haven't had much opportunity to associate with other girls your age."

"I don't mind."

Prudence smiled wryly. "It's because you're so accommodating that I have been able to take advantage of you."

"B-but you haven't taken advantage of me. I love helping with the children. Charlie and Charlotte are so cute. And little Janey is a princess. And Davy... He can be a real firecracker sometimes, but he's a good boy."

"And what do you think of Davy's brother?"

Prudence had intended to be more subtle, but the question popped out.

Sarah's cheeks flooded crimson. "M-Micah?"

"Yes, what do you think of Micah?"

"W-well he sure loves Davy."

"Yes, he does."

Sarah cleared her throat. "He seems determined to do right by the boy, coming all that way to fetch him."

"It shows a lot of character," Prudence agreed.

"Well I expect that's all I can say about him."

"I spoke with him earlier today."

"Y-you did?"

Prudence nodded. "He told me he's leaving tomorrow with Davy."

Tears smudged Sarah's pretty blue eyes. "He told me, too."

"Did he also tell you that he was going to ask me for permission to marry you?"

Sarah's face bloomed with color. "He did? He really asked you if he could marry me?"

From the young woman's ecstatic expression, there was little doubt in Prudence's mind that the girl would jump at the opportunity to become Mrs. Micah Bowcutt.

"You haven't known each other very long, Sarah. And you're very young," she added gently.

"I reckon that's true enough, but I love him and I'd be highly honored to become his wife."

The emotional words should have sounded ridiculous coming from someone sixteen years old. They didn't. Their simple honesty and dignity touched Prudence.

"How can you be so sure that you love him? Perhaps you're merely infatuated with him," Prudence suggested softly.

"I feel it in here." Sarah touched her heart. "It's a warm, steady feeling, and it tells me that even if times are hard, I can be happy with him. It's kind of like we belong together. And as long as we're together, everything is going to come out all right. I don't think I could ever feel this way about someone else. I don't want to feel this way about someone else."

Prudence was humbled that one so young could express such a depth of emotional maturity. It was uncanny how the girl's simple words summed up Prudence's feelings toward Sloan.

She loved him, and she never wanted to feel that same kind of love toward anyone else. She belonged to him in a fundamental way that made it impossible to even think of giving herself to another.

"I believe you sincerely care for Micah and he sincerely cares for you, Sarah. But I still think you need to wait. Marriage is a big step in a person's life. You and he can correspond for six months. If, at the end of that time, you still feel the way you do, I will travel with you by train to Arizona and witness your wedding vows to Micah."

"Six months is too long," the girl protested with an unusual display of independence.

"Not if you love each other."

"But I don't want to wait that long!"

"I'm sure you don't," Prudence said gently. "But I can't in good conscience let you leave with a boy you've only known a few days. Those six months may seem like forever, but they'll give you time to get to know each other. You need that time, honey. The waiting will make being with him all the sweeter."

Sarah jumped to her feet and began to pace. "My head says you're making sense. But my heart says I'll die if we're apart that long."

"You're sixteen, Sarah. I've given you my council. I believe you're responsible enough to make the right decision."

Sarah stopped pacing. "If my head and my heart said the same thing, I guess I'd be on that train tomorrow with Micah. But they don't, so I'll wait. For *four* months."

Prudence mentally conceded that a four-month delay was all the time she was going to get. Love had changed the shy, accommodating girl into a stubborn one.

"All right, Sarah. In four months I will travel with you to Arizona and see you married to Micah. If you haven't changed your mind, that is."

"I won't change my mind," the girl vowed with enough youthful passion to make even a cynic believe in true love.

After Sarah left, Prudence picked up the embroidery hoop. She stared at it a few moments, then set it aside. She wasn't in the mood to sew the delicate stitches required to finish God Bless our Happy Home to her own exacting standards.

*When my head and my heart say the same thing . . .*

Sarah's words returned to Prudence. She hated to admit how much sense they made.


The following afternoon Prudence and the children, along with Gladys, stood on the train platform, saying their final farewells to Davy. Prudence couldn't seem to keep her fingers from straying to the boy's unruly hair and brushing it from his forehead. The contact was bittersweet.

She prayed she was doing the right thing in letting him go. When she looked into Micah's purposeful gaze, she was reassured by his unshakable loyalty for the brother he'd come several hundred miles to reclaim. He was a fine young man, she thought. And he'd made a life for himself and Davy. But even that knowledge didn't lessen the anguish that squeezed her heart.

"Don't cry, Miss Prudence," Davy admonished, his brown eyes radiating the unusual maturity he'd reached at such a tender age.

"I can't help it," she confessed. "I'm going to miss you."

"I'm going to miss you, too, but I have to go with my brother. He came back for me, and I can't let him down."

Prudence's throat tightened. "No, you're right, you can't let him down."

"Remember you promised to come visit us," the boy reminded her, adjusting his slight weight against his crutch.

"We will," she told him. "You be good now and mind your brother."

"I don't have to mind Charlie," Charlotte retorted smugly, breaking into the conversation. "He can't make me do anything I don't want to."

"Who wants to boss around a girl?" Charlie asked with boyish disdain.

"Goodbye, young Davy," Gladys said, wiping her eyes with a handkerchief. "You're a fine boy and the world's a better place for having you in it. Now, you remember that!"

"I will, Miss Gladys. I promise."

The housekeeper bent down and enfolded the youth in a vigorous hug. A lot of promises were being made, Prudence noticed, glancing at Micah and Sarah as the couple exchanged a tentative, heart-breakingly innocent kiss.

The train whistle screamed, and everyone jumped.

"I guess it's time we go," Micah said, reaching out to help his brother step across the car's threshold.

Richard stepped forward and stuck out his hand with awkward self-consciousness. "Goodbye, Davy. It was nice knowing you."

Richard's unusual demonstrativeness pleased Prudence. The boy was beginning to emerge from his shell.

The whistle sounded again, this time accompanied by a blast of belching smoke. They left the platform and walked alongside the train, searching the row of windows until they saw Davy's excited face peering down at them.

Everyone waved and called out their last enthusiastic goodbyes. The engine roared to life and the great wheels began to turn. Giant puffs of steam shot out like blasts of cannon fire from beneath the moving cars.

The group moved farther back from the tracks. A growing sadness built inside Prudence with each revolution of the turning wheels. Evidently the others felt Davy's loss as much as she, because once the train was out of sight, a heavy silence engulfed them.

Prudence realized she wasn't the only one with tears in her eyes. "Well that's that, I suppose." Inane words offering meager solace. She cleared her throat. "I was thinking that as long as we are in town, we might visit Brubaker's Emporium and enjoy a sarsaparilla soda. How does that sound?"

She could tell how upset the others were at Davy's departure by the lackluster "okays" that greeted her suggestion.

The walk to the Emporium was a short one, and they proceeded in silence. From the corner of her eye, she noticed that Richard had stopped suddenly on the boardwalk. She turned and sent him a questioning glance.

"Is something wrong, Richard?"

A look of undisguised fear gripped his face. Prudence tensed, wondering what could have so terrified the boy.

"What is it?" she asked softly, her gaze scanning the busy street. Several wagons and buggies moved along the dusty road. The men and women strolling by looked entirely ordinary. She saw nothing to account for the stark terror bleeding the color from Richard's skin.

"Well ain't you going to give a howdy to yer daddy, boy?"

At the guttural question, Prudence's attention became riveted on a bandy-legged man who'd detached himself from a shadowed doorway. He was dressed in the dusty western garb of a cowpoke. Traditional battered Stetson. Checkered shirt. Travel-stained britches. Scuffed boots. The gun belt he wore looked as well used as the boots.

He should have looked like any other saddle tramp. He didn't. There was an aura of menace about the man's shadowed features that chilled the blood in her veins. His small, dark eyes hinted at a brutal nature, as did his twisted smile.

As if they, too, instinctively sensed the stranger was dangerous, the children drew back in silence. Prudence couldn't help contrasting their reaction to this man with the first time they met Sloan. With him, they'd instigated an unending barrage of conversation and questions, hardly giving him the opportunity to get a word in edgewise. Not so with the man who identified himself as Richard's father.

Richard said nothing and remained frozen to the spot where he'd stopped.

"Yer looking a mite peaked, boy. We'd best be on our way."

Richard trembled visibly. "I—I ain't going with you, Pa."

"Don't talk back, now, son. That ain't the way I raised you."

"Now, see here, Mr. Beck," Prudence began, stepping between the boy and the man. "Richard has—"

"Has run away from his daddy," the grizzled-haired man interrupted, then paused for a moment to relieve himself of a yellow mouthful of chewing tobacco. "And the name's Lemuel Beck. Most folks call me Lem."

Prudence's stomach rose to her throat. Lem Beck was a notorious gunman! Despite Sloan's stated opinion to the contrary, there were still violent men loose in the West. Lem Beck had killed most of his victims south of the border. In Texas, though, the border just wasn't that far away.

"I can tell by your expression you've heard of me," Lem said with a complacent smile that was probably the most frightening thing she'd ever witnessed. Deadlier than a rattlesnake. That's what folks said about Lem Beck.

"I've heard of you," she admitted quietly.

"Then you should know better than to get between me and my boy. Now, step aside."

There was nothing of human compassion or kindness in the man's small, dark eyes. She saw only cruelty. She tried to swallow and failed. How could this monster be Richard's father?

"Richard has found a home with us," she choked out tightly. Her knees were shaking so hard she didn't know how she remained standing.

"Well now, ain't that sweet. It appears to me that you've done gone and got yourself adopted by this here fine-looking woman. That was smart of you, boy. Ain't no reason to sleep in the dirt when you can have yerself a real bed."

Another stream of tobacco sailed into the air, landing precariously close to Prudence's hem. She worked her throat muscles to keep from retching. It occurred to her that she should get the children out of this killer's presence.

"Gladys, please take the children to the Emporium. Richard and I will meet you there."

"I'm not going to leave you with the likes of him," Gladys announced coldly.

Prudence turned her head from Beck and sent the housekeeper a beseeching look. "Take the children *now*."

Gladys stared at Prudence for a full minute before doing as she was asked. Sarah, Charlie, Charlotte and Janey followed the older woman with unaccustomed meekness. The fact that they had enough sense to be scared further heightened Prudence's tension. Nothing in her life had prepared her to handle a creature like Lem Beck.

"Well now, this is getting downright cozy," the evil man observed.

Prudence shuddered. "Mr. Beck—"

"Lem," he corrected her nastily.

"Lem, you have a fine son and he's become settled here in Port Dodd. He's going to school and—"

"Ah, hell, why'd you want to do that, boy? I told you there ain't nothing in a book that's worth knowing. All you have to do is listen to me and you'll learn everything you need to get by in this life."

"Lem," she forced herself to say, even though speaking the man's first name nauseated her. "I don't know what your plans are for Richard but—"

"My *plans* are that he becomes a man. You reckon you can teach him to be one?" His disgusting stare moved down her as if she was a piece of prime beef. "Well, maybe you could at that. He's old enough for a woman, that's fer sure. Is that what's going on, is my boy playing stud for you?"

"Mr. Beck!" She couldn't bear to speak his first name again. "That's a ghastly thing to imply!"

"'Cause if that's the case," he continued in his slimy voice, "you'd be better off with a man who's fully growed. I ain't going to be in town long, but I'm willing to plow your furrow for you."

The bile rose in her throat. That this man could defile something as pure and as wonderful as what she and Sloan had experienced seemed a loathsome blasphemy.

Again she wondered how this animal could have fathered a boy as special as Richard.

"Richard is not going anywhere with you," she said, her voice trembling.

"You can't rightly keep him from me. I'm his pa."

"You're a disgusting animal," she breathed through pinched nostrils, saying far more than she intended to the terrifying man, but unable to stop herself. "I would kill you before I'd let you take Richard."

Something hot and animalistic flickered in the man's beady eyes. Prudence shuddered again, but she refused to look away from him.

"Well now, that's pretty harsh talk coming from a woman." His next shot of tobacco splashed directly on her skirt. She flinched, but held her ground. "You ever killed a man before?"

"You would be the first."

He smiled, revealing yellowed, broken teeth. "I guess my boy's found himself a good home, after all. It'd be a shame to take him from it." The man tipped his hat, his feverish eyes lit with unnatural amusement. "I reckon I'll just have to leave without him."

"Wait, Pa." Richard stepped forward. "I'll go with you."

The naked terror in the boy's voice overwhelmed Prudence. She knew he was offering to go with his father to spare possible retribution from him.

"No, Richard." She put a restraining hand on his arm. "Everything will be all right. You don't need to be afraid."

"That's right, boy. You don't need to be afraid. Everything's settled just fine and dandy." The man turned from them, walking away as if he didn't have a care in the world. "Fine and dandy..."

"Oh, Miss Prudence, I'm sorry," Richard said, tears streaking his cheeks. "I didn't think he'd ever find me. I ran away in the middle of the night, and I kept running. For months. I thought I was safe here, but I've brought you trouble."

"Nonsense," Prudence said briskly. "I don't like to speak ill of others, but your father is a bully. When someone stands up to a bully, they invariably back down. It's been that way since the beginning of time."

"I should go with him," Richard said urgently. "He'll forget all about you if I go with him."

"You're not leaving with that man. I don't care if he is your father."

Richard scrubbed his eyes. "I thought . . . I thought if you ever found out who my pa was, you wouldn't want me around."

How many times could a heart break in one day?

"Richard, I fully expect you to remain with us until you're grown. Now, come along before the others drink up the Emporium's stock of sarsaparilla."

Prudence wished she'd had the foresight to have Sloan instruct her on the proper method of discharging firearms. She supposed it was a bit late to begin shooting lessons. It would probably be more practical to hire a gunman of her own.

Her thoughts went to Sloan. He'd assured both her and the children upon countless occasions that he was not a gunslinger, which was unfortunate. Because a gunslinger was exactly what she needed. A twenty-four-hour-a-day gunfighter who got along well with children.

That night, conversation around the supper table was sporadic. Invariably, Charlie or Charlotte or Janey would make a statement of some kind, and it would be left hanging in the air. It was as if, without Davy present to add his two cents, they had run out of things to say. Prudence knew that in a matter of a few days they would adjust to the boy's absence. Children were resilient. She wondered how long it would take the hole in her heart to begin to mend.

"George said that come Monday he was going to start running Warlord and Lord Triumph."

That news would have greatly excited Davy. Now, however, Charlie's announcement fell into the pool of silence that hung over the table.

Prudence pushed away her plate. "I suppose you're going to want to watch them race."

"Mr. Coltrane did invite us," Charlotte said.

"He invited the Reverend and Miss Marabelle, too," Janey added as she used the back of her hand to wipe a milk mustache from her upper lip. Such was Prudence's mood that she didn't chide the girl.

"Mrs. Curtis said she'd fix us a special supper," Charlie remarked around a mouthful of freshly baked bread. "She sure is a fine cook. Just like you, Miss Gladys," he finished with ingenuous charm.

The conversation lagged again. Prudence's gaze drifted first to Sarah, then to Richard. Both the older children were unusually quiet this evening, but then she supposed they had good reason to be lost in their own thoughts. Each had experienced a traumatic event today.

The meal continued to pass with interminable slowness, as did the rest of the evening. Long after the children had heard their stories and were asleep for the night, Prudence lay awake in her bed. The house seemed full of strange noises that prevented her from drifting off to sleep. Finally she gave up. What was the point of lying in bed with her eyes wide open? She wasn't the least bit sleepy.

Prudence got up and pulled on her robe. Before going downstairs, she put on Aunt Phoebe's silk slippers, the only article of apparel of the older woman's that fit her. Perhaps a cup of hot tea would settle her nerves.

She tried to move around the kitchen quietly, taking care not to add to the vague noises that periodically sounded in distant corners of the house. She surmised that a strong wind had come up and was responsible for the discordant creaks and thumps. As she sat at the table waiting for the water to come to a boil, she relived her day: Riding in the wagon with Davy and Micah to the train station. The emotional parting on the platform. The train shrinking in size until it finally disappeared. The run-in with Lem Beck. Beck's threatening presence, his cruelty. The wake of fear that remained even when she'd watched him ride out of town.

Sloan Coltrane was always at the back of her mind, as he had been for the past three days. It hurt that he hadn't sought out her company. He'd been so insistent that she become his wife, and now he was nowhere to be seen. How could a woman trust what a man said, when he roared into and out of her life like an unpredictable Texas twister?

The kettle shrieked, and Prudence rushed to the stove to remove it from the burner. She poured the steaming liquid into her cup and watched the tea leaves float to the surface before sinking again. She located the sugar bowl and carried it and the steaming cup to the table.

The night wind howled. She stirred her tea. The faint clatter of the spoon against the china cup seemed a soothing backdrop for her brooding reflections. She remembered her first encounter with Sloan. Looking back on the incident, it was obvious that he'd resented her and the children moving into Amos's house. Sloan had wanted this piece of property to add to the rest of the land his uncle had left him. She and the children had been in the way. In a manner surely typical of most men, Sloan had tried to rid himself of their unwanted presence by the expedient means of buying them out. When that had failed, he'd tried to get them to leave by threatening to build his racetrack around them.

A less honorable man would have followed through on those threats. Sloan hadn't. Instead, he'd redesigned his track and the accompanying buildings. He'd tolerated the children's unremitting curiosity about his thoroughbreds to the extent of allowing them to watch the horses be trained. George had spent hours with the children, explaining the fine points of handling the magnificent runners.

Prudence added a spoonful of sugar to her tea. When she thought of Sloan, she remembered the times he'd held her in his arms, the times he'd kissed her, the times he'd made love to her. She was reminded anew of his incredible tenderness in the face of the overwhelming passion that had erupted between them.

She sipped the tea. When she'd first met Sloan, she had thought he was one kind of person. Then she'd gotten to know him as intimately as a woman could know a man, and she'd discovered he was nothing like she'd originally thought. He was... Well, he was fine, and gentle and noble.

She marveled that her feelings could have changed so much. If he asked her to marry him one more time, she was surely going to accept. Her greatest fear was that he'd somehow lost interest in her, that having once possessed her, he no longer desired her, that he'd decided she wasn't what he wanted in a wife.

She realized all her doubts sprang from the simple fact that he hadn't chosen to visit her in the past three days. She supposed that, if she really thought him noble, she would trust him and trust his stated intention to wed her. The difficulty was, she wasn't precisely certain what it was that he saw in her. He didn't like the clothes she wore; he'd made that abundantly clear. He'd never spoken a word about loving her. He had a habit of becoming impatient with her. He...

She lowered her cup. He'd made love to her and then disappeared from her life. Oh, perhaps disappeared was a strong word. But the fact was she felt abandoned, and it was an uncomfortable feeling. In its own way it hurt as much as Davy's departure.

A long, sighing creak moved through the house. It sounded as if the wind were gathering in intensity. Prudence picked up the lantern from the kitchen table and stepped to the back door. All the animals were settled for the night, but her inner restlessness drove her to discover for herself what the rising wind was up to.

Sufficient moonlight filled the yard, enabling her to clearly view her surroundings, though she did have to squint to keep the flying dust from getting into her eyes. Almost immediately she realized that one of the intermittent thumps she'd been hearing was caused by the barn door not being securely anchored. She extinguished the lantern before setting it on the porch, lest the wind knock it over. Besides, she would need both hands free to shut the huge door.

She was midway across the yard, her robe and nightgown whipping around, when another sound brought her to a stop. Approaching hoofbeats. She turned in the direction of the rider and peeled back the hair that had blown into her eyes.

A frisson of cold terror gripped her until she saw that it was Sloan, not Lemuel Beck. Her relief was almost immediately crumbled beneath a wave of anxiety. Had he come to tell her he'd changed his mind, that he no longer wanted her to become his wife? Even as she berated herself for her self-doubt, she couldn't banish the sense of foreboding that washed over her.

He reined in his horse and smoothly dismounted. "What are you doing outside?"

The pebble of tension in her stomach began to relax. This was the Sloan she knew and loved. Blunt and bossy. She decided to counter his question with one of her own.

"What do you want?"

*Why didn't you come sooner?*

"I've given you all the time I'm going to give."

There was an edge to his voice that set her pulse racing.

"Now, answer my question," he growled softly. "Why are you out here alone?"

"The barn door didn't get fastened," she replied, scarcely paying any heed to her explanation. "It keeps banging in the wind."

The distance between herself and Sloan was eaten up with his bold strides. "So you decided to take care of it yourself."

"Why wake someone else up to do something I can do for myself?"

"When we're in bed together, I expect you to wake me up."

A tremor of anticipation rippled across her skin. "I shall make a point of doing so then."

He raised his hand and brushed it across her cheek. "I'm glad to see you've decided to be reasonable about this."

"Only to a certain extent."

He stepped closer. A strong blast of wind swirled around them, catching the barn door. It slammed against the side panels with a reverberating bang that made Prudence jump and the timbers shudder.

"First things first, honey. We better secure that door."

She walked alongside him to the barn. When they reached the entrance, his powerful arm closed around her waist, and he urged her inside the darkened building. What puny light there'd been disappeared when Sloan grabbed the door and used the inside latch to bolt it shut.

The pungent scents of hay and kept animals swirled around her. "I know this isn't what you had in mind, but I needed to be alone with you without the worry that one of the kids or Gladys would interrupt us."

She remembered the last time they'd been in a barn together. As if by magic, her breasts and the area between her thighs began to pulse with a new awareness.

"When you live in a household such as ours, there's always that possibility," she said in a shaky voice.

It was still pitch black in the barn. She wished she'd decided to bring the lantern with her.

"This way we'll have a chance to talk without being disturbed."

"I can't see a thing."

"You will in a minute" came Sloan's disembodied but reassuring voice. "Richard keeps this place in perfect order. There's a lantern on a hook right along this beam."

"You're very observant. I hadn't realized you'd ever been in the barn."

"This was one of the places I tried to find you when you didn't come with the children to see my thoroughbreds. I couldn't help but notice how neat Richard kept everything. The boy has the makings of a fine man."

With that observation, the barn was filled with a circle of light from the lantern Sloan was holding. He carefully returned it to the nail from which it usually hung.

"I knew you'd be beautiful in yellow."

His husky compliment came as a pleasant shock. In the excitement of seeing him again, she'd forgotten she was wearing a white nightgown and yellow robe. "You say the nicest things."

"They're all true, darlin'. That's the best part of—"

"Naw, the best part is what's going to happen next."

Prudence's heart leapt to her throat as Lemuel Beck's coarse voice echoed through the cavernous barn. She spun around in horror and watched the loathsome man materialize from a shadowy corner.

"Now, what say you take that gun you're packing and ease it nice and slow out of that holster?"

around in the barn, watched the roughness turn tender from a distance away.

"Here, what say you take this gun you're pointing and even it up with the law of the land of Sloan?"

# Chapter Eighteen

"Don't mess with me," Beck snarled when Sloan failed to do as he'd been ordered.

"Who the hell are you?" Sloan demanded, not sounding the least bit terrified.

"Why, I'm the daddy of that fine boy you were just praising." Beck stepped into the light, revealing more clearly the lethal gun pointed at Sloan's chest.

"So you're what he's been running from."

The raw contempt in Sloan's voice sizzled inside the barn's drafty interior.

"You might say we had a minor disagreement. The boy had no business riling me when I was in my cups. I knocked him around. When I woke up the next day, he'd flown the coop."

Prudence could tell from the plaintive tone with which Beck told his story that he considered himself the aggrieved party and expected sympathy for having a son who would cause him such grief.

"Well, a man has a right to knock some sense into his kid," he continued belligerently. "It wasn't right for him to run away. I raised him better than that."

Prudence guessed that the vile man had beaten his son on more than one occasion. She ached for the life Richard must have lived before he'd escaped his father's vicious control.

"You said Richard could remain with me," Prudence reminded him.

He laughed, almost choking on the wad of chewing tobacco he had in his mouth. "I was funnin' with you. If you was as smart as you think you are, you would have known that."

"You're Lem Beck, aren't you?" Sloan asked suddenly.

"I'm honored that you recognize me. Of course, my face is plastered all over this part of the country. But I never figured them wanted posters did my likeness up proper. Now, drop your gun, mister."

"The word is you're one of the fastest guns ever to ride through these parts."

Beck smiled widely, showing his yellow-filmed teeth to disgusting prominence. "What are you thinking, cowboy? That you'd like to test yourself against me?"

"If you're as good as they say, it probably won't be much of a contest." Sloan shrugged. "But a man likes to go out fighting. You know how it is."

"I do at that," Beck said agreeably. "The thing is, I'm not as fast as I used to be. I don't like unnecessary trouble, and my bones tell me you're trouble, mister." He cocked his gun. "Best die with a prayer on your lips. That way your Maker will be expecting you."

Prudence shook off the numbing paralysis that had gripped her and stepped forward.

"You can't shoot a man in cold blood!"

Beck chuckled as he drew out the horrible moment of terror.

"Just watch me."

Her mind raced frantically. "But—but there's no reason to kill Sloan. You don't even know him!"

"Men like him don't need a reason to kill," Sloan said with disquieting matter-of-factness. "Isn't that right, Beck?"

The gunslinger's eyes glittered with savage amusement. "You got anything tender you want to say to your lady before I shoot you full of lead?"

With a sickening flash of comprehension, Prudence realized the gunman was enjoying his vile sport.

"Nothing I'd care for you to hear," Sloan answered with continued casualness.

She wanted to scream at both men. How could they stand in this life-and-death situation and act as if they were exchanging the most ordinary of pleasantries?

Beck leveled the gun barrel directly at Sloan's chest. "Then I'd best finish this."

Not thinking, just reacting to the hideous drama unfolding before her, Prudence stepped forward. There had to be a way to stop this before—

Two shots roared simultaneously inside the barn, bruising her ears and filling the air with gun smoke. Both Sloan and Beck slumped to the ground with blood seeping through their shirts. She went to Sloan, fighting off a black cloud of dizziness. He couldn't be mortally wounded. He had to be all right.

She knelt beside him. In the harsh yellow stream of light provided by the overhead lantern, his face seemed terrifyingly pale. The blood was pumping in a crimson stream from a hole that had ripped through his side.

"Sloan. Oh, Sloan," she sobbed. "Don't you dare die."

His eyelids fluttered, then rose. "That's no way to ease a man's final moments."

She shrugged out of her robe and pressed the bunched-up fabric against his wound. "These are not your final moments."

"You're sure about that?"

She swiped away the tears. "Positive. I have no intention of letting you off the hook. You proposed to me, and you're going to live up to your obligations. I refuse to have my heart trifled with."

He closed his eyes. "I'm glad we got that settled."

"I love you," she whispered.

The barn door shook under several pounding blows. Prudence thought it was the wind gone wild, then realized the shots must have been heard from the house.

"Prudence, are you in there? Are you all right?" Gladys called out.

Prudence gently laid Sloan against the ground and rushed to open the door. If he was going to survive as she'd promised him, they needed to send for Dr. Sparks.

"Is he breathing?"

"I don't think so."

"That means he's dead."

"He doesn't look dead. He looks like he's sleeping."

"That's how dead people look, silly."

"Don't call me silly."

"You're a girl—all girls are silly. They can't help it."

"Well, all boys are dumb."

"Are not!"

"Are, too!"

"Children, come out of there now. Sloan needs his rest."

"See?" An angry whisper whisked by Sloan's ear. "I told you he wasn't dead."

There was the sound of shoes racing across a wood floor. Ah, the patter of little feet. He drifted, fairly certain he was alive. It hadn't been just the voices of Charlie and Charlotte that encouraged him to think he was going to live. A molten area of pain radiated from his side, indicating that his spirit was locked solidly inside his earthly tabernacle. It would be a mean trick if a person took their

bodily pains with them all the way to heaven. He didn't
figure God was up to those kinds of cruel high jinks.

Eventually he was able to open his eyes. He was reclin-
ing in a four-poster bed. Sunlight filtered through white
eyelet curtains into a room he'd never seen before. Slowly
he turned his head to investigate his surroundings. Next
to the bed was a mahogany nightstand upon which a por-
celain pitcher sat. Across the room was a well-polished
dresser. On it a clear glass vase rested, overflowing with
freshly cut bluebonnets. Their tart scent drifted pleasantly through the chamber. A ceramic clock clicked
somewhere to his left.

Obviously he was in someone's bedroom. He wondered whose. He'd heard Gladys's voice calling the children from the room, but he didn't think this was her
chamber. A faint scent of lilacs wafted from the pillow,
reminding him of Prudence. He smiled. Evidently she'd
managed to do what was necessary to save his hide.

And she'd agreed to marry him. He remembered that
quite clearly, even though a lot of his other thoughts were
scrambled. He didn't know if he'd killed Beck. He'd hit
him and seen him go down, but that didn't guarantee he'd
stayed down.

The door swung open. So did Sloan's heart. Crossing
into the chamber came Prudence, dressed in a pretty yellow dress that made her look like a schoolgirl. She was still
wearing her hair scrunched up on her head, but that only
made him look forward to taking it down.

As she got closer, Sloan noticed the dark circles beneath her eyes. Somehow they managed to make her
lovelier. She came to the side of the bed, fiddled with his
covers for a minute, then reached up to plump his pillow.
She was looking at him, but her thoughts were obviously
miles away. Absently her fingertips brushed back his hair.
Sloan's gut tightened. Her touch was soft and seductive.
He closed his eyes to better savor it.

The contact of her lips gently kissing his forehead made his eyes snap open. He was going to have to get her to work on her aim. He used the opportunity to sample the column of her exposed throat.

She jumped as if she'd been scalded, letting loose a small shriek. "Sloan! You're awake!"

"That I am, darlin'."

"Oh, Sloan." She gave a soft sob and began raining kisses across his face. Not a one of them landed on his mouth. He brought his hands up to grab her shoulders and point her in the right direction.

She moved out of his weakened grasp before he could succeed with his goal, however, and clutched his hands to her bosom. While it wasn't his original intention, he didn't mind the change in plan.

"I've been so worried about you."

"I guess Beck's reputation as a gunman was a deserved one. He was quick with the trigger and accurate," Sloan said, disgusted with himself for getting shot and making Prudence worry about him. "Did I kill him?"

Prudence's eyes darkened. "You shot him through the heart. He died instantly."

"How did Richard take it?"

"It's been hard for him. He was afraid of his father, so there's a sense of relief. But I think he's also feeling guilty. A boy's supposed to love his father, after all."

"Richard will come to terms with his feelings over time. When my father died, I felt guilty, too."

Her eyebrows rose in obvious surprise at his admission. "But he was killed in the war."

"Yeah, and he was a good man. But I kept thinking that if I'd been able to go in his place, he would have lived."

"You were only a boy."

"That's what my head told me, but my heart told me different."

At Sloan's words, Prudence's heart seemed to tumble over itself. She leaned forward and kissed his cheek. His hands appeared from nowhere and cupped her face. He pulled her mouth to his for a deep, soul-piercing kiss. She braced herself against his shoulders.

After a few moments, she drew back. "Sloan..."

"Yes?"

"You're much too weak for this kind of activity."

He laughed in a low, slithery tone that tickled her stomach. "Come closer and you'll find out I'm a lot stronger than I look."

"We need to talk," she informed him, smoothing the folds of her newly sewn dress. She wondered if he'd noticed she wasn't wearing one of the black dresses he'd taken such a dislike to.

"Has my family shown up yet?"

His question startled her. "Not that I know of. Why?"

"I sent a telegraph to them, asking them to come to Port Dodd." He tried to sit straighter in the bed. A grimace of pain tightened his features. "I wanted them here for our wedding. They'll be showing up any time now."

"You were that confident I would marry you?" She wasn't sure she liked him taking her for granted.

"You told me that you loved me," he said as if that settled the matter.

"I wasn't certain you'd heard me."

"Oh, I heard you all right," he breathed huskily. "After that there's no way you could have gotten out of becoming my wife."

What a singularly unromantic statement!

"Isn't there something you wish to tell me?" she prompted helpfully.

"There's something I want to get straight," he muttered, wincing as he rose to a sitting position.

"I don't think it's a good idea for you to move around so. You might reopen your wound."

"There's no way I'm going to be flat on my back during our wedding night."

Her cheeks warmed. Actually, the picture his words inspired wasn't all that unpleasant.

"A man likes to pull his share of the load," Sloan continued, eyeing her thoughtfully. "What are you blushing about now?"

"Nothing," she answered innocently.

His dark brows converged. "Did the doctor happen to mention how soon it would be before I'll be fit enough to get out of this bed?"

"It will be a few weeks before you're up and about."

Sloan's expression became ominous. "Hell."

"The time will pass quickly, you'll see."

"Is this your bed?" he asked suddenly.

She swallowed. "Yes."

"It's a big one."

"I believe it was Amos's."

"There's more than enough room for two people in it."

She didn't trust the sudden gleam in his eyes. "What do you have in mind?"

"A man needs some incentive, if he's going to mend quickly."

"What kind of incentive?"

"Maybe the kind that a visitor might bring if she came to his room late at night when the rest of the house was asleep."

"That would be—" she licked her lips "—not at all prudent."

"She could slip out of her nightgown and get under the covers with him," Sloan persisted. "Together they could make the long nights pass more pleasurably."

"Sloan, that's not going to happen. It would be far too dangerous for your recovery."

"It would probably be a lot more dangerous for me to get out of bed and try to find you in this big old house."

"Don't you think of anything but...but..." She broke off. It was eminently apparent to her that he was totally fixated with physical pleasure.

"I don't think of anything but you," he responded, his voice gritty. "I think of you in the morning, in the afternoon and at night. I think about standing beside you and cheering as our horse crosses the finish line. I think about you sitting across the supper table from me. I think about you holding our baby to your breast. I think about you...sharing a bed with me. I think about being inside you and you crying out in ecstasy. You're all there is."

Tears filled Prudence's eyes. She carefully pushed aside the coverlet so she could be close to Sloan. His arms came around her and he settled her head against his shoulder.

"There's something I started to tell you before," he said, kissing her temple. "I was going to tell you that I didn't want you agreeing to marry me just because I'd been hurt. You have a way of taking in wounded critters who need a place to live. I didn't want to be another stray you'd opened your door to."

She turned on her side to face him. It seemed entirely natural when he began unfastening the buttons that ran down the front of her bodice. It wasn't long before he freed her breast from her chemise with a gentleness that seemed almost reverent. His callused fingertip caressed her distended nipple. The sight of his dark hand touching her pink flesh made her tremble. She reached out to untie the string that fastened his nightshirt.

"I wasn't interested in being adopted by you," he continued huskily, leaning forward to touch her nipple with the tip of his tongue. "But now that I've reflected upon it, I've decided I'll take you any way I can get you."

Her stomach fluttered. "I see."

"I love you, Prudence Abercrombie."

Her heart soared. "I love you, too."

Footsteps sounded at the end of the hall. "Damnation," Sloan muttered.

Prudence slipped quickly from the bed and hurriedly rebuttoned her dress.

The door swung open just as she finished her hasty efforts.

Charlie barreled into the room. "Sloan! You're alive!"

"Yeah."

Charlotte entered the room a moment later. "See, I told you he wasn't dead."

"Well, he could have been," Charlie informed her loftily as he approached the bed. "But I'm sure glad you ain't."

"Aren't," Prudence and Charlotte corrected him simultaneously.

Charlie and Sloan exchanged astonishingly similar looks of male forbearance.

"What's my middle name?" Janey demanded, marching into the room, her face pinched with obvious concern.

"You must not have one, or you'd know what it is," Charlie told her. "I'm Charles Henry Williams," he announced with great relish.

"I'm Charlotte Marie Williams," his sister said with equal pride.

"You have a middle name," Prudence told Janey. "Your full name is Jane Susan Henspeter."

Janey's small face beamed with pleasure. "I like that." She turned to Sloan. "Do you have a middle name?"

"Sloan Travis Coltrane," he answered.

"Do you have a middle name, Miss Prudence?"

"Yes I do. Now I think it's time for us to run along and let Sloan get some rest. We mustn't tire him out."

The children moved toward the door.

"What is it?"

The question came from Sloan. She continued shepherding the children into the hall. "What's what?"

"Your middle name."

She looked over her shoulder at him. He looked like a man on the trail of a piece of information he had no intention of doing without. She sighed, supposing it was reasonable for him to want to know his future wife's full name.

"Britannia," she mumbled.

"What did you say?"

"My full name is Prudence Britannia Abercrombie," she snapped, not looking forward to his amused reaction to the unwieldy combination of names with which she'd been burdened at birth.

"You're not leaving, are you?"

"You need your rest," she reminded him.

"Don't I get a goodbye kiss?" he asked softly.

She stared at him from across the room. Then glanced down the hall. The children had already disappeared.

"I don't expect you to make fun of my name," she said stiffly as she closed the bedroom door and returned to his bedside.

She bent over him to bestow a chaste kiss on his cheek. Why wasn't she surprised when he encircled her with arms that could have easily been mistaken for bands of steel and drew her to him?

"I wouldn't do that," he said gravely. "I love your middle name. I'm going to start calling you by it."

"You're going to call me Britannia?" she asked in dismay.

"I'm going to call you Brit, honey. It suits you."

"All the time?" she demanded, not certain she liked the idea of going through life being called Brit.

"I'll save it for when we're in bed together," he said against her throat.

"Oh."

"Sometime later tonight..."

She found herself in bed with him, pressed against his uninjured side.

Several intense kisses ensued. Prudence shivered and shuddered and melted.

"I'm still not sure it's a good idea for me to disturb your rest."

He groaned in her ear. "Honey, I'm already disturbed. If I were any more disturbed, you'd have to take me out and shoot me to put me out of my misery."

"That makes no sense at all!"

"Maybe not to a woman, but believe me, it makes perfect sense to a man."

Several more hot, delicious kisses ensued.

"Sloan..."

"Hmm..."

"Are you going to be hiring any other men besides George to assist you with your horse-racing venture?"

The tip of his tongue investigated her ear. Her breath caught in her throat. Goodness, what an amazing sensation.

He stopped his marvelous assault. "Why do you want to know?"

"Well, it occurs to me that things are going splendidly for just about everyone. Davy's with his brother. Sarah will be joining them in a few months. Reverend Brown and Marabelle are most certainly going to be married. I'm sure they're going to want to adopt Janey. George and Junella seem to have been made for Charlie and Charlotte. And Richard is free from his father's pursuit."

"That just about sums up everyone's life. What has that got to do with me hiring men?"

She regarded him solemnly. "What about Gladys?"

Sloan's eyebrows knit. "You want me to find a man for your housekeeper?"

Prudence beamed. It was amazing how perceptive Sloan had become. "A husband is what I had in mind."

He blinked at her. "Isn't that something she can take care of herself?"

"The final decision will be hers, of course." Prudence snuggled closer. "I just feel that we need to help her along."

"Is it only Gladys we have to find a husband for, or am I expected to play matchmaker for the whole state of Texas?"

"Don't be rude."

"Because," Sloan continued, his voice becoming downright testy, "if you expect me to find someone to save Hortense Tittle from being an old maid, I'm telling you now that she's a man-hater, and I refuse to condemn some unfortunate soul to being shackled to her."

"You just don't approve of her because she told your sisters that you were going to hell in a hand basket," Prudence said soothingly, remembering that Alicia and Lenore had quoted the Taylorsville woman.

"You've never met the old biddy, so I'll overlook your opinion."

If he hadn't been grievously wounded, Prudence would have poked him. Instead, she caressed his cheek. "I'm sure she just hasn't found the right man yet."

Sloan coughed. "Let's hope the poor bastard's luck holds out."

"Sloan!"

"Honey, I'm trying really hard to be patient, but I don't want to hear another word about Hortense. Her tongue is sharp enough to peel the hide right off a man."

Realizing that she wasn't going to change Sloan's mind, Prudence decided to let the subject drop, but there was another one that needed to be discussed.

She took a deep breath. "Sloan..."

"What is it now?"

"I know that it looks as if only Richard is going to remain with us, but there's something we need to clarify."

"He's too young for me to find him a wife," Sloan said dryly.

Prudence forced herself not to smile. The issue was too serious. "It is all right with you that he lives with us, isn't it?"

Sloan's gaze softened. "Of course, it is, honey."

"And...and..."

This next question meant so much to her that she didn't know if she possessed the courage to ask it.

"Darlin', if there's a knock on our door, morning, noon or night, and someone's looking for somewhere to tuck an unwanted child, there will always be a place for that child in our home. I promise."

Prudence's eyes filled with tears. She hadn't known she could love someone as much as she loved Sloan.

"Thank you."

"And maybe, God willing, we'll have a few young'uns of our own."

Or that her love could continually grow. Second by second.

"I'd like that, though..."

"Though what?"

"This isn't the kind of life you envisioned having when you moved to Port Dodd." She stared at him in concern. "Are you sure this is what you want?"

"More than my next breath." He touched her cheek. "When I left the ranch, all I had on my mind was racing thoroughbreds and living the good life."

She suspected his definition of the "good life" was vastly different from hers. "And now you want more?"

"I'm still going to race my horses, darlin', but I've decided to do without the gambling casino." He smiled ruefully. "Somehow poker, whiskey and frisky women don't seem compatible with married life."

She beamed at him. He was a very perceptive man. "It's all for the best, Sloan."

"It is?"

She nodded gravely. "You really aren't the kind of man who would be content living a desultory life."

"I'm not?"

"Not at all," she assured him. "You wouldn't have spent so many years caring for your family if you weren't a responsible and honorable man."

"I'm glad you think so."

"It's the truth. A person can't run away from who they are."

He hugged her to him. "Believe me, I have no intention of running from you, honey."

She surrendered herself to his comforting embrace. Seconds slipped away as they sealed their feelings with the passionate force of their trembling bodies.

The house shook with a rumble that had nothing to do with what was happening between them.

Prudence came up for air. "Goodness, what was that?"

His embrace tightened. "Sounded like thunder."

"Another summer storm must be on the way."

He strung hot kisses along her jawline. "There's nothing to worry about, Brit. It's just a little Texas thunder."

As Prudence gave herself up to Sloan's tender caresses, she thought about the coming night and shivered. There was so much to look forward to.

A lifetime of loving.

A lifetime of Sloan . . . the Magnificent.

\* \* \* \* \*

## _Harlequin®_
## _Historical_

## WOMEN OF THE WEST

Exciting stories of the old West and the women whose dreams
and passions shaped a new land!

Join Harlequin Historicals every month as we bring you
these unforgettable tales.

May 1995 #270—**JUSTIN'S BRIDE**
Susan Macias w/a Susan Mallery

June 1995 #273—**SADDLE THE WIND**
Pat Tracy

July 1995 #277—**ADDIE'S LAMENT**
DeLoras Scott

August 1995 #279—**TRUSTING SARAH**
Cassandra Austin

September 1995 #286—**CECILIA AND THE STRANGER**
Liz Ireland

October 1995 #288—**SAINT OR SINNER**
Cheryl St.John

November 1995 #294—**LYDIA**
Elizabeth Lane

Don't miss any of our **Women of the West!**

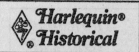

# Harlequin® Historical

## From award-winning author
## Theresa Michaels

Harlequin brings you—The Kincaids

A series with all the Romance and Adventure of the Old West

July 1995

**ONCE A MAVERICK HH #276**
Former fast gun Ty Kincaid helps a beautiful young gambler track down the man who killed her father.

Winter 1995

**ONCE AN OUTLAW**
No one but the strong-willed widow could lure Logan Kincaid off the outlaw trail.

Spring 1996

**ONCE A LAWMAN**
Sheriff Conner Kincaid finds more that he bargained for when he helps a feisty woman look for her missing brother.

Follow the saga of the unforgettable Kincaid brothers in Theresa Michaels's dramatic new trilogy from Harlequin Historicals.

## Harlequin® Historical

### What do A.E. Maxwell, Miranda Jarrett, Merline Lovelace and Cassandra Austin have in common?

They are all part of Harlequin Historical's efforts to bring you longer books by some of your favorite authors. Pick up one of these upcoming titles today and see what a difference an historical from Harlequin can make!

**REDWOOD EMPIRE—A.E. Maxwell** Don't miss the reissue of this exciting saga from award-winning authors Ann and Evan Maxwell, coming in May 1995.

**SPARHAWK'S LADY—Miranda Jarrett** From this popular author comes another sweeping **Sparhawk** adventure full of passion and emotion in June 1995.

**HIS LADY'S RANSOM—Merline Lovelace** A gripping Medieval tale from the talented author of the **Destiny's Women** series that is sure to delight, coming in July 1995.

**TRUSTING SARAH—Cassandra Austin** And in August 1995, the long-awaited new Western by the author whose *Wait for the Sunrise* touched readers' hearts.

Watch for them this spring and summer wherever Harlequin Historicals are sold.

ANNOUNCING THE

# PRIZE SURPRISE SWEEPSTAKES!

This month's prize:

# L-A-R-G-E—SCREEN PANASONIC TV!

This month, as a special surprise, we're giving away a fabulous FREE TV!

Imagine how delighted you and your family will be to own this brand-new 31" Panasonic** television! It comes with all the latest high-tech features, like a SuperFlat picture tube for a clear, crisp picture...unified remote control...closed-caption decoder...clock and sleep timer, and much more!

The facing page contains two Entry Coupons (as does every book you received this shipment). Complete and return *all* the entry coupons; **the more times you enter, the better your chances of winning the TV!**

Then keep your fingers crossed, because you'll find out by July 15, 1995 if you're the winner!

Remember: The more times you enter, the better your chances of winning!*

*NO PURCHASE OR OBLIGATION TO CONTINUE BEING A SUBSCRIBER NECESSARY TO ENTER. SEE THE REVERSE SIDE OF ANY ENTRY COUPON FOR ALTERNATE MEANS OF ENTRY.

**THE PROPRIETORS OF THE TRADEMARK ARE NOT ASSOCIATED WITH THIS PROMOTION.

PTV KAL

## PRIZE SURPRISE
### SWEEPSTAKES

## OFFICIAL ENTRY COUPON

This entry must be received by: JUNE 30, 1995
This month's winner will be notified by: JULY 15, 1995

**YES,** I want to win the Panasonic 31" TV! Please enter me in the drawing and let me know if I've won!

Name_____

Address _____ Apt. _____

City                    State/Prov.              Zip/Postal Code

Account #_____

Return entry with invoice in reply envelope.

© 1995 HARLEQUIN ENTERPRISES LTD.                    CTV KAL

---

## PRIZE SURPRISE
### SWEEPSTAKES

## OFFICIAL ENTRY COUPON

This entry must be received by: JUNE 30, 1995
This month's winner will be notified by: JULY 15, 1995

**YES,** I want to win the Panasonic 31" TV! Please enter me in the drawing and let me know if I've won!

Name_____

Address _____ Apt. _____

City                    State/Prov.              Zip/Postal Code

Account #_____

Return entry with invoice in reply envelope.

© 1995 HARLEQUIN ENTERPRISES LTD.                    CTV KAL

# OFFICIAL RULES

## PRIZE SURPRISE SWEEPSTAKES 3448

### NO PURCHASE OR OBLIGATION NECESSARY

Three Harlequin Reader Service 1995 shipments will contain respectively, coupons for entry into three different prize drawings, one for a Panasonic 31" wide-screen TV, another for a 5-piece Wedgwood china service for eight and the third for a Sharp ViewCam camcorder. To enter any drawing using an Entry Coupon, simply complete and mail according to directions.

There is no obligation to continue using the Reader Service to enter and be eligible for any prize drawing. You may also enter any drawing by hand printing the words "Prize Surprise," your name and address on a 3"x5" card and the name of the prize you wish that entry to be considered for (i.e., Panasonic wide-screen TV, Wedgwood china or Sharp ViewCam). Send your 3"x5" entries via first-class mail (limit: one per envelope) to: Prize Surprise Sweepstakes 3448, c/o the prize you wish that entry to be considered for, P.O. Box 1315, Buffalo, NY 14269-1315, USA or P.O. Box 610, Fort Erie, Ontario L2A 5X3, Canada.

To be eligible for the Panasonic wide-screen TV, entries must be received by 6/30/95; for the Wedgwood china, 8/30/95; and for the Sharp ViewCam, 10/30/95.

Winners will be determined in random drawings conducted under the supervision of D.L. Blair, Inc., an independent judging organization whose decisions are final, from among all eligible entries received for that drawing. Approximate prize values are as follows: Panasonic wide-screen TV ($1,800); Wedgwood china ($840) and Sharp ViewCam ($2,000). Sweepstakes open to residents of the U.S. (except Puerto Rico) and Canada, 18 years of age or older. Employees and immediate family members of Harlequin Enterprises, Ltd., D.L. Blair, Inc., their affiliates, subsidiaries and all other agencies, entities and persons connected with the use, marketing or conduct of this sweepstakes are not eligible. Odds of winning a prize are dependent upon the number of eligible entries received for that drawing. Prize drawing and winner notification for each drawing will occur no later than 15 days after deadline for entry eligibility for that drawing. Limit: one prize to an individual, family or organization. All applicable laws and regulations apply. Sweepstakes offer void wherever prohibited by law. Any litigation within the province of Quebec respecting the conduct and awarding of the prizes in this sweepstakes must be submitted to the Regies des loteries et Courses du Quebec. In order to win a prize, residents of Canada will be required to correctly answer a time-limited arithmetical skill-testing question. Value of prizes are in U.S. currency.

Winners will be obligated to sign and return an Affidavit of Eligibility within 30 days of notification. In the event of noncompliance within this time period, prize may not be awarded. If any prize or prize notification is returned as undeliverable, that prize will not be awarded. By acceptance of a prize, winner consents to use of his/her name, photograph or other likeness for purposes of advertising, trade and promotion on behalf of Harlequin Enterprises, Ltd., without further compensation, unless prohibited by law.

For the names of prizewinners (available after 12/31/95), send a self-addressed, stamped envelope to: Prize Surprise Sweepstakes 3448 Winners, P.O. Box 4200, Blair, NE 68009.

RPZ KAL